ROSE CITY

ALSO BY MICHAEL POOL

Debt Crusher
Texas Two-Step

MICHAEL POOL

ROSE CITY
A Teller County Novel

Copyright © 2019 by Michael Pool

All rights reserved. No part of the book may be reproduced in any form or by any electronic or mechanical means, including information storage and retrieval systems, without permission in writing from the publisher, except by a reviewer who may quote brief passages in a review.

Down & Out Books
3959 Van Dyke Road, Suite 265
Lutz, FL 33558
DownAndOutBooks.com

The characters and events in this book are fictitious. Any similarity to real persons, living or dead, is coincidental and not intended by the author.

Cover design by Zach McCain

ISBN: 1-948235-67-6
ISBN-13: 978-1-948235-67-9

CHAPTER ONE

Cole Quick stood at the edge of the burial plot while the preacher gave his sermon from underneath the cheap green and white awning. Sweat poured down the side of his face, soaked through his faded button-down shirt, and collected at the waist of his old wrangler jeans. He hoped it was even hotter in that chrome and ebony casket, shaded though it was by the awning.

Chester Quick had always despised heat. Not even a lifetime working in the oil fields could change that. Chester had never liked much of anything, tell the truth. The goddamn casket had to be worth more than the rest of Chester's entire life had been. Cole had almost lost himself in that irony before the preacher's voice snapped him back into the moment.

"For a thousand years in your sight are but as yesterday, which passes like a watch in the night. You sweep them away like a dream; they fade away suddenly like the grass. In the morning it is green and flourishes, in the evening it is dried up and withered."

The wrinkled old preacher paused, closed his Bible over his right index finger and wiped sweat from his forehead with the back of his left arm, then opened the Bible again and continued.

"We consume away at your displeasure. We are afraid at your wrathful indignation. You have set our misdeeds before you and our secret sins in the light of your countenance. When you are angry, all our days are gone. Our years come to an end like a sigh."

The preacher closed his Bible and scanned each of the other three attendee's faces, then Cole's. Finally, he spoke again.

"It's hard to find an explanation when tragedy strikes. Satan would have us forsake our faith due to a lack of perspective on death. But death is Christ our Lord's promise, his gateway for the transformation to everlasting light. In each death there is both tragedy and triumph. We must focus on the triumph if we seek perspective. Chester Quick has been taken from us in a horrifying accident, but we must take comfort that in the Lord's light there are no accidents. Even our deaths are the Lord's will. Today, we commit Chester back to the earth so that he can be one again with the Father in heaven."

The preacher turned and picked up the arrangement of yellow roses from the top of the casket. He laid them on a table next to the speaking podium and nodded to an attendant in pale green coveralls. The attendant stepped on a pedal connected to the casket-lowering device and lowered Chester Quick into the dirt. Cole peered over the edge and down into the hole. He still couldn't get past the irony of burying a man like Chester in a casket like that. They'd have done him as much honor to burn his body and scatter the ashes at a sewage plant. Tradition and ceremony had meant almost nothing to Chester Quick.

After the casket had been lowered out of sight, Cole turned and headed back toward his ragged grey Chevy Silverado, the only truck he'd ever owned. When he was seventeen he'd paid the former owner more than it was probably worth in cash. The man had assured him the truck would last forever if he treated it right. Cole couldn't vouch for the treatment, but the truck had held true the past thirteen years since he'd last left Teller County.

"Mr. Quick," the preacher called out from behind him as he opened the driver's side door. "Cole Quick, could you wait up just a moment?"

Cole pushed the half-open door shut and turned to face the

preacher. The pudgy little man waddled toward him with the yellow roses in his arms. It took him longer than it should have to make his way up the slight incline to the cemetery's main driveway. By the time he stopped in front of Cole his red face had a sweat-sheen and his breathing came out labored.

The preacher said, "Mr. Quick, I'm Calvin Roach. I'm the pastor at Rose Meadows Baptist Church here in Teller. I preside over most all of the funeral services provided by Ambrose Oil Company's employee life insurance policy."

"Pleasure to meet you," Cole said, digging in his pocket for his pack of smokes. He lit up a cigarette as Roach caught his breath. Roach pushed the flower arrangement forward like a peace offering. Cole made no move to accept it.

"I thought I'd see if you wanted to keep the casket arrangement, as a keepsake of your father?"

Cole shook his head. "No, thank you," he replied. "I appreciate the thought, though."

"I realize times like these can be tough, Mr. Quick. Perhaps I'll take it back to my office in case you feel like retrieving it later. I'd also be happy to sit with you and discuss your father's death anytime you feel the need. Death takes its toll on the best of us, you know."

Cole wiped the sweat from his forehead, starting now to get irritated with the man's superficial formality. Teller County was nothing if not superficial.

"Yes sir, it does. I'm just saying that if you need someone to talk to, the entire congregation at Rose Meadows is here for you. Accidents like these are…challenging for the family. I spoke to your father's foreman over at Ambrose, and he assured me your father was a professional man who will be missed on the job. Even the best workers sometimes make mistakes."

Cole took a last pull on his cigarette and put it out on the bottom of his boot. Chester would have just tossed it off among the gravestones. "I appreciate the thought," he finally said. "Really, I do. Chester was a lot of things, but I'm not sure missed will be one of them."

Cole pulled the dented truck door open and climbed into the cab. He unscrewed the cap on a half-empty Dr. Pepper bottle and put the cigarette butt in, then screwed it back on. Calvin Roach set the flower arrangement down on the hood of the truck and dug out a business card from his wallet before starting in again.

"I understand you must be grieving, Mr. Quick. If you decide you have some things on your mind, I'd be happy to listen to them. I hope to hear from you."

He handed Cole the card through the open truck window, then lifted the arrangement off the hood.

"Take care," Cole said as he fired up the truck's engine and shifted into gear. He drove slowly past the rows of gravestones around the cemetery's circular driveway and out under the wrought iron gateway, turned east down Highway 19 toward the thirty-acre farm where Chester Quick had raised him.

He scanned the stations on the radio as he drove, trying to remember call signs ten years removed from his mind. He tuned to 97.5 to find that the local classic rock station hadn't changed. The first notes of La Grange came through the speakers and he turned up the volume.

Back when he was a teenager he'd driven this highway drunk and high so many times it was a wonder he'd lived long enough to escape this place without wrapping the truck around a pine tree. As he drove he noticed that half the pristine pasture he remembered had either been chopped into housing developments or was now littered with oil derricks pumping the day away to make one of the local oil companies like Ambrose Oil richer.

It had always amazed him that people hoarded more than they could spend in a lifetime while their neighbors all but starved not two farms over. It came as no surprise they had to steal or deal drugs to support their families. He'd once done the same when left to fend for himself.

As the drums kicked in on La Grange, flashing red and blue lights appeared in his rearview mirror. He wondered how long the officer had been back there. His heart beat a little faster as he drove another quarter mile before finding a safe spot to pull off on the shoulder of the two-lane highway. He dropped the transmission into park and shut off the engine.

The cruiser's door opened in the truck's side-view mirror. A stout sheriff's deputy with a thick black beard got out and shut the door behind him. His boot heels echoed off the asphalt as he approached the truck. Cole kept his left hand on the wheel as he fished in the visor above him for his expired insurance card and license.

"License and insurance," the deputy said when he got to the window.

"Is there something I did, officer?" Cole said. "I don't think I was speeding or anything like that."

"Get your license and insurance out, and shut your goddamned mouth." The deputy's hairy face showed no emotion with his eyes hidden behind mirrored Ray-Bans.

Cole handed over his license and insurance card. The deputy, Desmond Charles by his nametag, raised his glasses with the tip of his index finger and studied the license.

"Mr. Quick?" he asked.

"Yes sir. That's me."

"Is this address in Grand Junction, Colorado, current?"

"I moved out before I came down here for my daddy's funeral. You just caught me leaving the service, actually."

"Mr. Quick, go ahead and step out of the truck for me." Deputy Charles pulled the exterior door handle and the truck's door swung open.

"What's this all about?"

Without responding, Charles grabbed him by the collar and yanked him out the door. He landed with a grunt on the hot asphalt.

"What the hell—" Cole started to say, but Charles kicked him in the ribs before he could finish the sentence. Cole wheezed for breath and rolled to his knees. Charles snatched him up with a headlock and slammed him face-first into the truck's doorframe. A small cut opened above Cole's eye. Blood dripped down his cheek. Charles twisted Cole's right arm around his back and attached cuffs to his wrist, then did the same with the left.

"What the hell's going on? What'd I do?" Cole gasped as jolts of electricity shot up his right shoulder. Charles lifted up on the handcuff chains from behind Cole's back.

"Move," he said. "Now."

Cole put one foot in front of the other toward the cruiser, every step searing the nerves in his shoulder. Charles opened the rear door and pushed down on Cole's head to force him into the back seat, then slammed the door behind him. Blood trickled down the side of Cole's face. He tried to wipe it with his shoulder.

"The prodigal son has returned," a familiar voice said from the front seat of the cruiser. "Cole Motherfucking Quick. How you been, Cole?" Big Zach Ellis turned his gigantic torso and looked Cole in the eyes like a dog he was trying to intimidate. "Folks round here was starting to think you might have died. Or maybe that was just wishful thinking on my part."

Cole exhaled a deep breath and let himself sink back into the cruiser's worn leather seats.

"You thought I wouldn't notice you coming back for your daddy's funeral, is that it?" Big Zach grinned and shrugged like they were having a casual conversation that had nothing to do with the seventeen thousand dollars of stolen cocaine Cole owed him for.

"Listen, Zach, I'm sure you're angry," Cole began.

Zach cut him off. "Cole, if you think angry is all I am, you've lost your fucking mind."

"I got robbed, man. And I got scared. I shouldn't have run, but I was young and stupid. Hell, it's been thirteen years, man. I ain't the same person I was then."

Zach's smile flexed into a snarl. "You better start talking more sense than that or you ain't ever gonna be the same person again, either. Surely I don't have to tell you what kind of shit you've stepped into coming back here."

Cole considered his situation before he replied. "I guess you're going stronger than ever if you got a Sheriff's deputy driving you around to do your dirty work. How's Bobby, anyway? I saw he was playing ball down at UT and almost went pro before he got in that accident. Saw some other controversy with him and Troy on the news a year or so back. He still work for Jack Gables like you?"

Zack frowned, which made his cheeks sag. He didn't look all that much older after thirteen years, but somehow he looked meaner. Rumor had it he'd done some hard time.

"I'd be careful whose name you put in your mouth," Zach said. "It might rot your teeth out. I did five years down in Huntsville and never once said that name out loud to anyone, now here you are spitting it out like a sunflower seed, not caring if it breaks some of your teeth."

Cole exhaled. He needed to cool it, but his temper was starting to get the best of him. "Listen, Zach," he started, looking for words that would keep his body out of a ditch. "I know I fucked you over when I left, and I realize I owe more than y'all are likely to let me pay back. That is what it is, words won't change it. For what it's worth, and I know that ain't much, I reckon I made you ten times that number in the time we worked together. But I get it. If you're gonna kill me there ain't much I can do or say about it. You've got me dead to rights and a damn good reason to do it. That won't get you paid though, right? So I'm thinking, maybe we can make a deal?"

"First of all, watch your fucking mouth, Cole. In a perfect world I'd be pulling your teeth out one at a time with a pair of pliers right now, no conversation required. But I've got orders and they mention you by name. Consider it a favor that I'm letting you know that much. In return for that favor you're gonna sign over the deed to your daddy's farm to my associates once your inheritance comes through. That won't keep you alive all on its own, but it's a start, which is more than you've got now."

Cole blinked. He hadn't even considered Chester's farm yet. Even knowing he was Chester's only living relative didn't give him much confidence that Chester would leave him the farm, especially after Cole had left town without saying a word. He leaned forward and wiped the blood from his cheek with his shoulder again before he spoke.

"Chester's farm...What in the hell would anyone want with that dump? And anyway, Lord knows if Chester even left the farm to me, Zach. I thought folks might have noticed over the years how much he hated my guts. He might have gambled that thing away years ago for all I know."

"You better hope he left it to you, Cole. The only reason you ain't on your way to the bottom of Lake Strongbow right now is someone important thinks he did. The meter's been running on your life. That farm's a drop in the bucket of what you owe. I've got it on good authority that he didn't gamble it away. Consider this your lucky day."

"What in the world would y'all want with some raggedy-ass redneck farm? Chicken bones all over the back yard and bunch of junk scattered all through the weeds. Hell, I don't even want it." Cole laughed at the memory of his stubborn father throwing chicken bones outside, yelling off the porch that he hoped every coyote in the county choked to death on them.

"I want what's owed me, but I owe other people first. Besides, ain't nobody got to look at you twice to know it's all you've fucking got. Much as it would please me to crack your head open and see what you been thinking about all these years, I've got orders. They're giving you a week to settle your affairs and sign the farm over, otherwise you're shit out of luck. Understand Cole, there's eyes all over you everywhere you go in this town. You try to run off this time you won't make it past the county line. Things have changed, Cole. Nobody fucks around with lowlifes like you anymore. Pay up and see if you can put the past behind you. Your other options ain't too good."

Zach motioned to Deputy Charles and the lawman opened

the cruiser's back door. Cole managed to stand up, his right arm numb now from the cuffs. Charles turned Cole around and slammed him over the trunk. He unlocked the handcuffs and Cole shook out his arms, the right one so stiff it wouldn't bend back straight.

"I'll be in touch in a few days, Cole. Settle your business and be ready to sign when I come calling." Charles shut the door and got back in the driver's seat. The cruiser's rear tires kicked up loose gravel on Cole as it sped off down the highway.

Cole dusted himself off and climbed back into his truck. He lit up a cigarette and dug under the seat for the bourbon he kept there. He took a generous pull and wheezed the heat out through his teeth, then replaced the flask where he found it. As he shifted the truck into drive a black Mercedes SUV he'd seen parked back at the cemetery pulled up beside him and stopped in the middle of the highway as if it were a parking lot. The sun's reflection in the passenger window kept him from seeing who was inside at first. The reflection faded off as the window lowered.

"Cole Quick. The man, the mystery, all grown up."

Cole leaned out of the truck's window and squinted.

"Mr. Calvert?" Cole shifted back into park and sat back. "How are you, sir? How's Jimmy?"

James Calvert leaned farther across his passenger seat to speak. "I'm all right, I guess. Old. I heard about your father dying. I'm sorry for your loss."

"Not necessary, but I appreciate it. Glad to see you. I was planning on looking Jimmy up while I'm in town."

"Well then, we probably ought to talk, but I need to get off this highway. You free right now?"

"Actually, I was about to stop in down the road at Vernon's Barbecue for some food. You wanna follow me down there and catch up over lunch?"

"That's the black barbecue joint down the road here another couple miles?"

"Yes sir, it is."

I've heard for years that he's got the best brisket in the county, but I've never been in myself."

"Sometimes there's some rough folks in there, but you heard right about the food. Unless he's slipped since I've been gone. I'll meet you down there. I haven't heard a word about Jimmy in years."

James Calvert nodded. "I'll meet you down there," he said.

The window slid back into place as the Mercedes pulled away. Cole massaged his temples and marveled at how fast the past was catching up with him now that he was back in Teller County. He put the truck back into gear and waited for a minivan coming over the hill to pass. He pulled out onto the highway behind it.

He'd only regretted two things about leaving Teller. One was leaving Jimmy behind, the other was not saying goodbye to Vernon and Millie Miles. If he had to get sucked back in with Zach Ellis, at least he got to reach out and try to make things right with them. He hadn't dared to contact them when he and Kerrie left all those years ago, in part out of fear they might get dragged into his mess with Zach, but also because he'd been worried that word would get back to Kerrie's parents, and they would stop her from leaving with him. It all seemed so long ago. Especially now that Kerrie was dead and gone.

CHAPTER TWO

"I figured you'd turn up, but I don't believe my damn eyes," Vernon Miles said as he moved out from behind the dingy barbeque restaurant's counter and pulled Cole into a bear hug that lifted him off the ground. "That really you, Cole?"

The corners of Cole's mouth turned up as Vernon released him. He stepped back.

"I suppose it is, Vernon. How you been?" Cole inhaled a deep breath of the familiar smell, a mixture of smoked meat, grease, and stale beer. Vernon looked mostly the same, except the lines in his dark leather skin had dug in deeper. The tattered and stained white apron he wore could have been the same one, though. He'd always been bald in the time Cole had known him.

"Shit. Nothin' ever changes 'round this place," Vernon said. "Folks comin' and goin', dyin' out."

He grinned and leaned back against the counter. He looked past Cole to James Calvert, who still hung back near the restaurant's entrance, looking out of place in his suit jacket, pressed jeans and shiny cowboy boots. Stockier than Cole remembered him. Chester had always called that type of getup a Texas tuxedo, said you couldn't trust a man dressed that way. In truth it was Chester himself who couldn't be trusted, though Cole had never had the courage to say that to his father.

"Who's your friend? He don't need to be shy, ain't nobody

gon' bite him," Vernon said.

"Vernon, this is James Calvert. His son Jimmy is an old friend of mine."

"I remember Jimmy, used to come in with you late nights lookin' for a hot plate. A pleasure to meet you, Mr. Calvert. My condolences about your son. Terrible business that was."

Cole shifted his eyes to James Calvert. "What's he talking about, terrible business?"

"Let's have a seat, Cole," Calvert said. "And thank you, Vernon."

Vernon's grin faded like he'd spoken out of line. "I'll bring you fellas over a pitcher of Shiner on the house. You want me to fix you up a Hunger Hanger, Cole?"

"I don't think I've ever eaten anything else off your menu."

Vernon laughed. "Yo daddy was the same way with my pulled pork. Drank himself under the table here every night for fifteen years, never even tried nothing else. I know you probably don't want to hear it, but I'm sorry about Chester, too, Cole."

"Yeah, well, Chester wasn't much for change, unless it was in his pocket. I'm not all that sorry."

"I know you ain't, and that's all right. What 'bout you, Mr. Calvert? Can I get you some food?"

"No thanks, Vernon, I already ate."

"Suit yourself." Vernon headed off toward the kitchen. Cole and James Calvert settled into the same corner booth in which Cole had spent countless hours of his childhood. The grout between the table's patterned tiles was stained maroon from spilled barbecue sauce, and the brown leather seats had cracks and tears in the same places. It gave Cole the odd feeling that he might have been in only yesterday.

The table's familiarity after ten years away stung, like he'd missed out on something he couldn't quite pin down. It brought back memories of the nights he'd spent hunkered down in that booth eating Hunger Hangers, waiting for Chester to drink himself into a sufficiently passive state to be helped to the truck and driven home. Chester might have been a drunk, but he never drove afterwards. It had been maybe his only rule. When you worked for a big company like Ambrose, a DWI meant unemployment, and for all Chester's faults he'd never missed a day of work in his life. The man had been too stubborn to get hung over.

The rest of the place hadn't changed much either. Smoke-stained walls with old beer signs nailed to them in some parts, covered by sheet metal in others. Random rusted tools mounted like pictures at various intervals. A few neon signs advertising Shiner Bock, Budweiser and Lone Star.

Vernon had a thing for carrying Texas beers, though if you asked most people they would tell you it was Millie who really insisted on it. The two pool tables at the back of the big open room had stained-glass light fixtures hanging over them, which cast the players in a colorful light while they bet their workweek away on games of 8-ball.

"What was Vernon talking about when he said 'terrible business,' Mr. Calvert?" Cole said.

"Please, Cole, call me James. We're both grown men," James Calvert replied.

"All right, James. What's going on with Jimmy?"

Calvert exhaled and sat back into the booth's ripped red cushion. "He's dead, Cole. I wish I had something better to tell you than that."

Cole sucked in his breath. "Dead?" He tried to digest the word, and what it meant. "When? I hadn't heard anything about that."

"Considering you dropped him like a bad habit when you left town, that doesn't surprise me. It ain't pretty, either."

"I didn't drop him, at least not like you're making it sound. I had no other choice but to get out of town. I thought contacting Jimmy would just pull him into my mess. Wasn't anything to do with him. He was always a good friend."

"So you're saying you left him here to circle the toilet bowl alone for his own good?" James crossed his arms in front of his chest.

"Look, it wasn't like that," Cole said. "We were both out of control, partying all the time. I got tangled up in a mess that the only way to untangle was to get out of town and stay there." Cole crossed his own arms, felt the weight of truth in his long lost best friend's father's words.

"That business with the deputy back there have anything to do with what you're talking about?" Calvert asked.

"Unfortunately, yeah." Cole shook his head, having one conversation out loud and another entirely in his mind. "I can't believe Jimmy's dead," he added. "You said it wasn't pretty. What's that mean?"

"The neighbors found him dead of a gunshot wound to the head. You ever know a girl named Caroline Ambrose? Her father Tim owns Ambrose Oil?"

"I bet everyone in town knows the name. Chester worked for them most of my life. I never knew Caroline though. How old is she?"

"Twenty."

Cole whistled. "He never did see the value of a woman his same age, I guess."

"Jimmy never saw the value in a woman who wasn't out of her damn mind." Calvert rapped his knuckle on the table for effect.

"Doesn't sound too far off, I guess."

"Anyhow, she's dead too. Her body was strung up like a deer carcass from a pine tree out back of our lake house. Jimmy's was on the ground right next to it. Her body had been…mutilated, I guess would be the word. Sheriff's detectives said Jimmy must have strung her up in a drug-induced rage, then shot himself when he come down."

Cole swallowed hard in a dry throat as Vernon arrived with the pitcher of Shiner Bock and two pint glasses.

"There you go, gentlemen," he said, setting the pitcher on the table before wandering off to attend to other customers. Vernon had always had a good sense of when to interrupt and when to move on.

"When did all this happen?" Cole asked. He poured beer into the glasses, then took a big pull off his own glass to clear the lump in his throat.

"About a month ago." Calvert paused, as if considering what to say next. "Jimmy was messed up, but I don't think he could have done what they're saying he did, Cole."

Cole took another drink of beer. "Drugs do crazy things to people," he said, digging his pack of cigarettes out and stuffing one between his lips.

James Calvert eyed the cigarette, but said nothing. "I know that, Cole. There's more to it, though. About six months ago I had the trustee on Jimmy's trust cut him off. He was killing himself drinking and drugging, and the Ambrose girl made good company for it. Her folks did the same thing to her, too. She was the Rose Queen last year, and from what I heard, her behavior at the festival embarrassed damn near everyone in town, not to mention her father. He cut her off, but unlucky for the both of them, she had Jimmy to fall back on."

"What happened at the festival?" Cole asked.

"I don't know, exactly. I moved to a ranch out near Crockett five years ago, so everything that happens around Teller I get secondhand. I heard they had to throw her in the pool to sober her up the morning of the parade, and had to have a bucket on the float for her to puke in. Imagine that. Girl in a fifty-thousand-dollar handmade dress getting vomit all over herself, shooting the finger at the crowd between heaves."

"Sounds like a good start to me," Cole said. "There's lots of people around here I'd like to give the finger to myself."

"Be that as it may, I heard the scene she made really upset her father. He had to be taken to the hospital afterwards with chest pains. Imagine how he must have felt when he found out his daughter died that way."

"I'm sorry, James, I really am." Cole took another big gulp

from his beer. "It doesn't ring true to what I know about Jimmy, but I'll tell you firsthand, people can get pretty far out there on some cocaine." Cole refilled his glass from the pitcher and set both on the table in front of him.

"Jimmy couldn't have done this, Cole," Calvert said. "I think someone killed them and made it look like a murder-suicide. From what I can put together, Jimmy and Caroline might have run up a massive drug debt with someone."

Cole watched what he said now, careful with his questions. "Even if he ran up a debt, why would anyone want to kill him before he paid? I can tell you from my own situation that isn't usually how it works."

Calvert leaned his elbows on the table. "I don't know," he said, "But I intend to find out. I have a confession to make. I didn't run up on you by coincidence back there on the highway. I followed you from the cemetery."

"I figured. I was pretty sure I'd seen your car back at the cemetery, that reflective tint really stands out."

"I wanted to catch you there but I lost my nerve when I saw how small the crowd was. It was a lucky guess that you'd be there at all. Truth is, I need your help. I was hoping you'd maybe be willing to poke around a bit, ask some questions in your old running circles. See if you can figure out where Jimmy was getting his dope, how much, that kind of thing."

"I'm not sure that's a good idea," Cole started, "I've got a few debts myself. I don't think the people I owe want me asking questions about anything that has to do with drugs."

Calvert sighed. "I get it, Cole. I do. But this is important to me. Money's not an issue. How about this. You look into it for me, and I'll pay your debt off, whatever it costs."

Cole raised an eyebrow. "I think you're underestimating how deep my problem is."

"He was fucked up, Cole, but he was my son. I can't explain it, but I know he didn't do this. Jimmy was too much of a coward to shoot himself, for one thing. And he wasn't capable of hacking that girl up that way. I'd wager every last penny I have to prove it. I can't just sit and let my only son's legacy be that of a psychopath."

Cole sat back and put his hands on top of his head as two country boys walked in the front door and over to the counter. Could have been the same people who'd hung out there back when he'd left. The only changes he'd seen in Teller so far were nothing and no one.

He agreed that Jimmy wasn't the kind of guy who could cut up a girl. For all his loud mouthing and showing off, Jimmy had always shied in the opposite direction from violence. Cole himself had done most of the fighting for the two as teenagers. Even if Jimmy had started nearly all of it. But crazy things happened when drug addicts were involved, and he had his own problems to deal with. It had nothing to do with the guilt he felt about leaving his best friend behind without a word.

"I need some time to think," he finally said, lighting the cigarette between his lips. "I just got into town ten minutes before Chester's funeral. My hope was to get in and out without most people taking notice. It didn't take fifteen minutes for that plan to go to shit."

"I understand. And I'm sorry to dump this on you right after your father's death. Jimmy loved you. I don't think he ever really got over you disappearing like that. If you won't do it for your own benefit, do it for Jimmy. You said yourself he always did right by you. Can you say the same?"

Cole drained his glass and filled it again from the pitcher. Just then Vernon pushed through the swinging kitchen doors with Cole's gigantic brisket and sausage sandwich, set it in front of him.

"There you are, Cole. One Hunger Hanger, extra pickle and onion, just like you like it." Vernon smiled.

"Thanks, Vernon. I've been craving one of these every day for the last thirteen years."

"Well then make sure it ain't thirteen more years before you have the next one." Vernon winked and retreated back to the bar.

"So what do you think, Cole? Can we work this out somehow?" James leaned in on his elbows again.

Cole exhaled smoke and stubbed out his cigarette in a small tin ashtray, still taking everything in. "Like I said, I need to think on it. My life is already in the shitter. I'm not sure I can keep a grip on it and deal with all this stuff."

"I know you and your father had problems. When you run off with the Ferris girl like you did, half the town was talking about it. Nobody blamed you for getting away from your daddy. What ever happened between you and the Ferris girl, anyway?"

"We got married," Cole said. "Had a nice life for a while. Unfortunately, she passed away six months ago. Breast cancer." Cole looked down at the stained table.

"Oh," Calvert said, "I didn't realize. I heard she passed. They used her maiden name in the paper. I assumed you'd split at some point."

"Doesn't surprise me. Her parents hate me more than Chester ever did. They cut her off when we left, then when she died they showed up with a gang of lawyers and took her body away like they owned her. They had a will for her that said she was to be buried in the family cemetery, five lawyers and a coroner saying the same. Nothing I could do."

Calvert held his palms out in front of him. "I'm sorry for bringing it up, Cole. Really."

Cole shook his head. "It's all right. I've been trying to make peace with it every day since. Had about as much luck as I did making peace with Chester, but that's life."

"I understand," Calvert said. "When I got the call about Jimmy, it was like I'd been expecting it. Not *this*, but something bad. I don't know what the hell happened to him."

"There was always something about Jimmy," Cole said. "Like he was waiting to drop an anvil on himself, like in a cartoon. We had that in common for a long time. Maybe we still do."

"He never really got over you taking off like that, Cole. You were one of the only real friends he ever had. How can a boy be so goddamn sociable and still do nothing but make enemies everywhere he goes?"

Cole actually smiled at that, thinking about all the crazy shit he'd seen Jimmy do to the socialites he'd been forced to grow up with. "It's harder than it looks to get out of your own way, I guess," he said.

James Calvert seemed to think about that for a moment. He stood up as if he'd forgotten he had to be somewhere, took out his wallet, threw a twenty on the table, and pulled out a business card. He hadn't even touched the glass of beer in front of him.

"Go ahead and eat your food, Cole, my treat. That's my cell at the bottom of my card. I'm at the Rose City Motel tonight. Heading back to the ranch tomorrow. You decide you want to help me with this, just call or stop in, and I'll gather up cash to cover your debt. Money's not an issue for me. The issue here is Jimmy. I want justice. This county never had nearly enough of that."

Cole took the card and stood up. It struck him as ironic that a man like Calvert would feel like he couldn't get justice in Teller County. In Cole's experience people with money were the only ones who ever did. He didn't mention it. "I'll call you in the morning," he said instead. "Thanks for the meal and the conversation. Take care."

"That might be better advice for yourself." James Calvert turned and strode back out the front door, leaving Cole with a plate of his favorite food but hardly any appetite for eating it.

Vernon came over after Calvert left and sat across from Cole in his place.

"Boy, where you been all this time?" he asked.

"Away from Chester, I guess. A bunch of places. Maybe you, me, and Millie can sit down soon and I'll tell y'all about it. Right now it's been one hell of a rough day and I'm all talked out about the past, no offense."

"I know it has. Was sorry to have missed Chester's funeral.

Millie go down to Huntsville to see Jamal on Saturdays. He been down there 'bout two years now, so I got to cover the restaurant when she there."

Cole raised his eyebrows. "Jamal's in prison? What happened?"

"Aw, you know, drug stuff. I tell you all about it when we get that conversation you promising. Millie gonna lose her mind when she see your face. She asked Chester 'bout you so much after you gone that he liked to have stopped coming in. I had to back her off."

"Trust me, it wasn't anything to do with you and Millie."

"Ain't never thought it was. Listen, I gotta get back to work. Come back and see us tomorrow, Millie be in then."

"Will do, Vern," Cole said. Vernon stood and went back behind the counter. By the time Cole finished his second glass, the place had started to fill up for happy hour, so he poured another. Nothing would befit Chester Quick's memory better than getting good and goddamn drunk, so that's what he decided to do.

CHAPTER THREE

The two-track dirt road wound through the pine trees and sandy loam clearings to the interior of the thirty-acre farm. The Silverado's headlights shone through the brush and reflected off the pine boughs that formed a tunnel overhead, illuminating a few sets of bright red eyes huddled out in the thickets.

These woods had been his kingdom as a child, and he'd filled them with forts and secret places to hide when Chester got drunk and lost his temper. Driving through them he realized they still felt like home in a way he hadn't anticipated.

Beyond the road's final curve, the forested parts of the property gave way to a clearing with a dilapidated ranch-style house planted in the middle, the house where Cole had lived all his life before leaving Teller County in the dead of night. Where the paint had once been chipping, now it had faded into a dull grey color that absorbed the light from the headlights.

Cole switched off the engine but stayed sitting in the truck with the windows down, sticky night air in his lungs. Insects buzzed and called out all around him. He lit a cigarette and blew a chest full of smoke into the cracked windshield. Then another. The smoke coagulated with condensation on the inside of the glass to form a web of white residue. Two pitchers of Shiner deep, he had to squint to try and make out the pattern.

Back in high school he used to hang out in the truck, just like this, dealing dime bags of pot, and then later ounces of cocaine, safe and sound down the long dirt road with Chester passed out cold in his recliner fifty feet away. He'd spent many nights lying in the Silvarado's bed, looking up at the stars with girls, pressing for sex and occasionally getting it, other times getting nothing but a couple wet fingers and a severe case of blue balls.

He'd never brought Kerrie here, though. Not one time. In fact, he'd been terrified that this classy, gorgeous girl, whose parents were the elite of the debutant elite, would run far and fast if she ever met Chester Quick, ever saw the squalor Cole had existed in his entire life.

In the end it hadn't mattered. She'd been just as in love with him as he was with her. She'd had to give up far more to be with him than he'd given up to be with her, and that thought had stuck with him more than ever when she was lying there dying in the hospital.

God, he missed her now. In spite of being a loaner most of his life, he still never could have imagined feeling as alone as he had since she died.

He snagged his duffle out of the extended cab behind the seat and climbed out of the truck. The lone flood lamp above the driveway hadn't worked since he was a boy, but the half-moon above gave enough light to see. He could have made his way onto the porch in complete darkness from memory anyway.

The front door was locked. He searched around the porch for a spare key, knowing there wouldn't be one. He lit his lighter and held it up to the truck's key ring, found the faded gold key he'd almost forgotten he had, slid it into the lock. The door opened with a creak and released the familiar smell of stale smoke and rotten wood paneling.

Cole flipped the switch just inside the doorframe. Chester had never changed the locks, and the interior of the house had received even less attention. The floral wallpaper in the entry hall that his mother had put up when he was five had come off in strips, revealing the dull sheetrock underneath. It surprised him that her presence still radiated from it after all these years, as if the wallpaper, like all the other seeds she'd planted in this house before she passed, had also withered away without her there to nurture it.

The plaid couch at the center of the living room looked like an animal had torn half the stuffing from the cushions. Adjacent to that, the corduroy recliner that Chester had slept in for years after an accident broke four of his ribs sat in two pieces, its fabric frayed at the seams and worn down to holes at various stress points.

Cole tossed the keys along with his pack of smokes on the cracked Formica counter in the kitchen. He opened the fridge out of old habit. A single can of Lone Star and a bottle of Kentucky Deluxe both lay on their sides on the top shelf. The bottom shelf held a brackish jar of dill pickles and an empty bottle of ketchup. He shut the door and moved past the sink full of dishes, through the living room toward the small bedrooms in the back of the house.

He slid past Chester's half-open door as if Chester might still be in there, then continued down the tiny hallway to his own room. The door creaked when he opened it, and a gust of stale air blew into his face. A thin coat of dust covered everything. The room looked as if it'd been sealed the day he left. The same single mattress right on the floor, a crate for a night stand, a small desk in the corner that Chester had picked up off the side of the road when Cole was twelve.

The threadbare baby blue sheets he'd slept on almost his entire childhood still stretched across the mattress. Even his pillow was still there, waiting for his head as if it'd only been a night since the last time he slept here. He dropped the duffle on the floor and sat on the edge of the bed to pull his boots off. He was out cold as soon as his head hit the dusty pillow.

* * *

Cole awakened in the morning to a rooster crowing on the next property over. A thin shaft of sunlight filtered through the paisley curtains his mother had sewn. He didn't have a lot of memories of her anymore, other than her sitting around sewing all the time. Looking back, it was probably to keep Chester out of her face, though Chester hadn't been quite as bad back then. After she died he'd really gone off the deep end.

Cole sat up and sneezed. His clothes had soaked through with sweat during the night and were covered now in a dust paste. He brushed a salty strand of hair out of his face, stood up and unbuttoned his pearl snap. He took it off and peeled off his jeans with it, then pulled the sheets off the bed and took the whole pile to the utility room off the kitchen, wearing nothing but his tighty-whities.

The washing machine had been pulled out from the wall. It took only a quick inspection for Cole to discover it probably hadn't worked in a while. Knowing Chester, he probably wore everything he had five or six times before taking it to the laundromat. The drainage hose was ripped out of the back of the machine, and the lid had somehow come unattached. From the looks of it, Chester had tried to rig it back on, then given up and delivered the machine a beating instead.

Chester had never been much for fixing what he could just beat the tar out of instead, including Cole. Cole dropped the pile of clothes and sheets on the floor and went back to his bedroom. He dug a towel and his dopp kit out of his duffle, went into the bathroom to take a shower.

The showerhead had been pulled from its mount and the hot water never warmed up. He showered beneath a pulsing stream of water that sprayed from the headless shower pipe. Afterward, he brushed his teeth in front of the cracked mirror above the single porcelain sink.

He was just getting dressed when a sharp knock on the door filled the empty house. He pulled on a fresh pair of jeans and buttoned up a plaid Lou Casey shirt on his way to the door. He opened it just as an Excel Energy truck finished turning around in the clearing. The truck rattled off down the bumpy dirt track out toward the highway. A notice hung from the doorknob that said the house's electricity would be cut off on Friday if the bill hadn't been paid by then.

Chester had almost never paid his bills on time, dead or alive. By the time Cole was in high school he'd started paying them himself just to make sure he didn't come home to no electricity after football practice or after a shift sweeping floors at Crenshaw's Grocery Store Warehouse—before he figured out selling drugs was more lucrative.

He went back inside and picked up his smokes off the counter, came back out on the porch and lit one. The tall grass that had grown up around the house shone with dew.

Before long he was thinking about Jimmy again. In a lot of ways James Calvert had been right: Cole had run off and left Jimmy. Back then he'd been twisted off on cocaine in his own right, just like Jimmy. Jimmy's problem had been that he never ran out of money. Cole's had been that he had so much of it around it was hard not to dip into it all the time.

That is, right up until he got robbed. He'd snorted up or otherwise blown most of the profits by then. In fact, he'd been well on his way to becoming just like his father before he met Kerrie. He'd needed to get away from Jimmy because he'd known even back then that Jimmy would never get straight. His debt to Zach had been just the excuse he needed to leave. He could have worked it off if he'd really wanted. Zach had liked him, he was certain of that.

To this day his mind still went around in circles, wondering what would have happened if he'd just stayed. If Kerrie might still be alive, if there had been some way they might have stayed together and made a home here.

Her parents would never have accepted him, though. He'd been right to think that. But luring her away only to have her die estranged from her family, made him feel like a worthless piece of garbage every time he thought about it. He'd always pushed her to reconnect with them, but she'd always insisted there was nothing in Teller worth returning to. And yet here he was, right back where they'd started. What was it Zach had said? *The prodigal son returned.* He didn't like the sound of that the second time, either.

He'd slid James Calvert's business card into the cellophane of his cigarettes the night before. He pulled it out and studied the letters on the card while he smoked.

He went back into the house and picked up the phone receiver on the wall next the kitchen cabinet. It had no dial tone. Cole hadn't had a cell phone in months. He'd let his lapse after Kerrie died. They'd lived a quiet life these last thirteen years. She'd had her friends from work most places, and he'd gone out for beers with the boys after hard days on the job. But they'd spent most of their time together, put a wall up to everything else in the world except each other. *Introverted love birds*, Kerrie had joked. Now she was gone and he was an introverted lone bird. The loneliness had been consuming him one day at a time ever since.

He snagged his truck keys off the counter and headed back out the door. A mile down the road he stopped at the Nu-Way and grabbed a roll of powdered donuts and a chocolate milk, a ritual he'd repeated every morning back in high school. Chester hadn't given so much as a thought to feeding him once he was able to drive.

He ate as he drove into town and across it toward the north side. Clean streets and businesses gave way to dilapidated old houses and red brick streets that had been built a century earlier. Black faces watched from porches as he cut through the neighborhoods over to Finney Avenue, where the Rose Hill Motel was located.

It was odd for a man like James Calvert to stay in a crack den like that. Cole had always known wealthy people to be cheap, but there was a difference between cheap and squalid. The only thing he could figure was that the motel held close proximity to

Jimmy's house on Lake Strongbow.

Maybe Calvert's instinct was to be somewhat close to the place, even if he couldn't stand to sleep there. Or maybe he just didn't want to run into anyone he knew after what had happened with Jimmy. That was always a likely motivation in a place like Teller.

Calvert's Mercedes was parked right outside room 10. It looked hotter than a mound of fire ants parked in that rundown parking lot. That the windows had not been bashed out and the chrome rims zipped off was as close to a miracle as either of them would probably come today. The motel had always been a magnet for criminal activity.

Cole parked next to the Mercedes and got out of the truck. As he approached room 108 the door opened and James Calvert emerged.

"Cole, glad you decided to come," Calvert said, as if he'd been waiting on Cole. "Hotter than hell in these crappy rooms. I was just headed out to grab a bite to eat. You had breakfast?"

"Sort of. Ate some powdered donuts on the way over."

"Well hell, that's no kind of breakfast. Why don't you let me take you out?"

"I'll come sit with you, I guess." Cole shifted his weight from one foot to the other, never comfortable feeling like he was doing or being done a favor. "Let me ask you something," he added. "Were you serious about what you said last night, paying my debt if I ask around about Jimmy for you?"

The plastic smile on Calvert's face darkened. "Serious as a heart attack, Cole."

"It's a big number. Probably bigger than you think."

"I doubt it. I figure it had to be big for you to run off and leave your entire life behind."

"Wasn't just for that. Anyway, we're talking *seventeen-thousand* big. Still interested, knowing that?"

Calvert whistled. "I see why you ran. I can swing that, but I need assurances you'll do what I'm paying you for and not just run off again."

"I'm not a thief. Way back when, I got robbed and I got scared. That's the main reason I ran."

Calvert frowned. "Jimmy said you were up to your eyeballs with trouble. You don't mind my asking, who was it you got into a jam with?"

"We can talk about it over breakfast," Cole said.

"Atta-boy. Why don't you follow me to Jenkins's, over on Front Street."

Calvert climbed into the Mercedes SUV. Cole hopped back into his truck and followed him out of the parking lot onto Finney Parkway.

Jenkins's was tucked in a choppy asphalt parking lot across from the drainage ditch that had run down the middle of Front Street for the last fifty years. At one time Jenkins's had been a mainstay in Teller, but that was back before white flight had migrated south and left everyone that remained, including a few longtime businesses, to flounder. Now the faded-brick façade had chips and cracks in the paint, and there were three cars in the parking lot at a prime breakfast hour.

Calvert parked at the back of the parking lot away from the entrance. Cole eased the Silverado into a spot right in front of the restaurant. The oppressive late-summer heat had jumped at least ten degrees between the motel and the restaurant. Cole waited by the front door as Calvert made his way across the parking lot.

"You need some exercise or something?" Cole called out.

"Don't want people chipping my doors," Calvert replied.

Cole shook his head and led the way inside the restaurant. A woman with frosted curls that hung to the collar of her plaid waitress uniform nodded as they stepped up to the cashier's counter.

"Be with y'all in a minute," she said.

The restaurant had a line of beige booths against the front window and tables of various sizes scattered evenly across the cracked linoleum. Worn-in industrial carpet covered the dining-room floor. An old man in overalls and his wife, who looked to be fresh from the beauty shop, occupied the booth in the far front corner. They each had a plate full of biscuits, gravy, bacon, and eggs. Against the far wall adjacent to them were two buffet carts filled with various breakfast items where an almost-identical couple stood filling their plates.

"Ma'am, do you think we could grab this one?" James Calvert put his hand on the waitress's shoulder as she passed and indicated the booth closest to them. The waitress looked at his hand but didn't move to shake it off or correct him. She sighed.

"I don't see why not."

"Thank you." Calvert slid in so he faced the front door. Cole took the seat across from him and leaned on the table with his hands folded.

"Get y'all something to drink?" the waitress asked.

"Sweet tea."

"Coffee and water," Cole said.

"Be right back." The waitress wandered off toward her station.

"So, you were just about to tell me whose meat grinder you got your ass stuck in, before hunger overcame your better judgment."

James Calvert looked Cole dead in the eyes now. Cole put his palms flat on the table and leaned back.

"I'm not totally sure it's something I should talk about in public," he said, looking around. "Let's just say my trouble is likely to have ears around town."

"Anybody Jimmy would have known?"

"I never introduced anyone to my supplier when I was selling. In fact, they forbid it. But these guys have a bit of a reputation anyway, so yeah, you and Jimmy probably both know them." Cole looked around again. "You ever hear of a guy named Big Zach Ellis, big ol' country boy?"

Calvert looked around, too, before he answered. "Matter of fact, I have. Bastard son of Walter Burnell, right?"

"That's right."

"I went to high school with his half-brother Troy. Every single one of them Burnell boys was trouble. The rumor was always that Zach's momma was a hooker who dropped him off on Walter's porch at thirteen and disappeared."

"Well then, it won't surprise you to learn that he took to the family business." Cole lowered his voice even more. "It's always been rumored that they got Jack Gables backing them up, too."

"Wouldn't surprise me. I didn't trust his department's investigation of Jimmy and Caroline's murders as far as I could throw the husky son of a bitch. He's always had a rotten reputation. Almost got rolled up in some crazy drug deal gone wrong with a Texas Ranger about a year and a half ago, actually. Troy Burnell got himself dead in the process."

"I saw that on the national news," Cole said. "You got any idea how Jack Gables squirmed out of it?"

"No evidence, I guess."

Both men sat back as the waitress returned with their drinks and set them on the table.

"Y'all can help yourself to the buffet whenever you get a mind to," she said.

They both nodded and thanked her. Cole waited until she was out of earshot to continue.

"The Burnells are like redneck mafia, always have been."

"I remember that Troy's uncle Ricky did some time back in the seventies, but nobody ever knew why. That family has a way of controlling all the information about them, if you know what I mean."

Cole did. "Trust me, I do. I used to go out to their pool hall out on Teller County Highway to pick up my stash. I'm pretty sure they had coke and a whole bunch of other stuff coming in and out of Troy's ranch by the semi-load, though I never saw any of it. I can tell you I've seen Zach pistol-whip a man unconscious more than once."

"You said you got robbed, what happened to you?"

Cole sat back. He didn't want to think about that time anymore after the last few days. He sighed. "My stash disappeared from my house. Honestly, I was partying so hard back then that I started sucking most of the profits up my nose anyhow. After a while I didn't have the money to re-up anymore, so Zach started fronting me. I got my shit together after I met Kerrie. I needed money, so like an idiot I convinced Zach to cuff me one last big re-up. It almost worked. I sold everything off and had a good pile of money to go on stashed in this compartment under my dresser where I'd stashed everything for years. Came home the next day and it was gone. Dresser moved back into place and everything, just no cash."

Calvert wiped his mouth with a napkin, swallowed a big bite of food. "Ever get any idea who took it?" he asked.

"I knew right away who took it. It just didn't matter, because first thing he did was twist off to the boats up in Shreveport and gamble it all away."

"You mean your father?"

"Yes sir."

"He admitted it to you?"

"He didn't have to. My money disappears, and he disappears along with it, don't show back up for three days. Meanwhile I'm sweating it hard, trying to figure out what to do. We never spoke a word about it, but I know it was him. I left the day after he got back. Never saw him again, as it turned out."

Calvert shifted in his seat as if it had become uncomfortable. "That's quite a tale," he said. "Where'd you go when you run off?"

"Colorado. And New Mexico, a little bit. Worked some farms up in Paonia, took work at ski resorts, that kind of stuff. I've damn well done every kind of job you can think of by now."

"Let me know if y'all need anything," the waitress said as she passed by their table.

"Guess we ought to eat before she worries herself sick," Calvert said.

Cole followed Calvert over to the buffet. Calvert loaded his plate up with two biscuits, several sausage patties, and a scoop of eggs, then poured two ladles of country gravy on top of it all.

Cole took four pieces of bacon and a scoop of scrambled eggs, opted for toast with gravy instead of a biscuit. They sat back down and dug into their food.

"So, what exactly would you need me to do on this Jimmy deal?" Cole asked, his mouth half-full of toast and gravy.

"Talk to some old acquaintances. Buy some drinks. Rekindle some old friendships. Maybe see if you hear anything about who Jimmy was getting his dope from, or if there was some other nonsense he got tied up in that the police don't know about."

"And there's no way Jimmy could have done this thing?" Cole asked. He hated to do it, but he needed to know what the man really thought.

Calvert frowned. "I knew my son, Cole. If anything, he was too soft to do something like that. He hated fishing because he had to handle the fish. He just about fainted at the sight of blood the time I took him hunting. Jimmy came out of the womb as neurotic and picky as any person who has ever lived."

"Is it possible he just lost his mind with jealousy?"

Calvert sighed and put down his fork. "Anything's possible, Cole. But you didn't see the crime scene. There's something animalistic about it that doesn't make sense to me. It reeked of cruelty in a way Jimmy wasn't capable of. Whoever did it must have hated that poor girl."

"How so?"

"I don't know how to explain it. I'll take you over to the lake house after this so you can see the house for yourself. I haven't moved a thing. It's…strange. My lawyer got me copies of the crime scene photos through a lady friend at the Sheriff's Office. You can have them, if you want to see them. I've got copies at home in the safe." Calvert shoveled the last of his biscuits and gravy into his mouth without saying anything else. Before long he stood and headed back to the buffet to fill his plate again.

CHAPTER FOUR

The lake house was mostly how Cole remembered it, same contemporary country furniture and decorations, same vaulted ceilings in the living area. Same pine trees looming around the property, though they were even bigger now.

However, most of the furniture had been turned over as if there'd been a struggle. Pictures had been knocked from the walls and smashed on the floor.

"I know I should've had it cleaned up by now." Calvert said. "I just keep hoping there's some sort of clue here that the police missed. My understanding is the Sheriff's deputies weren't here ten minutes before all this talk of murder-suicide started dominating the conversation."

Cole took in the wrecked room. "It does look like they had a fight or something."

Calvert put his hand in the left pocket of his jeans. "You ever see Jimmy lay a hand on anyone? Ever see him break anything in frustration?"

Cole shrugged. "I guess not, no. But maybe he got desperate, or dope-sick. Thought she stole his stash or something. I've heard of people flying off the handle when they get their stash jacked. It sure made me take off."

Calvert sighed. "Maybe. But I don't think so."

"Was there any sign of a fight on Jimmy's body?"

"That's one of the things that didn't make sense. The autopsy showed he'd been hit over the head pretty hard. Cops said she must have fought back when he attacked her. Girl was five-two and Jimmy almost six foot, but they just assume she can hit him with that kind of force right over the top of his skull."

"It doesn't make complete sense, I can see that."

"Goddamn sheriff's detective just shrugged like it had no bearing."

"What if they're right?" Cole met Calvert's eyes and a flash of pain registered in them before the man's poker face kicked back in. "I don't want to think that about Jimmy either, but I'm just saying, *what if?*" he added.

"You can't stand in this house and hear what I'm telling you without at least having some questions, right? The sheriff's detectives refused to even consider the possibility that this was anything other than murder-suicide. That makes me suspicious of the whole thing. You ask me, I think Tim Ambrose wanted to put it to bed ASAP, start making distance from the scandal in double time. People hearing about his daughter getting killed that way makes it hard to maintain appearances. I don't have to tell you that appearances are all that matter to most of the people around here.

"I tried to reach out to Tim about what happened and all I got was a letter from the family lawyer telling me they'd run me out of the county if I ever tried to contact him again."

"You said they'd both been cut off from their trusts. So, her family was aware she had a problem, right?"

Calvert put his hands on his hips and stared at Cole. "Well hell yes they knew," he said. "There's a big difference between knowing and acknowledging it in public. This is Teller County, lest you forget. Randall Harrington up at Bank of Teller was the last trustee on the trust Jimmy's mother and I set up for him before we split. Had three other trustees recuse themselves in one year. I had to dig into Randall's father Don to persuade Randall to cut Jimmy off. The two were buddies, and I'm pretty sure Randall let Jimmy do as he pleased until his daddy stepped in.

"It's a weird choice for trustee," Cole said.

"You know Randall?"

"I knew him a little. Professionally, if you know what I mean. I knew a time where he wasn't much better off than me and Jimmy."

"Maybe he grew up, I don't know. But anyway, Jimmy's using only got worse after we cut him off. That says to me someone was bankrolling his habit. He wasn't seeing squat from the trust, I guarantee you that much. I've known Don Harrington since I was a kid, so he knew I'd make a stink if he didn't stick to it. From the rate Jimmy was spending before I cut him off, six months was enough time to run up plenty of debt, easily. He was heavy into it, and so was the Ambrose girl. This house looks to me like someone was looking for something."

Cole thought that over. A lot of what Calvert said made sense. But none of what he'd shown so far was enough to back his assumption that Jimmy and Caroline were murdered by someone else.

Calvert led him through the rest of the house, which was in much the same state as the living room. Broken lamps and vases, holes busted into the walls at various places. In the kitchen the refrigerator had been dumped over. The more he saw, the more Cole got the feeling that maybe someone *had* been looking for something. Whether that was Jimmy looking for an old stash, a dealer looking for the same, or just a violent fight, Cole couldn't tell.

They went through the sliding glass doors onto the back deck. Sunlight reflected off the lake's glassy surface. Cole's eyes locked onto a bloodstain in the dirt at the base of the pine tree just off the deck. Though he knew some details of the deaths, he wasn't prepared for so much dried blood to still be there. His stomach turned as Calvert watched him take it all in.

"A lot of blood, right? I thought the same thing when I saw it. It looks like someone gutted a white tail. But this is tame.

Wait until you see the pictures. They're horrifying. I'll grab the file from the car before...Actually, what time is it?" Calvert checked the Rolex on his left arm. "You know what? I've got to hit the road. I've got a meeting with a private investigator back on my ranch this afternoon. He's been running down some other stuff for me.

"Come with me to the car, I've also got a key to the place and an opener to the front gates you can use. If you don't have anywhere else to stay, you're welcome to stay here. Can't promise you'll be comfortable, though. I don't think I'd ever be able to sleep in this house again. Way this town talks, I'll probably never sell it either."

"I stayed at Chester's last night," Cole said. "It makes this place look sane, actually. But I'm not sure I can sleep here either."

Calvert nodded as if he understood. "I figured I'd offer. There's one more thing, though. I can't make it back to Teller for a week at least, but I need to pay you. I'll toss an extra five hundred to you if you can drive out to my ranch near Crockett to pick it up tomorrow. That should give you some operating cash. I'll write the directions on the front of the file."

Calvert opened the door to his Mercedes and took a manila file folder off the passenger seat. He dug a pen from the console and scribbled an address across the front, then handed it over to Cole along with an automatic gate remote and key. Cole tried to take the file, but Calvert held onto it.

"Feel free to come and go as you please," he said. "You've got my number. Come by the ranch anytime tomorrow afternoon and I'll have the money for you in cash. This is important, Cole. Consider it a chance to make things right with Jimmy. You've been gone, but people in that scene know you. They might tell you things they won't tell me or the police."

"A lot of those people would rather not see my face."

"Tomorrow you'll have what you need to make amends."

There were some things no amount of money could make amends for. James Calvert probably knew that, so Cole let it be.

As the Mercedes drove back up the winding drive to the road, Cole couldn't shake the feeling that he'd gotten himself knee deep in something serious. Coming back to Teller had been a poor choice, but he'd had nowhere else to go. He had nothing left to lose anyway.

CHAPTER FIVE

Cole wandered a circle around the inside of the lake house remembering times long past. Parties, benders, sexual encounters he'd experienced down on the dock as a teenager.

They'd blown enough money on cocaine to feed a village in Peru for a year. It was hard to imagine that scenario could end any other way than the wrecked, haunted house around him. Jimmy had always been the life of the party, sharp-tongued with plenty of money to do as he pleased. The money had always brought a lot of leaches around. Jimmy just shrugged anytime Cole pointed that out and said, "It's worth it for a good time."

Leaving Teller with Kerrie had been cathartic. Col recognized that feeling only by its absence as he stood in this hopeless place. The night they'd first met, Kerry had asked him why he and Jimmy partied all the time. Didn't they have things they wanted outside of that?

Cole had never considered there could be anything else before she asked. That had been the thing he loved most about Kerrie. She knew how to ask the questions he could never quite ask of himself, and she could do it without making them sound like accusations.

He'd stopped having goals when he quit the football team sophomore year to work as a stock boy at the grocery warehouse. When she asked the question that night, the two of them sitting alone out on the dock, his only goal had been to avoid the ass whippings and constant criticisms Chester heaped on him day after day. After that night his only goal had been making Kerrie his own, and he would have done anything to achieve it.

He walked back into the living room as if he might find something other than the chaos he'd already seen. He tried to recreate the struggle that happened there in his head. He was still trying when the front door's hinges creaked and someone gave three slight knocks.

"Hello?" a female voice called out. "Is somebody here?" The voice had a thick East Texas drawl that radiated a mixture of innocent girlie talk and firm Southern lady. Heels clicked against the granite tile floor in the entry hall.

Cole headed to the hallway to greet whoever it was. As he rounded the corner he almost knocked down the gorgeous blonde headed the opposite direction. Her soft hand caught his forearm to stay on her feet. She wore a short, pleated pink dress, accented at the waist by a white belt with a golden-rose buckle and a tight, white button-down blouse that showed off her assets without exposing them.

"Goodness. You scared the bejeezus out of me," she said, extending her hand. "I'm Mandy Ambrose. And you are? Wait...You're Cole, right?"

"How did you know that?" Cole asked.

She smiled to reveal a mouth full of perfect white teeth. He'd forgotten that about Teller girls. Whether by braces or birth, they all had perfect teeth.

"We went to school together. Well, not *together*. You were a few years older than me. I think you went to school somewhere outside of town or something, right? I never forget a face."

"Now I recognize you. When we were seniors you and some other freshman girls used to come to our pasture parties."

Cole could suddenly picture her at fifteen, put together like she'd been twenty-five, just like the rest of her friends.

"We did. Five bucks a cup." Her blue eyes looked over his

shoulder, deeper into the house. She stayed like that long enough to make Cole feel like he was stopping her from exploring farther.

"What brings you down here, Mandy?" Cole asked.

"The gate up at the road hasn't been open since...Well, you probably know."

Her face shifted, and the bags she'd covered up with makeup showed under her eyes. She looked for half a second like she might tear up, but it passed just as quickly. "I guess I wanted to see if it was as bad down here as everyone says. Why are you here, you casing the place?" She smiled, but it was forced.

"Jimmy was my, well, I hadn't seen him in a long time, but he used to be my best friend. Yesterday was the first time I've stepped foot in Teller in almost thirteen years."

"You haven't missed much. Except, well, *this* obviously. Some friend. Teller hasn't seen a scandal like this in decades. All the little old Sunday school ladies are thrilled."

"I guess I wouldn't know about that. You said Ambrose is your name? So, wait then, the girl who died here, she was..."

"My little sister, Caroline." Mandy's face contorted, then straightened so fast it might not have happened. "Daddy's little girl."

"I'm so sorry for your loss. I didn't make the connection at first. You came down out of curiosity, then, I suppose."

"I don't really know why I came, actually. I just saw the open gate as I was driving by and followed the driveway down without thinking."

"Have you been here before?"

"I've hung out at this house lots of times. Jimmy was always having parties and barbecues out here, and I live right down the road. Caroline met him at one of them, I think. But not since the...well, anyway. So, what brings you back to town?" She changed the subject with the precision of a professional socialite.

"My father passed away. I came to town for his funeral. I ran into Jimmy's dad and he told me what happened. He just left. I wasn't far from doing the same."

"I'm sorry," she said.

"Don't be."

"Still, I am. It's incredible."

"What is?"

"Just, like, what drug addiction can do," she said. "I think I could use a drink now that I'm seeing it."

"I think anybody who comes within fifty yards of this place probably could," Cole said.

"Anything in the fridge?"

"It's been dumped over, so I doubt it."

"You checked the boat house?"

"I haven't checked anything. I've just been thinking back on some old times and looking around."

Mandy's demeanor changed. "You ask me, the whole world ought to forget Jimmy ever existed, after what he did to my sister." She paused as the anger seeped into her tone, seemed to mentally straighten herself up. "I'm sorry," she said after a couple of seconds, "this whole thing has just been really jarring for my family. As you can imagine, I'm still pretty emotional. Apparently embarrassing my family was my sister's unique purpose in life. I never would have thought it would cause something like this, though."

"I assume she didn't think it would either?"

"Yeah, well. She could start a fight in an empty house. Anyway, about the boathouse. There's a fridge down there. Care to join me on the dock? I need some air."

She pushed past him through the house and onto the back patio. Cole turned and followed her out, not really sure why, maybe because of his own recent loss and the mixed emotions it brought with it.

Plus, it wasn't his job to keep her out. Mandy had the same look in her eyes he saw whenever he looked in the mirror. Sadness and anger buried beneath a calm exterior. He had no intention of standing in her way if she wanted to see where her sister had lost her life.

She froze at the sight of the bloodstain, then walked by as if she hadn't seen it. So much for curiosity. Flashes of the struggle that must have happened there mingled in Cole's mind. He wondered if Mandy was picturing what had happened to her sister, too, but she showed no emotion.

Bright fuchsia Azaleas lined the path down to the boathouse. Her slender shape floated down it in tune with the click of her black heels.

Murky brown lake water lapped against the edges of the dock. Bugs buzzed in the grassy shallows at the lake's perimeter. Out on the lake, a couple of old fishermen trawled a slow arc across the small bay, stopping at various spots to cast their lines. Fishing for bass, most likely. Like the main house, the boathouse hadn't changed much in the time he'd been away. The things it held had changed. A fluorescent green-and-black Supra with a tall ski tower had replaced the old Sport Nautique they'd prowled the lake in years ago, but otherwise the same old fishing décor hung from the chipboard walls, same cheesy 1980s poster of a man cutting a blade through glassed water on a fat slalom ski.

A hundred fresh memories flooded Cole's mind all at once. He had a hard time giving context to any one, all of them tiny threads of the fabric that had been his friendship with Jimmy Calvert. He allowed himself to feel the weight of death for a moment, then forced it back down where he'd been keeping all his other feelings since Kerrie had died. It would be disrespectful to reminisce about a guy who might have murdered this girl's sister, and he already regretted having mentioned it at all.

Mandy opened the fridge and came back with two sweating Lone Stars.

"All there is," she said.

"Good with me."

"I'm not much for beer unless it's hot out like this. Makes me bloated. Lone Star tastes like crap either way."

"It ain't so bad," Cole said as he twisted off the cap and took a long pull. "I kind of missed the taste, to be honest."

"Did you miss Teller after you left?"

"Nah. A few people, maybe, but never the place itself."

"Yeah, well, I hope Jimmy wasn't one of them. What he did to my sister was just—"

Cole held his free hand in front of him as if to stop her advance. "Look, I understand how you must feel. I'm not here to defend Jimmy or anybody else. I got plenty of problems of my own."

"You understand how I must feel? Has your little sister ever been carved up like a wild hog so the whole town can talk about it for months afterward? You don't want to know the kinds of things people are saying about my family. Has your family been humiliated in front of everyone they've ever known or respected and had to grieve the loss of someone they loved in the process?"

"I wasn't trying to step on your tail," Cole said, pulling his cigarettes from his back pocket and tapping out a smoke. "Of course, there's no way I can understand."

Mandy exhaled and took a drink of her beer. "It's all right, you didn't do anything. I've just been a mess since it happened, is all. Sorry if I seem intense or bipolar. My father looks like he's aged ten years in two months." She hesitated, as if unsure, then added, "Can I get one of those?"

Cole tapped out another cigarette and passed it over. He lit hers and then his own. Mandy took a long drag on her cigarette and exhaled, coughed a little.

"Thanks," she said, clearing her throat. "I don't really smoke, but yours looked good. You mentioned your father passed, but y'all weren't close. Is that why you've been away so long, to stay away from him?"

Cole took another drink. "You could say that, yeah. And also no. Lot of things I don't care for about this place, never did."

"What will you do now that your father's gone? Is your mother still alive? Where's home?"

"Home is here, I guess. For now. I got laid off a few months ago from my last job back in Colorado. My mom died when I was twelve. Anyway, I've kinda been struggling since..." Cole drained his bottle and trailed off without finishing the thought.

"Since what?"

"Since my wife Kerrie passed away."

Mandy sucked in her breath just an inch, caught herself. "Now I'm the one who can't believe I didn't put something together right away."

"Put what together?"

"It's been so long, I forgot that was you. You ran off and married Kerrie Ferris. That was big-time drama back when it happened, but there's always something new to gossip about. I can't wait until something comes along to replace this scandal, honestly."

"That's true, I did."

"And she died six months ago."

Cole winced, but tried not to show it. "She did. I've been sort of drifting since," he said.

Mandy took a drink of her own. "*Drifting*. My father hates that word. Says it's another way of saying lazy. No offense, of course."

"None taken. I understand what he means. Freedom's nice, but it can get old."

"I suppose it can, if you have any." Mandy finished her beer. Cole looked at his feet as she kneeled down and submerged the bottle beneath the water, then released it and let it sink.

"Listen, Cole, I've gotta go," she said. "It's been nice talking with you, though. I'm hosting a gala for this year's Rose Festival at my house night after tomorrow, and I've got some things to get done for that. Actually, given the circumstances, I think you should consider coming to the party. I live seven houses down from here," she gestured down the lake's shore with her hand, "My house is just around the cove there, the big red brick house with iron gates out front. Gala starts at eight, but be there by seven-thirty if you come."

"Why would you think I should go to something like that?"

Cole asked. They both knew it was well above his station in Teller. Rose Festival parties were something he'd only heard about from Kerrie. He couldn't imagine anyone letting him within two-hundred yards of one, unless he was setting up the tables.

"Because it's being held in memory of your late wife." Without another word, Mandy Ambrose turned and walked back up the dock leaving Cole standing there too dumbfounded to ask any of the dozens of questions that would overwhelm him not five minutes later.

CHAPTER SIX

The rowdy sounds of Vernon's happy hour carried across the full parking lot, getting louder as Cole opened the door and stepped inside. The booths and tables were full of construction workers and roughnecks, men in Carhart overalls wearing sleeveless T-shirts and huddled around pitchers of Shiner Bock and Lone Star.

Vernon was behind the counter taking orders and stringing the tickets up above the window to the kitchen. His wife Millie came out of the swinging kitchen doors with a tray full of baby-back ribs balanced between her hand and her hip. She stopped in place and grinned when she saw Cole.

"Good lord, I don't believe it," she said. "Vernon told me you come by yesterday, but I said he were making it up for sure. Now I see it was me had it wrong. Colton, a grown man back after all these years."

Cole smiled. "Hell, Millie. You know Vernon's never told a lie in his life."

"Now I know you done grown up. Nuthin' but nonsense coming out yo mouth." Millie set down the tray on the end of the bar and wrapped him in her strong, wide frame. When she released him, she held him by the tips of his shoulders and looked him over again.

"It's good to see you, Miss Millie," Cole said.

"And it's sure good to see you, too, Cole. I'm so sorry about your daddy. I been missing you, but that don't mean I wanna see you on terms like these."

"Well, you know Chester, everything was always on his terms."

"Some men ain't got no sense. Don't you be one of 'em, you hear?"

"I hear you. And I'm trying. Seeing your face is worth a hundred Chesters."

"If you trying to sweet talk me into a Hunger Hanger sandwich, you on the right track. Go tell Vernon what you want and grab a seat at one of them tables. I'm busy as hell jus now, but I wanna hear for myself about what you been up to all these years."

"Will do. Thank you, Millie."

"It ain't nothin," she said as she picked up the tray of ribs and waddled off across the restaurant.

Cole stood in line while Vernon refilled a couple of pitchers and took a few orders. Vernon smiled and nodded to Cole when he saw him, but kept working. A few minutes later Cole made it to the front of the line.

"Hey hey, Cole," Vernon said. "I seen Millie already got to you. Hope she didn't smother you."

"Millie? Never. Happiest I've been to see someone's face in years."

"That's cause you ain't married to her." Vernon chuckled. "You want a Hunger Hanger sandwich?"

"You know it. And a pitcher of Shiner Bock."

"You got any other folks with you?"

"Nope. But it's been one hell of a heavy day, and I'm ready to get good and Goddamn drunk."

"You sound like yo daddy when you talk like that."

"Guess I had the right teacher."

"Ain't no count to be like that," Vernon said as he filled up the pitcher.

"So listen, Vernon. Are any of Chester's crazy old running

crew still bouncing in and out of your place?"

"You know. Same-ole, same-ole. There go yo daddy's gambling buddy Sheldon Johnson right over there." Vernon pointed toward the pool table in the back corner.

Sure enough, there was Sheldon, looking not that much older than the baby-faced hustler who could have been mistaken for Cole's age back in the day, years ago, though he had at least a decade on Cole. Sheldon had a crowd of people around him, listening to him talk shit, just like he always did.

Chester had gambled so much money back and forth with Sheldon that it was a wonder one of them hadn't tried to kill the other. Threats had been made, at least by Chester.

The group standing around Sheldon erupted with laughter. Vernon set the pitcher and a pint glass down on the counter in front of Cole.

"I'll be damned. I forgot all about Sheldon," Cole said. "I'm gonna step over and say hello. I'll just be at one of those tables, you and Millie come on over whenever you get a break."

"Will do," Vernon said.

Cole picked up the pitcher and pint glass and wandered over toward the pool tables. As he approached, Sheldon's words came clear.

"I told that bitch, 'not me, I ain't the one to be chasing yo nappy-ass pussy all over town...'" Sheldon noticed Cole and stopped talking mid-sentence. Finally, he said, "Now look at this little white motherfucker right here. If I ain't know better I'd think you Chester Quick's boy, all growed up. But you can't be no dead-ass Chester's son. You too fucking pretty for that."

"Whaddaya say, Sheldon," Cole said. "Been a long time."

"Man, I thought I must of beat yo daddy so bad he sold you into slavery or some shit. Where you been?"

"I guess Chester never mentioned it."

"Hell naw, he ain't said nothing about you. I figured you got away from his crazy ass like everybody else. Only reason I let him around me were cause he so willing to hand over that paper."

Sheldon smiled a big, bright smile, with several silver-capped teeth. "You look just like his stupid white ass."

"I guess I'm fucked then."

Sheldon snickered. "I like your attitude. I were just finishing up with these wannabe pool sharks. They gettin' tired of giving me they checks anyway. You bring that beer over for me?" Sheldon gestured to the pitcher.

"I did if you'll come over and fill me in on what Chester was up to the last few years."

"I done a lot of things, Cole, but keeping up with Chester Quick's bullshit ain't one of 'em. But anyway, I get finished up over here, I'll come over and sit with you."

"So be it. Thanks."

"Thank yourself." Sheldon grinned and winked. He shuffled around the table for his next shot. Two guys got up from the booth Cole usually sat in, so Cole headed over and took their spot. The table still had an empty pitcher, two glasses and two used plates on it. He stacked them at the corner of the table.

He'd already drunk the first pint-and-a-half of the pitcher before Millie brought out the sandwich.

"Here you go, hon. I can't believe how handsome you is, all grown up. You look strong as your daddy ever was."

"Thank you, Millie. Have a seat if you want."

"I let you get that sandwich ate first. Be back soon, though." Millie collected the empty pitcher and dishes on her tray. As she left, Sheldon sauntered over to Cole's table.

"Pour me some of that honky beer you got there," he said, brandishing an empty glass as he slid into the booth opposite Cole.

Cole took it and filled it from the pitcher. "What makes it honky beer?" he asked.

"Shit's expensive and will fuck a nigga up. That what make it honky beer."

Cole shrugged. "Works for me."

"Work for everyone, cause it's true. Now what you wanna

know 'bout yo daddy?"

"I don't know, really. Just, how was he, these last few years?"

"You really ain't talk to him?"

"Not a word."

Sheldon whistled.

Cole shrugged. "I had my reasons."

"I don't doubt that," Sheldon said. He sucked down half his glass before he continued. "He were the same. Bitter. I ain't gotta tell you that. Chester were a man who the sun never once shone on his pasty white ass."

"If you're saying he wasn't a ball of cheer, I agree."

"I'll give Chester's stupid ass this. Motherfucker must have been a tireless worker, the amount of cash he always losing."

"How often did he gamble with you?"

"Two, three nights a week. Y'all white folks love you some cards."

"You think he ran himself broke, or what?"

"I look like a banker?" Sheldon sipped his beer. "He never stopped playing, so I doubt it. Usually motherfucker runs out of money, he don't keep playing long before he get his ass shot off. Even aggressive crackers like Chester."

"Did he mention any debts, anything like that?"

"Nah. He always pay up at the end of the night, win or lose. He straight like that. He act like a piece of shit, but Chester always pay. One thing though. Last couple weeks before he died, he all talking 'bout some big payoff he 'bout to have. Said we was all gon' be kissing his rich-ass feet, escorting him around like Driving Miss Chester or some shit. I just figured he were bullshitting."

"What kind of payoff?"

"Shit Cole, how the fuck I know? He be keepin' his cards close. He was yo daddy, maybe y'all had some cracker-ass relative die or something."

"Chester didn't have any living family, except me."

"Well fuck it then, I guess. All I know is he were shootin' off his mouth 'bout never having to work again. Damn near everybody made fun of his ass behind his back, too. People thinkin' he lost his mind. Don't nobody live happily ever after on this side of town. Specially not Chester Fucking Quick."

Cole took a couple of bites of his sandwich. Millie caught his eye, and he held up the empty pitcher for her. She nodded and moved to fill a new one.

"Now," Sheldon said, taking a deck of cards out of his back pocket, "we gonna piss and moan all night 'bout Chester's dead ass, or you wanna play some cards?"

"I think you've probably had enough Quick money, Sheldon," Cole replied. "Besides, I'm half broke. Thanks anyway for talking with me though."

"Thank yoself, motherfucker. Imma head back over here and shake these bitches down for some more pool money then, if you don't mind." Sheldon stood to head back to the pool table.

"I don't. But Sheldon?"

"Yeah?"

"Did Chester ever try to gamble the deed to his farm, that you know of?"

"Nah. Never that I seen. He were an asshole but he weren't that stupid. 'Round here a nice piece of land ain't nothin' to gamble with, specially a family farm. These rich-ass crackers done bought up or stole all the good land."

"Good talking to you, Sheldon."

"Later, Little Chester." Sheldon strutted over to the pool table again and started to heckle two roughnecks who'd taken it over, both still in their coveralls. Millie brought over the fresh pitcher and two shot glasses of whiskey, along with a single extra pint glass.

"Here you go, Cole. This one on me, but I'm gon' help you with it. Finally got this place under control for the evening. Don't take me wrong, we needs the business. Times been hard. But some nights I feel too old for all this prancing around, waiting on folks. Specially the ones come in here."

"This place never was much but hard times for folks like us."

Millie's face contorted. "Like us? I got love for you Colton, but you obviously ain't looked in a mirror lately."

"I didn't mean it like that, Millie. I know half the folks around here are racists, and most of that is the rich half. I'm just saying for people who came up poor. Seems like no matter how good the money is, we always find a way to give it all back."

"That just life, Cole. Folks everywhere fall all over theyselves giving it back, too."

"Sometimes it feels like the game's so rigged it's hardly worth playing."

Millie raised an eyebrow. "What you mean by that? You depressed or something, Cole?"

Cole sighed. "I don't know what I am. Jaded, I guess. Ready for something else, but that something is already long gone."

"What you been up to all this time?"

"Ran off to Colorado with Kerrie. Got married. Almost got the life I wanted, I guess. But she died."

"Oh, my lord," Millie said, concern now in her eyes. "I'm sorry to hear that, Cole. You loved her?"

"She was just about the only good thing that ever happened to me. Good heart, smart, and gentle. When we were together it was like all the anger inside me dried up. Been about six months now. Might as well have been yesterday." Cole fought back tears, the booze lowering his ability to keep them in check.

"Lost my momma the same way. Hard watching 'em shrivel. Look like God done forgot about 'em at the end."

"Millie, if there's a God, he forgot about us all."

"That sound like Satan talking, Cole. Don't let he get all in your business like that."

"I got nothing against the idea of God. But you don't ask the ant to give praise to the man with the magnifying glass." Cole was starting to get a little intoxicated now, which made his feelings from talking about Kerrie come out sour.

"The ant and the what?" Millie said. "That what you think,

Cole? God taking a special interest in torturing you?"

"Maybe. I don't know."

"Don't you never give up on grace, Cole Quick. Redemption neither. They out there, and they real. But you ain't gonna find 'em lookin' down at your feet."

Cole took a bite of his sandwich and wiped his mouth with a napkin as he chewed. "Maybe you're right. I never got a chance to say thanks to you, as it were."

"Thanks for what?"

"All those nights you looked after me, sat with me when Chester was out of his mind on the booze and pills. Kept him from whipping my ass in front of the entire place more times than I can count. You and Vernon looked after me, fed me, spoke to me with respect. First people I ever met who did that, and it changed me. Y'all treated me like family. I felt awful to leave without saying goodbye, but I just had to go."

"You don't give that another thought, Cole. Life is hard. We help those in need, just like the good Lord said to do. I ain't never faulted nobody for jumping in front of the train if that's what it took to get on board. You done the right thing to get away from Chester. I know he was your daddy, but that man had problems can't nobody ever have fixed."

Millie picked up one of the shot glasses of whiskey and motioned for Cole to do the same.

"We toasting to Chester?" Cole asked.

"Hell no, Cole. We cheersing to you. Welcome back. You always was a good boy, and I always knew you would find a way out of this place."

"How 'bout we toast to you and Vernon, Millie. If I gave you guys a thousand plates of food, we still wouldn't be square."

They both tossed back the shots. Cole chased his with a gulp of beer but Millie's might as well have been water.

"Life ain't about being square, Cole. It's about being happy. You wanna be happy, you got to face yourself every day and tell the truth about what you see. You don't like what come looking back at you, change."

"You think Chester changed after I left?"

Millie frowned. "Nah. Not Chester. He had pain, deep pain. Sometimes the poison run so deep can't nobody suck it back out."

"He was damn good at spreading it around." Cole drained his glass. "Sometimes I feel his venom like I just saw him yesterday."

"That's the stuff can't never be taken all the way out, Cole. We all got it inside us. You got to turn away from the dark if you want to live in the light."

"I know. And I do want to. Or I did, at least. I was *there*, Millie, *right* on the edge of that, until Kerrie died."

"You hush all that talk, Cole. You was a good boy, and you a good man. Everything gon' work out just fine, you'll see."

"I wish I knew what I was supposed to do in the meantime. By the way, did Chester ever mention some sort of big payoff he might have had coming to him?"

Millie sat back in her chair and crossed her arms. "I don't remember it if he did. He was always going on about something, but I never gave much thought to most of it. He were tight as hell most of the time he spent here." Millie sat up straight as a loud noise interrupted her thought.

"The fuck'd you just say to me?" one of the roughnecks over by the pool tables yelled.

He and Sheldon had been playing pool but were now squared off in each other's faces.

"You heard me, motherfucker," Sheldon said. "Now back up out my fuckin face."

The roughneck had a pot belly and greasy grey hair, outweighed Sheldon by at least forty pounds. Sheldon sucker punched him anyway. The man absorbed the punch and flung Sheldon up on top of the pool table, gave him a much harder one in return.

"Y'all take that shit outside, dammit!" Vernon yelled from behind the counter.

They ignored him and continued rolling around on the pool

table. The man's friend swung a pool cue wildly in Sheldon's direction, eventually splintering it on the pool table next to Sheldon's head.

Vernon reached under the counter and came up with a sap, was headed around the counter when Cole sprang to his feet and rushed across the room. Cole caught the one with the pool cue from the side with a straight right to the chin. The man crumpled to the floor and the pool cue's stub rolled across the floor toward Sheldon, who'd managed to get back to his feet.

The roughneck looked up to see what had happened to his friend only to get cold-cocked in the chin with the broken cue. The man hit the floor and was on his way back up when Sheldon brought the broken pool cue down on top of his head, knocking him out cold. Sheldon turned just as Vernon was about to bring the sap down on his skull.

"Easy nigga, easy Vernon," Sheldon said. "We done man, we done. These motherfuckers tried to jump me. It ain't my fault."

"It ain't never your fault," Vernon said. "Maybe if you kept your mouth shut this bullshit wouldn't happen all the time. Now gather your shit and get the fuck up out my restaurant." Vernon turned to Cole. "Boy, you lost your goddamn mind? You gon' get yo head caved in jumping up in some bullshit that don't concern you."

Cole looked beyond Vernon to see Millie with her hand under the counter, where he knew they kept a sawed-off shotgun. "He could've killed Sheldon with that pool cue," Cole said. "I saw that, and I just jumped in without thinking. I'm sorry."

"Well next time think, goddammit. I don't need this bullshit in my place. I run a clean business, least as much as I can. I don't need bodies on my conscience and especially not yours."

Sheldon wiped blood off his lip and turned to Cole. "Thanks, Little Chester. You all right, man," he said.

"It's all good," Cole said. "You ought to check the odds before you square off next time though."

Vernon interrupted them. "You got to go, Sheldon. That's

enough for one night. Pay your bill and get the fuck out." Vernon turned to the last three people still nursing drinks over by the bar. "In fact, all of you get out, we closed."

"I ain't got no ride, Vernon," Sheldon said. "How the fuck I'm supposed to get home? My cousin ain't gonna be here to pick me up for a minute still." Cousin could mean literally any casual acquaintance to Sheldon, but Vernon probably knew that.

"Figure it out, not my problem," Vernon said. "I've about had all this bullshit I'm gon' take, Sheldon."

"I'll give him a ride," Cole said. "I'm sorry. I shouldn't have jumped in. It was instinct, that's all. Let me get him out of here for you, Vernon."

"Shit, I'm glad you jumped in," Sheldon said.

Vernon gave Sheldon a dirty look in return, nodded to Cole. "Go on and get him out of here then. Me and you ain't got no trouble, Cole, I just had enough for today. I mean it, everybody out. Pay your tabs and get gone."

Cole walked back over and dropped two twenties on the table where he'd been eating, poured the rest of the beer from the pitcher and drained it from his glass. Millie leaned over the men on the floor out of curiosity more than caring. They were starting to come to their senses but were still dazed. Cole motioned to Sheldon and headed to the front door.

"Much obliged, Vernon. I'll see you soon," Cole said.

Vernon nodded and turned to Sheldon, tapping the sap against his palm. "Next time you come back here you best have your shit together, understand?" He turned back toward the two roughnecks. "Millie, make sure these gentlemen pay for the pool cue they broke on they way out."

Sheldon grinned a bright smile as he walked out into the humid night.

Cole fired up the Silverado's engine as Sheldon climbed into his passenger seat. A Hank Williams tune filtered out from the truck's speakers as Cole shifted into drive.

"Ain't you got anything but honky music?" Sheldon asked,

eying the radio.

"Put on whatever you want," Cole said.

Sheldon fumbled with the dials as various snippets of music shuffled through the radio. He stopped on an R&B song Cole had never heard before.

"This my shit right here," Sheldon said, bobbing his head as he dug in his pocket for something. He came out with a single house key and a miniature bag of white powder. He untwisted the top, dipped the key down in it and brought it up to his nose with a sniff.

"You want some of this yack, Little Chester?"

Cole eyed the bag. All those years with Kerrie he'd never touched it again. But she was gone, and nothing could bring her back. Besides, it would sober him up for the drive.

"Fuck it," he said, taking the bag and key from Sheldon. He took a few key bumps and handed it back to Sheldon as the faint smell of gasoline wafted over everything and a familiar thundering electricity pumped through his veins to the pulse of the music.

CHAPTER SEVEN

Sheldon lived on the north side of town. They drove past the line of roach motels on Finney Avenue and across Fenton Parkway, which may as well have been the Mason-Dixon line as far as most people in Teller were concerned.

Some of the streetlights had been shot out. Others, perhaps, had burned out without the city bothering to replace them. Even without the lights the streets were still scattered with clumps of people. A cherry burned orange in the darkness between two men standing in the gutter just off the side of the road. Heads turned and tracked Cole's truck as it passed.

"You sure it's all good for me to be over here at night?" he asked Sheldon.

Sheldon grinned, passed Cole back the blunt they'd been smoking, which was now about three-fourths smoked.

"This still America, and you still white, right? Sound like you got a right to be wherever you want."

"Having a right and defending that right are two different things," Cole replied. "It's a piece of shit, but I'd like for this to continue to be my truck for a little while longer."

"Ain't nobody gonna try to steal your old busted-ass truck. You act like this a fucking Lincoln. Better than I got, but that ain't sayin' much."

Cole pulled hard on the blunt and blew the smoke out the

window. The rap song on the radio had been slowed down so that the voices sounded deep and hollow and tired. His heart thumped ahead of the beat from the cocaine, making him feel antsy. The rush was already starting to fade, making him want more.

"Go left up there." Sheldon indicated the turn with a nod as Cole handed him back the blunt. Sheldon pulled on it long and hard, choked once and pulled again, then tossed the last inch of it out the window.

"There my crib, go right there," he said, pointing to a peeling, brown ranch-style house with no lights on and foot-high grass in the front yard. Cole pulled the truck into the driveway and shut off the lights, but kept the engine running.

"Goddamn, Sheldon. You need a machete to get in the house or what? This is as bad as Chester's place."

"Mind your business, Cole. Right now, you all right, don't spoil the shit."

Cole turned down the radio some more.

"Point taken," he said. "Listen. You got any more of that chach I could pick up off you?"

"Ahh, you like that, right? White boys always callin' it chach. You get it from me it called yayo." Sheldon elbowed him in the shoulder. "You just like yo daddy. He loved him some drugs. Any drugs."

"Probably some truth to that. You got anything extra, or not?"

Sheldon smiled. "Hell yeah, I got somethin'. I always be hustlin', Cole. What you want, a gee?"

"How much?"

"Sixty-five. Three for a buck-fiddy."

"You lace it with gold or something?" Cole said.

"Fuck off with that bullshit Chester Quick talk, Cole. You want it or not? I ain't got all night to be sittin' in this truck, and you ain't my type if I did."

Cole got out his wallet and counted out the money, even

though it was most of what he had left.

"I'll take three, I guess. You know I used to sell eightballs for a bill on the nose?"

"Yeah? How'd that work out for you, motherfucker? Times has changed. Call it inflation. Be right back."

Sheldon got out of the truck and sauntered up the narrow, overgrown walkway to the front door. He unlocked the door after some fumbling and disappeared inside. Cole smoked a cigarette and waited, then another. He was thinking about whether he would have to kick in the door and get his money back when Sheldon slipped back outside and made his way back to the passenger window of the truck.

"There you go," he said, tossing three small baggies on the seat. Don't stop at no stop signs on your way back out the neighborhood." Sheldon almost doubled over with laughter as he backed away from the truck. Cole put the coke in the glove box, rolled up the window and backed into the street.

He took his time driving back across town, careful not to exceed the speed limit, stopping behind the white line at every red light. It took twenty minutes to make his way back out the southeastern end of town toward Chester's farm.

He pulled up to the farmhouse almost itching for another bump. He took the flask of whiskey from under his seat into the house with him, found a hunting magazine on the counter in the kitchen and dumped a pile from one of the baggies onto it.

He used a card from his wallet to break down the rocks into lines, forming half of the pile into one long line at one edge of the magazine. He used a rolled-up bill from his wallet to take down the big line, then almost wretched afterwards. His throat went numb as a wave of euphoria rushed over him. New ripples came over him every time it dripped down his throat.

Cole drained the rest of his whiskey flask and lit a cigarette. He got the bottle of Kentucky Deluxe out of the fridge and held it by the neck as he wandered into Chester's old room, heart pumping like an oil derrick.

The bed had filthy sheets half-pulled off to reveal a large sweat stain on the mattress, which suggested that at some point Chester had started sleeping in the bed again.

A hamper full of work coveralls and dirty socks sat adjacent to the bed. The huge oak dresser his mother and father had once shared still sat against the front wall. All the drawers that had been his mothers had been ripped out at some point, and now there were empty spaces where they'd been.

In the closet a few more sets of coveralls hung next to a few old pairs of wranglers and some pearl-snap shirts. A pile of old worn-out boots covered the floor, but otherwise it looked like Chester hadn't bought a single piece of clothing since Cole had left.

Certainly, the same belt he'd always kept was curled up on the shelf. At times, Chester had used it to beat the snot out of Cole almost daily. Cole set the bottle of Kentucky Deluxe on the shelf next to the belt and turned back to the dresser. He found Chester's .40 caliber pistol in the top drawer. San Antonio official police-issue Glock, full clip with one already in the chamber.

Cole turned the pistol over in his hands. He'd forgotten his father had it, could still remember the day Chester bought it at a gun show that came through at The Cotton Coliseum. Cole pointed the pistol at the reflection of himself in the cracked mirror above the dresser.

Sheldon was right. He did look like Chester. In fact, now he could see the same look in his eyes that had been in Chester's since the day Cole's mother died. Back then he'd thought it was hate, but just now he could see it was anguish.

Part of him felt sorry for Chester. Sorry for abandoning his father to this squalid shit heap. He understood in that moment how much his father had been hurting at the loss of his wife.

But Cole had been hurting, too. He'd lost his mother, the person he loved the most in the world until he met Kerrie. Anyway, Chester could have looked out for him. Nothing could make up for the things he'd done in the years that followed.

Especially stealing the money Cole had owed to Big Zach. He'd known right away it was Chester. No signs of forced entry, no way anyone else could have known about his stash spot. After the fact, Cole had actually felt a sort of amazement that it hadn't happened before.

He wondered if Chester had missed him all these years, or maybe regretted the things he'd done to drive Cole away. Probably not.

Cole squeezed the trigger and the mirror shattered. The report made his ears ring in the small space. He squeezed it again, then again, then again. He unloaded the clip into the mirror as glass and splinters blew everywhere. He had to close his eyes to keep from getting glass in them, but he kept pulling the trigger until it clicked. When he opened them there was nothing left of the mirror, and a haze of gun smoke and wood dust hung over the entire room.

He tucked the empty pistol into his back waistband, then ripped the remaining drawers out of the dresser and slammed them one at a time on the floor, stomping them until they were completely flat. He took out his pocketknife and stabbed the mattress right in the center of Chester's sweat stain, then dragged it all the way to the bottom, ripping through springs and fabric in a blind rage, as if to search for the money he knew Chester had taken, as if it would still be stashed there and not sitting in some Shreveport casino's bank account these last thirteen years.

He upended the mattress with such force that it knocked the ceiling fan from the ceiling and left it hanging by the wires. As he prepared to smash the bedframe he noticed a small beige file tucked into a slit that had been cut into the box spring. He pulled it out, opened it up and tried to read what was inside, but the whiskey and cocaine had made his eyes too blurry.

He closed the file and retrieved the bottle of whiskey from the shelf in the closet. He moved out into the kitchen and tried to sit at the table with the file, but he stumbled and turned the chair over, breaking it and spilling whiskey all down his shirt.

He sat up on his haunches on the torn linoleum and drained the last three inches of the whiskey, then stood and took down the three remaining lines of cocaine off the plate. Only the devil could have said what he did after that, because he blacked out.

CHAPTER EIGHT

He woke up soaked at noon, the air inside Chester's house so stuffy that he knew right away the power company had cut off the power. He was naked on the floor of the kitchen, his clothes piled beside him for some reason. His shoulder ached from sleeping with his arm cradled under his head like a pillow. When he sat up, his head rippled in pain.

He stumbled into the bathroom and looked in the cracked mirror. Bloodshot eyes. His nose burned, and his left powder-caked nostril was completely clogged, so much that it took four tries to blow it out into the toilet.

He rinsed his face in the sink, went back in the bedroom and found some new clothes to wear in his duffle, a plain black T-shirt and some boot-cut jeans. He'd planned to get on the road early and retrieve the money from James Calvert out at his ranch. He eyed the folder he'd found the night before, still on the table. He decided he'd look into it after he got back from paying Big Zach.

He dug his sunglasses out of the glove box and put them over pulsing eyeballs so he could check the address Calvert had given him as he pulled out of the driveway.

He stopped at the NuWay and got a cup of awful coffee, a road map, and a new pack of smokes. He lit a smoke and studied the map, figuring out the route down to Calvert's ranch.

He made the two-hour drive with the radio off and the windows down, humid air blowing in his face. He had to stop about an hour into the drive to puke on the side of the highway for a few minutes, aftereffects of the coffee mixed with his fragile stomach.

He wiped his mouth on his sleeve as he got back into the truck and continued on out into the sandy loam countryside spotted with oil derricks pumping in repetitive motion here and there.

He made it to Crockett in just under two hours, where he stopped at a gas station to get more specific directions, then headed west out of town. Calvert's ranch was tucked a couple of miles down a caliche rock road on what looked to be at least several hundred acres, assuming all of it was his.

Cole pulled across a cattle guard and parked in front of a red brick two-story house with a white picket fence surrounding it. The style made it look as if someone had stolen a house out of one of Teller's country club neighborhoods and trucked it out to the spot where it now sat.

Cole shut off the truck and got out. The noon sun beat down on him like a hammer, turned his stomach so sour he almost puked on the front porch as he knocked. He didn't hear anything inside.

He knocked again and waited, dying from the heat. He sighed and sat on a porch swing adjacent to the front porch with his stomach churning and threatening to spill over again.

For once he didn't even want another cigarette, but before long he found himself sucking one down anyway. It made him have to lean over the railing of the porch and dry heave the rest of his stomach into the bushes.

He sat up wiping his mouth with his sleeve to see Calvert's black Mercedes SUV coming down the dusty white road. He waved, but couldn't see whether Calvert waved back because of the glare off the windshield. Calvert's SUV pulled up and parked next to the Silverado. Calvert got out and shut the door, a bank bag in his hands.

"Whadaya say there, Cole? Good timing. Just got back from

the bank." Calvert held up the bank bag for proof, gave him a smile. "You look like hell. Everything all right?"

"I had too much to drink last night, is all. Been sick all morning."

"I appreciate you coming all the way out here in that condition. I don't make it into Teller much anymore. Especially since Jimmy died."

"I understand. Nice place you got here."

"It ain't all that much. The older I get, the less I want to see of people. This was about as far as I could get. I didn't get a whole lot of visitors even when I still lived in Teller. We had the money but not the name for that town.

Calvert unlocked the front door to a small entry hall with dark wood floors. "You'll have to excuse me if I didn't get a chance to clean up inside."

"If you saw Chester's place, you wouldn't bother to bring it up," Cole said.

The hallway opened up to a vaulted living room that encompassed both stories of the house, had a balcony above it. The walls held a mixture of enormous whitetail deer heads and a caribou head so big that the builder probably had to design the room around it.

"Killed that in Alaska about ten years back," Calvert said, noticing Cole eying the caribou. Tried to get Jimmy to go on that trip, but there's a lot of blood when you quarter a caribou."

"I remembered that about him after you said it. One time I saw him cut his hand on a broken bottle and he almost fainted. At the time I thought it was probably the drugs, but it makes sense."

"I killed my first deer when I was young. Six, maybe. My daddy and his brothers wiped its blood all over my face, made me help dress it out." Calvert laughed. "I nicked the stomach with the tip of my knife and the goddamn stink was so bad I thought my father was gonna jack-slap me, damn corn and bile getting all over the place. I never could have tried that with Jimmy. Can I get you something to drink? Iced tea, maybe?"

"Water, thanks. I don't think I can hold anything else down."

He followed Calvert into the kitchen. Calvert took a glass down from the cabinet and filled it with water from a two-gallon plastic jug on the counter.

"Goddamn well water out here is half brackish," he said, handing Cole the glass.

Cole took a sip and followed him back into the living room. Calvert sat down in a leather recliner and kicked his shiny loafers off to reveal bare feet, no socks. Cole sat on a plaid-patterned couch, took another sip of water.

"So," Calvert began, picking up the bank bag from where he'd set it on an end table next to the recliner, "Here's your money." He unzipped the bag and took two stacks of cash out of it, both all in hundreds. "You can count it if you like, but I've got eighteen-thousand in there, plus another five-hundred dollars for a little spending money in case you need to buy some drinks, loosen people up for information."

Cole marveled at the money. It was more than he'd seen at one time in years. "I'm sure it's all there," he said. "I gotta be honest though, I still don't see what I can do for it. I haven't seen or spoken to any of these people in more than a decade."

"See, to me that's an advantage. It won't be weird, you asking them a lot of questions. You'll come off curious, like you're catching up, not snooping."

"I'm just worried I won't come up with anything and you'll feel like you wasted the money. It's a lot, at least for me."

"I have no plans to stop pursuing this thing just because it gets expensive. I realize it's too late to save Jimmy's reputation, but I'd like to at least get this mess off his memory so he can rest in peace."

"So long as we both understand what's what, I'll do it," Cole said.

Calvert nodded and passed the bag to him. Cole counted out five one-hundred-dollar bills and tucked them away in his back pocket. He zipped up the bag, still so focused on the money that

Calvert said something he didn't catch.

"Say what?" he asked.

"You sure are hard up today, I can see that. I asked you to keep me updated on your progress," Calvert said. "Really. No matter how small it is. You've already got my info, but I put another business card in the bag just in case. I pulled some strings and spoke with a P.I. yesterday who used to be a Texas Ranger. I don't know if he'll take the case, but I'll put you in touch if he does, in case he needs anything. You find any information, he may want to interview you. The more I can give him, the better."

"I'll do whatever I can to help. Any idea where I ought to start?"

"I know Jimmy used to hang out up at Jackson's on the Square a whole bunch. Might be you'll find some old running buddies up there. Nobody would talk to me when I tried. You believe that? I've known the owner for forty years and now he walks right by like he's never seen me before. I walked in that place and you've never seen a room full of people pay their checks and leave so fast."

Cole headed toward the front door, hoping to get out of there without puking on Calvert's rug. "Jackson's, got it," he said. "I've been there before, I think. I'll let you know what I come up with. Is that same number you gave me a good one to reach you on?"

"Best I got. I don't keep a house phone out here, and cells don't work. That's how I like it. Nice and quiet."

"I'll do my best to call you."

"Feel free to stop back by anytime, day or night. I want justice for Jimmy, whatever it takes."

Cole dragged himself back out into the noon heat. He didn't have the heart to tell Calvert that he might already have gotten all the justice either of them was going to get.

CHAPTER NINE

He arrived back in Teller with the three o'clock sun grinding him into the truck's seat. The truck's AC had been broken for years. If that had been a mild discomfort up in Colorado, it was almost unfathomable in Texas. Cole was thinking about that as he drove up Highway 19 when the red and blue lights appeared in his rearview again.

He pulled over, not seeing anything else he could do. He told himself to stay calm. He'd needed to go see Zach anyway, now that he had the money. This might even save the trouble of figuring out how to find him. Deputy Charles climbed out of the Sheriff's Department cruiser and strutted over to the car.

"Well looky, looky. How you doin' today, Mr. Quick?"

"Just about dying from this heat," Cole caught his own reflection in Charles' mirrored Ray Bans. It didn't look good.

"Interesting turn of phrase. So?"

"So what?" Cole asked, squinting against the sun.

"So do I need to drag your dumb ass out of this truck again, or do you want to get the fuck out and come with me on your own? It's too goddamn hot today, like you said, so save us both the trouble."

Cole held his palms up in front of him in surrender and unbuckled his seatbelt as he said, "I was just gonna come find Zach anyway with the money I owe. I don't want to reach for it just now, but it's in a bank bag tucked under the seat."

"Smart thinkin'. Now get out. You can tell him all about it in the cruiser."

Cole eased the door open and tried to keep his distance from Charles as he climbed out of the truck. He looked back on his way to the cruiser to see Deputy Charles leaning across the floorboard to retrieve the moneybag. He'd hoped to pay Zach off in a more neutral situation, one where he could plan some sort of exit strategy. Now they had him by the short-and-curlies, as Chester would have said.

"I misjudged you, Cole," Big Zach said. "I figured for sure you'd run again. In fact, I was looking forward to it."

"Zach," Cole said. "As fun as these reunions are for me, let's cut right to it. I've got your money. Your man Charles over there has it in that bank bag, in cash." Cole gestured through the metal grate toward Deputy Charles, who was coming back to the car with the bank bag in his hand.

"No shit? Zach asked.

"No shit. See for yourself."

Deputy Charles opened the driver's side door and leaned inside.

"Found this on the floor of his truck," he said, not getting in. "It's full of cash, nothing but fresh hundreds, like they just came from the bank."

Zach took the bag and looked inside. He whistled.

"Goddamn Cole, you are just full of surprises. How in the fuck did you get your hands on this kind of cash?"

"I borrowed it from a friend. It's all there."

Zach nodded to Charles, who closed the door, leaving them alone again. "Well aren't you just full of fucking surprises," he said again. "I'd have taken ten-to-one odds you didn't have a friend left within a hundred miles of here."

"You never know, I guess," Cole said.

Zach gave a fake laugh and gored Cole with his eyes. "You might as well drop the bullshit half-bravado," he said. "I got bad news for you. This don't mean shit. Call it a down payment. You figure out the situation with your daddy's farm yet?"

Cole sighed. "You don't need the potential heat from stomping on a bug like me, do you?" he said. "Can't we be square now, forget we ever knew each other?"

"Shut your bullshit mouth," Zach said. "Here's what's going to happen. Our guy is drawing up all the legal paperwork, deed transfer, all that shit. He'll be dropping it off in the next few days. You lay your ass low and don't pull any bullshit until then, you might just make it through the weekend. Come Friday you can sign the paperwork and take your ass out of Teller County in one piece, lungs all full of air and everything. Deviate from that plan and you're dead. Understand?"

Cole nodded. "I have no intention of running. I'm sitting here right now, right? I'm doing what I gotta do. I don't give a good goddamn about that farm anyway. Ain't never been nothing but misery for me there. Y'all can have it."

"Ain't nobody asking. And I'm not the one who ought to be worried. Try this on for size: It ain't me you'll be signing the farm over to."

"Then who is it?"

"You'll be signing it over to Sheriff Jack Gables. Do I have your goddamn attention now?"

"You've had my attention since I got into town, Zach. But what the hell does Jack Gables want with Chester's farm? He's got that big-ass ranch out south of town, or at least he used to."

"None of your goddamn business what he wants. You've got thirty-six hours to handle your shit, starting now. You don't turn up, you won't be showing up anywhere else either. Got it?"

"Yeah, I got it," Cole said. "Can I go now?"

"Can you go... Cole, if you're not out of my sight in the next thirty seconds, I'll say fuck Jack Gables and scatter your tiny portion of grey matter all over the side of this here highway." Zach reached across the front seat and knocked on the driver's side window, jerked his thumb toward the back door. Charles opened it and Cole got out.

"Don't fuck around, Cole. You ain't never been in this deep, I promise," Zach said.

Cole didn't say anything. Deputy Charles shut the door and flinched his shoulders at Cole as if he were going to head-butt him. Cole jerked backward and fell onto his ass on the hot asphalt. Deputy Charles laughed.

"Have a good day now, you hear?" he said in a mock-professional voice.

Cole walked a wide arc around him back toward his truck. The cruiser's passenger-side mirror missed his elbow by inches as it pulled onto the highway and drove away.

These roadside meetings were already dangerous. Now they'd just become expensive, too. He needed to figure out whether Chester had left any sort of will anywhere, and what was supposed to become of his property.

He'd forgotten about the cocaine and the pistol until he walked back into Chester's house and saw them sitting on top of the file on the kitchen table. In some ways the sight turned his stomach, yet he found himself sliding into the chair and dumping some of the chunky white powder out of the second bag onto the table.

His nostril was sore, so the cocaine burned going up, but the pain faded off into electric numbness after a few seconds. His heart beat in rhythm with the drug, vessels and veins constricting as an energy wave washed over him.

He lit a smoke, picked up the file and flipped open the cover. The top sheet was a letter from a local LAN man named Bobby Hendon, detailing steps he'd taken in determining that Chester had inherited the mineral rights to the farm from his father, Herman, who had died when Cole was a toddler, leaving a legacy of anti-social behavior that dwarfed even Chester's. Or so Cole had been told.

The second sheet was a copy of an exploration lease Chester had signed with Ambrose Oil, dating back nine months. He ground his teeth as he thumbed through the pages. It looked like Ambrose had found some sort of well underneath the back twenty acres of the thirty-acre farm. He didn't understand all the details, but it made no sense, given that there were no rigs set up on the property, and not once had anyone ever even breathed the possibility of oil in seventy-five years of ownership.

Then again, Chester, like Herman before him, had been vicious about keeping others off his property, had shown his pistol to more than one person who wandered up the road on some business errand or other.

This explained what Jack Gables would want with the farm, though. But how would he even know about it to begin with? He needed to look up this Hendon guy and see what he had to say.

Cole cut out another line and sucked it up. He found the single Lone Star in the fridge and popped it open, thinking about how he needed to make a run to the county line for more booze. Should've stopped on the way back from Calvert's place, but he'd felt too bad then.

After all these years Teller County was still dry. He'd forgotten what a pain in the ass that could be, although it had provided him with ample opportunities to bootleg at the end of high school.

The first couple of sips of the Lone Star tasted like poison, but the cocaine helped his body begin to recover from the hangover.

Cole stubbed out his cigarette in the ashtray on the counter and pocketed Bobby Hendon's card. He wasn't sure how to proceed, but talking to Bobby Hendon might help figure that out.

Chester might have been telling the truth when he'd bragged around Vernon's about coming into money. But given that Chester had always spent money faster than he could make it, Cole didn't understand why he wouldn't have acted on something like this. It made him think there was some sort of catch he wasn't seeing.

It could be just more of Chester's stubborn bullshit, but the only thing that had consumed Chester more than his stubbornness was his greed and gambling addiction. Cole was missing something.

He polished off the last of the beer and decided he was ready for more. He put the full cocaine baggie in a bowl in the cupboard and the pistol next to it. He pocketed the bag he'd just been dipping into, picked up his keys and headed out the door for the county line.

CHAPTER TEN

It took him forty-five minutes to get out to the county line and pick up a case of Shiner Bock and a fifth of Wild Turkey, then drive back to Chester's farm.

He'd almost forgotten about the case file James Calvert had given him at Jimmy's lake house, wouldn't have remembered it again if it hadn't stuck to the case of Shiner he'd set on top of it when he picked the case up to take it inside.

He took the beer and bourbon into the house and set them on the table, went back out and retrieved the file. Back inside, he put the beer in the otherwise empty fridge and sat down at the table with a sweating Shiner. What he saw when he opened the file startled him.

On top was a picture of Caroline Ambrose, or rather what had once been Caroline. Blond hair, maybe not natural though. A slender shape with curvy hips and a couple handfuls of breasts.

She had been beautiful, no question. But in the pictures below that one she had become more nightmare than dream. She'd been stripped naked, her wrists bound with yellow nylon rope, each drawn up by the rope and attached to the bottom branch of the pine tree just off the back deck at Jimmy's lake house.

Her hands hung limp above their bindings, bloody fingernails on contorted fingers. She'd fought back, that much was clear from the pictures, though it had been obvious at the crime scene, too.

Bruises ran up her arms and legs. One deep gash in her right bicep exposed the muscle beneath. Her stomach had been cut open with the intestines piled on the ground in front of her, the source of all the blood. Her throat had been cut for good measure.

The tops of her toes dangled just off the ground.

Cole's first thought was that whoever had done this had to be a monster. His second was that the Jimmy he'd known was totally incapable of doing something like this. Whoever had done this had been as interested in humiliating the poor girl as killing her.

Cole had to open the Wild Turkey and take a good swig before he could look at the rest of the pictures, which detailed the carnage in more intimate, up-close shots. He ended up thumbing past most of them just to keep from getting sick.

He flipped past a closeup of the slit across Caroline's throat and sucked in his breath at the next page. It was Jimmy, or what was left of him. Half his head had been blown off. The half of his face that remained looked older, plastic, more gaunt than the Jimmy Cole remembered.

His body was too thin, and he had pock-marks up and down his arms. A pistol sat next to his right hand, which didn't make sense. Jimmy had been left-handed, and proud of it. But he'd also always bragged about how ambidextrous being left-handed made him.

Cole stared at the picture for what felt like hours; so this is what he had abandoned his best friend to become.

He flipped back to the first picture and tried to take it all in again. Without warning he wretched, then heaved, turned his head just in time to puke on the floor next to his feet. His head was swimming, palms sweating.

What had he gotten himself involved in?

Cole retrieved the pistol from where he'd stashed it in the cabinet and dug through Chester's closet until he found a box of shells. He refilled the clip he'd emptied the night before.

Whatever he did from here on out, he planned on having the pistol with him just in case. Whoever had done this was capable of violence he didn't want to experience firsthand. Besides, he was in plenty of danger all on his own. Not that shooting a cop would do much to save him.

He tried a little more whiskey but it made him sick again, so he went to lie down instead.

Just as he started to doze, someone knocked on the door. He opened his eyes to brown stains on the popcorn ceiling of his old room and daylight streaming through the curtains. His head pounded in rhythm to the raps against the kitchen door, which had always served as the house's front door due to positioning.

Cole sat up and swung his legs off the bed, shirtless down to his wranglers, socks still on. The knocking stopped as he made his way through the house to the kitchen door.

Sunlight swallowed him whole when he opened the door. He had to shield his eyes to see the man in a black suit and gator-skin shoes making his way back to a black Cadillac Escalade with a briefcase in his right hand.

Cole cleared his throat. "Something I can help you with, mister?" he managed.

The man looked back over his shoulder, then turned back to face him.

"I'm sorry. I knocked but assumed nobody was home. Are you Colton Quick, son of the recently deceased Chester Quick?"

Cole looked the man up and down as his eyes started to adjust to the sunlight now. "Depends on what you're about to say, I guess."

The man tilted his head, apparently confused by the response. "That was a yes," Cole reassured him. The man seemed to relax, straightened his head.

"Oh, well then, good. Mr. Quick my name is Gerald Watts. I'm an attorney for Ambrose Oil. If you've got a moment, I'd like to go over and finalize some paperwork for your father's estate with you."

Cole snickered.

"Did I say something funny?" Watts asked.

"Nah. It's just, you know, does this look like an estate to you? I just thought it was a funny way to put it. I guess it's no more ridiculous than Chester calling it a farm all these years, either. He never grew anything in his life, that I know of."

"Be that as it may, I have some paperwork you'll need to sign as his heir. Your father left you this…farm, as you called it. Once you sign some paperwork I can file it and have the deed transferred into your name. There was a matter of some back property taxes, but Ambrose Oil has decided to take care of those in light of the circumstances of your father's passing."

"Circumstances," Cole repeated, as if trying out the word. "You can come inside, but I can't promise you'll find it comfortable."

The man came back onto the porch and followed Cole inside the squalid farmhouse. If the general chaos inside bothered him, he was careful not to show it.

"Get you something to drink?" Cole asked, gesturing the rancid sink of dishes. They each took adjacent seats at the kitchen table, which still had the open file from the night before on it. The plate with cocaine residue was sitting right next to it.

Cole caught Hamilton stealing a glance at the pictures before he was able to shut the file and set it on top of the plate. In turn, Hamilton flipped the snaps on his leather briefcase and raised the lid. He set out two neat stacks of paperwork, each of varying thickness, but neither thicker than about ten pages. Once he had them arranged to his liking, he folded his hands and leaned on his elbows in front of them.

"I guess we can go ahead and get right to it, if that suits you?"

Cole nodded. "It does."

"Good. So these papers," he said, gesturing to the stack on his left, "Are regarding your father's estate. He owned the farm free-and-clear, but as you probably know, not much else. That is, of course, beyond the back taxes, which Ambrose has already taken care of. You can feel free to look it over, and when you're done I just need you to sign in the spots marked with the stickers, and all this will be yours." He mock gestured at the squalor around him.

Cole let the slight go and read through the paperwork instead. Chester had taken the time to name him as beneficiary of his will. Cole sat back, crossed his arms as if it would somehow help him to understand it.

"So he set this all up himself, of his own accord?" Cole asked. "How'd you know I'd be here?"

"Well, I can't say for sure in your father's case, but Ambrose likes for their longtime employees to keep their affairs in order whenever possible. It's likely that someone at some point counseled him about the dangers of not having a last will and testament. We didn't have any contact info for you so this seemed like the obvious place to start searching."

"Well I'll be goddamned. The pen must have singed the hair off his fingers," Cole said.

Watts looked at him as if he didn't understand, but he probably heard all kinds of family nonsense anyway.

"If you'll notice, the last page is the deed transfer. Once you sign that and I file it with the county, this will be your farm, free and clear."

"Free and clear? You sure someone ain't put you up to coming out here like this?"

Watts fidgeted with his tie. He looked uncomfortable with the question. "It's my job as Ambrose Oil's man, so you might say your father's employer put me up to it."

Cole shook his head, figuring the guy wouldn't say either way. "Anything else you got for me? I just got up from a nap and I need a shower."

"There is one more thing. This second set of documents relates to your father's severance payout. Ambrose keeps life insurance on all its long-term employees, a portion of which goes to the family as beneficiaries. We've taken care of your property taxes as well as your father's burial costs. The remaining portion of your payout is four thousand dollars. It's all in there, itemized and explained. Sign those documents and I'll leave you the check now."

Hamilton reached inside his coat pocket and fished out a check that was already made out to Cole by a computer. Cole started to look through the documents regarding the payout, but decided he had enough on his plate; he could use the four thousand more than he needed to worry about whether Chester Quick got a fair shake from his long-time employer. He signed the documents where indicated, and Hamilton slid the check across the table to him.

"I'll leave the copies of all the paperwork here so you have a copy. In the meantime, if you have any questions, please don't hesitate to give me a call."

"All right then," Cole said, not really listening as he continued to look through the documents. Ten seconds later the man was out the door and sweating his way back to his Escalade in that ridiculous suit, which must have felt like a wearable oven.

After looking through the paperwork a while longer, Cole closed the file and put it on top of the others in his stack. In all the hungover confusion yesterday, he'd almost forgotten about the gala being held tonight in memory of Kerrie, which Mandy Ambrose had invited him to. He wanted to show up looking respectable, if possible, which meant he needed some better clothes.

He drove into town and over to Western Mart, used some of the five hundred from James Calvert to buy himself a respectable pair of tan Wranglers and a nice button-down shirt, as well as a decent belt. He picked up a shining kit off the checkout counter for his work boots. Afterward, he went to Walgreens and bought some soap, a razor, and some shampoo, took it all back to Chester's farm.

He shined up his boots as best he could, shaved, and tried to scrub himself as clean as possible. No matter what he did he would stand out, but given who he'd be facing there, he needed to try.

All the while his mind turned in circles. Knowing he was about to face Kerrie's parents for exactly the third time in his life reminded him that the only way to get respect in the world was to get money.

He considered who else might know about the oil under Chester's farm as he drove down the highway back into town, humid summer air already dissolving the clean smell from his hair. Things would probably get even hotter at the gala, though he promised himself he'd at least try not to make a scene.

CHAPTER ELEVEN

Cole had several hours before the benefit was supposed to begin, giving him some time to look into things for James Calvert beforehand. He still had no idea what Calvert thought he might be able to add to the situation, but he needed to do something, especially since the money was already gone and had done nothing but fan the flames of his problems.

He headed over to Jackson's, the place Calvert had suggested he start. Jackson's had at one time been owned by a sitting mayor's brother, maybe still was. It was the closest thing to an elite gathering place that Teller had to offer, and a lot of the wealthy businessmen who kept offices in one or the other of Teller's two high-rise office buildings downtown hung out there.

Cole couldn't guarantee he'd run into anyone Jimmy hung out with, but he had to start somewhere. Maybe someone there knew something about who Jimmy had scored his cocaine from. Cole could use the cocaine in his pocket to get them talking, if need be.

Jackson's was a two-story brick building with a false-façade third floor at the top. It sat adjacent to the county courthouse, which served as the center of the town square. The owner had made obvious efforts to modernize the front exterior, but mostly it still looked like any building on any town square anywhere in Texas, the kind of place where million-dollar deals might go down over a glass of bourbon. Jackson's served high-dollar food in portions so small you had to go eat a second dinner after you'd finished.

He had insisted on taking Kerrie there for dinner once when they first started dating, and only realized it was a bad idea after they ran into virtually every one of her parents' friends. It wasn't long afterward that her parents got word she had been seeing Cole and tried to shut it down.

A man in a suit coat, boots and jeans was having his white Cadillac DeVille valet parked as Cole stepped inside the place. The dim lighting inside made it difficult to see the faces of the people at the five or six small tables scattered across the refinished original wood floors built a hundred years before.

A few people looked up at Cole, not because he stuck out, although he realized he probably shouldn't have rolled up the sleeves on his shirt, but most likely because they didn't recognize him.

He tried to get a look at each of their faces without being too obvious about it as he made his way to the bar. So far, he didn't recognize anyone. He ordered a Jack and Coke from the bartender, who wore black dress pants with a white button-down shirt and a black vest that matched the pants.

When the man brought the drink back Cole slapped a ten on the bar and told him to keep it. From the look on the guy's face it hadn't been much of a tip, so he dropped another single on the bar and carried the sweaty drink through a glass door onto the side patio, which stretched out between Jackson's and the next building over.

A series of fans hummed on the patio as a guitarist up on stage played an acoustic rendition of some country-pop song that had been all over the radio back in Junction.

The porch had an upper-level deck wrapped with a waist-high wrought-iron rail, which led to a set of stairs to a lower level, with round cocktail tables and chairs crammed into it. They were about a quarter full, but Cole still didn't see anyone he recognized, so he sat at an empty table off to the side. He kicked back, sipped his drink and listened to the music, which wasn't half bad, for a while.

Some men at a table across the floor from him started whooping and hollering after the song finished, and he realized that he actually knew one of them. Their eyes met and Cole saw a flash of recognition roll across the guy's face. Randall Harrington. Jimmy's trustee, according to James Calvert.

He'd met Randall a few times partying with Jimmy, which made it hard to imagine they'd ever allowed him to oversee Jimmy's trust at the bank. Randall stood up and headed over to Cole's table. Cole nodded as Randall approached.

"Randall, right?" he said.

"Yeah. You're Cole, right?" Saying it like it was news to both of them. "Been a long time, almost didn't recognize you."

"Yeah man, you know, ain't been around for a while. How are ya? Pull up a seat?"

"Sure, I guess so. Hell, I'm doing good. Man, your face is just a blast from the past for me. You used to run with Jimmy Calvert all the time, always the guy who supplied the party."

"I've been getting a lot of that lately."

"Where you at these days? I haven't seen you in years."

"Colorado, mostly. Right now I'm back here in Teller. My daddy just passed away."

"Oh," Randall said, sitting back and taking a drink of his beer. "Sorry to hear that."

"What about you? What are you up to these days?" Cole said.

"Working for the Bank of Teller. I'm branch manager for the motor bank over by the hospital. You need a home loan or wanna open a checking account or something, you come see me." Randall winked and smiled, just lightening the mood, working his charm.

"I might just take you up on that. You got a card?"

"They'd run my ass out of town if I didn't." Randall took out his wallet and passed a card across the table to Cole, visibly more interested in the conversation now that there might be business involved. Cole took it and put it in his own wallet.

"Say, you remember that time we was out at the whoop-de-doos and Jimmy set that tree on fire, then you climbed it for fifty bucks?"

"I do," Cole said.

"I never seen someone's face turn so sour as when the tree fell over five seconds after you got off it. That shit was crazy."

Cole hated that memory. He'd been nervous around all those socialites, trying to show off. Someone could have gotten hurt, not that you'd have known it the way those rich assholes had been egging him on, throwing twenty-dollar bills in the pot.

"Anyway," Cole said, "I've only been back in town a couple of days, but I heard about what happened with Jimmy. Kind of blew my mind. Did you still keep up with him?"

Randall frowned. He seemed to take account of where he was in space by looking around, leaned in and rested his elbows on the table. He let out a loud exhale.

"That was some nasty-ass business, wasn't it? I don't know anybody who ever heard of something like that happening around here."

"Maybe they forgot to mention it." Cole took a drink, then went on. "I can't get it out of my mind. Hard to imagine Jimmy doing something like that."

"I hung out with him here and there the last few years, parties at his place every now and again. I know his father was in and out of the bank dealing with Jimmy's trust all the time. Somehow, I ended up as the trustee, which put me in an awkward position with Jimmy. He was hemorrhaging money and staying throwed off on the drugs. I had to stop hanging out with him to keep my reputation good up at the bank. I recall you used to be knee-deep in that kind of mess with him."

"That's true, I was. If I remember right, so were you."

Randall smiled a little. "Hell, that's true." He leaned in closer and added, "You still get into that kind of stuff?"

Cole eyed him while trying to appear casual. It was hard to tell where he was headed with such a question, and it seemed a bit forward, but he'd obviously had a few beers already, so it might have loosened him up.

"You know how it is. The more things change, the more they stay the same," he said. "What about you? Bank got you on the straight and narrow now, or you still like to have some fun?"

"I've been known to dip my toe in the water from time to time, when I come across a puddle. Nothing like Jimmy, though. Mostly just low-key cutting loose after work, sobering up before I go home to the wife and kid."

Cole took a shot, hoped he'd read things right. "If I told you there was a puddle right around here, would you get your toes wet now?"

He was starting to get a good idea of how Jimmy had managed to go so long getting high off his trust. The trustee had been getting high off it, too, most likely.

Randall eyed him with a cheeky grin. "Why, you got something worth dipping it in?"

"It ain't much, but it's a little something. If you want, we could step off in the bathroom and have us an old-time reunion?"

"Can't roll quite like that anymore, bubba, too much risk with the job the way people talk in this town. But we could step out to my car, if you want? They let me park out back instead of using the valet. That work for you?"

"I'm game for it," Cole said.

"Well hell, yeah. I'm glad I came over, it's been a hell of a day and I could use some booger sugar. How about you head inside like you're looking to get another drink, and then just go out the side door instead. I'll just tell these guys at my table I've got to get something out of my car for a business deal and meet you back there. It's a black five series BMW, you can't miss it."

"Perfect," Cole said. He stood up and projected his voice for effect. "I got to get going, but it was great seeing you, Randall," he said, making a show of it.

"You too," Randall replied as they shook hands. Cole made his way inside, but instead of turning to the bar he went out the back door. He found Randall's car right away, was leaning on it and smoking a cigarette when Randall finally came out the gate to the back porch. The BMW's parking lights flashed and the interior dome light faded on. It was almost dusk now. Cole hopped in the passenger seat and Randall got in the driver's seat next to him.

"Appreciate you humoring me there," Randall said as he shut the door. "People act like a guy can't do his job and have a good time too."

"No problem, I understand. As you get older the stakes get bigger and you start to have things to lose."

"Exactly. That's exactly right. It doesn't mean a man can't have a good time, he just has to be careful to protect his image, am I right?"

"Right as rain," Cole said, digging the cocaine out of the front pocket of his shirt. "Mind if I see a key real quick?"

Randall passed his keys over to Cole. He dipped one into the bag, got a good pile on the tip and snorted it off the key, then repeated the process twice before he passed the bag and key over to Randall. It was going to get his teeth chattering, but he wanted to set the tone so that Randall got good and high, see if it would get him talking out of school maybe.

"Shit," Randall said as he sucked the third key-bump up. "Not fucking bad, Cole. Where'd you get this?"

"I ran into an old buddy happened to have some extra. I was actually kind of hoping you might know where to find more."

"Me? Shit, I got one or two guys I call. I try to get it indirect from the actual dealers. You know how it is. I don't need any bullshit. I might could help you out with a little something though. Looks like you're doing fine so far."

"Just thinking about down the road sometime. Hey, by the way," Cole said, changing the subject. "I need to open a local bank account up. I've got some inheritance coming. If I stop up there tomorrow could we make that happen?"

"That would be great, Cole. We take good care of our customers. Stop in, I'll be happy to help get you squared away." Randall's eyes dilated as he hit another bump. He sniffed hard and wiped his nose. Cole did the same, then sat back.

His throat had gone numb and his heart felt like a thunderstorm. Now was as good a time as he would get to ask a few more questions.

"You think Jimmy Calvert was dealing this stuff?" he asked. "I mean, you get the impression he was taking enough out of his trust to maybe get a little side hustle going?"

"You're pretty interested in that, huh?" Randall replied. "Tell you the truth, I can't really talk about it because of privacy laws. I can tell you he had enough money that there wasn't much reason to deal. What made you ask that?"

"Just trying to make sense of his behavior, maybe hoping someone else did the deed instead of him. It's thrown me for a loop. The Jimmy I remember wasn't capable of that kind of violence."

"I didn't notice that he was anything other than the same party-boy maniac he'd always been. I sort of had the same reaction as you when I heard about it. I don't think he was selling drugs because he sure loved to share them for free. I don't know a lot of dealers who act like that. I've sat in this exact spot doing this exact thing with him many times. Probably not a good idea, given the trust situation, but you know how it is, the older you get, you got less and less people you can do this kind of thing with."

"I do. You think Caroline had another lover or something?"

"Maybe. She had a reputation for being a whore. I can't imagine anyone killing for her, though."

Cole sensed that Randall didn't want to keep talking about Jimmy, so he let the conversation die there and they reminisced about people they'd known in common instead, which didn't turn out to be very many beyond Jimmy.

Not that Cole was surprised. Eventually Randall felony-checked himself in the rearview and said he needed to get back inside, as visibly bored with the conversation as he was visibly high.

"It was sure good seeing you, Cole," he said over the top of the car as they got out.

"Likewise," Cole replied. "I'm gonna stop by the bank and open that account sometime tomorrow, hopefully."

"Looking forward to it," Randall replied. Fuck, I might still be awake after this. Thanks for the good times, Cole, I'll have to get you back."

"Anytime, man, just let me know."

"Sounds good. Adios, amigo. My goddamn mouth's so dry I can taste the dust."

Adios," Cole parroted.

On the walk back to the truck he tried to pull himself together and prepare for the benefit gala. His nerves were a mess now from the coke. He probably hadn't needed to go that far with it, but it was too late now.

If his time back in town so far had taught him anything, it was that his baggage was guaranteed to come up. He didn't know what he wanted to say to Kerrie's parents, or if he would even speak to them at all. But he had an intense desire to be close to anything that had to do with Kerrie, anything that might remind him of what he'd once had, even if that remembrance would only lead him to see, even more, just how much he'd lost.

CHAPTER TWELVE

The iron gates out front were open when he drove up to Mandy Ambrose's house. Various makes of luxury cars were parked in neat formation along the sides of the country-style road, with a few stacked along the edges of the long, red-brick driveway.

The driveway's brick matched the brick used to build the house, which Mandy had mentioned in her description of it. She'd failed to mention the size. Enormous didn't begin to describe the sprawling, two-story house with big bay windows at intervals along the second story, complete with flower boxes full of blooming roses. As he pulled up to the edge of the driveway a valet in a tuxedo approached his window. Cole rolled it down and nodded at the man, who smirked in return.

"Good evening, is there something I can assist you with, sir?" the valet asked.

"I'm here for the gala." Cole said, still sniffling, his voice a little shaky.

"I see," the valet said, eyeing his busted-up Silverado. "Do you happen to have your invitation on hand?"

"I didn't get one, so no. I'm a friend of Mandy Ambrose's. We ran into each other the other day and she invited me, kinda spur-of-the-moment."

"I see. And could I get your name, sir?"

"Cole Quick," he said.

"One moment please." The valet moved just out of earshot from the truck. He spoke into an earpiece attached to a walkie-talkie he had on the back of his belt.

Cole took the opportunity to stash the baggie of Coke in the glove compartment and smooth the front of his shirt. He hoped he didn't look as sweaty and high as he felt.

The valet appeared at his window again. "I'd be happy to park your truck for you, Mr. Quick. Ms. Ambrose has been expecting you. My apologies for the delay."

"Don't mention it," Cole said. He stepped out and made a sweeping motion with his arm toward the truck. "She's all yours," he said.

"Of course," the valet said. He lingered there between the open door and the truck's seat until Cole realized he wanted a tip.

"Huh," Cole said, patting his shirt pocket. "I must have left my cash in my Mercedes."

He turned before the valet could reply and headed down the driveway toward the house. He stopped halfway when he noticed that none other than Jack Gables himself was working security at the front door.

Cole had never seen Gables in person, but anyone in Teller County would recognize his iconic moustache, neatly trimmed with stiff white bristles. Jack Gables was the kind of man who stood out in any crowd, a man you didn't need to look at long to see he was as dangerous as he was charismatic. Dangerous not just because of what he might do with his hands, but also what he could do with his mouth. He'd been the uncontested sheriff of Teller County for more than thirty years, despite every single year being riddled with rumors of corruption and criminal activity. His most recent scandal had even made national news, yet here he stood.

He had on elephant-skin boots that had probably been illegal for decades, form-fitting black jeans and a starched red Lou Casey shirt on which was affixed an old-west-style circle-capped star badge. His State of Texas belt buckle matched the bolo tie hanging between the lapels of a black vest. An old school .357 Lawman pistol was strapped into a holster on his right side—the quintessential cowboy sheriff in all his glory.

Cole considered turning back, but it was too late to do so without making it obvious. Instead, he tried to approach the entrance looking casual. There was no reason to think that Jack Gables had ever seen a picture of him. All he needed to do was nod politely and walk past him. When they made eye contact Cole's pulse spiked.

"Evening," Gables said, giving no indication that he recognized Cole in any way.

"Evening," Cole mumbled. As quick as Gables had focused his attention on Cole he placed it somewhere else as an elderly black man in a tuxedo opened the front door for Cole.

The elaborate entry hall opened up into a main foyer with ceiling-to-floor windows off the back of the house that looked out on Lake Strongbow. A stage had been set up on the back lawn with rose-themed decorations all around. There was a vase of long-stem roses on each of the cocktail tables in front of the stage.

Cole made his way through the house and out the double French doors that led to the back lawn. He located one of several complimentary bars off to the side and wandered over to it. People were dressed to the nines, and he felt even more out of place than he'd anticipated.

The cocaine had made him nervous and sweaty, not talkative or sarcastic like he'd been before he saw Jack Gables at the door. He realized that he'd come here to make some sort of scene, but found himself hoping to avoid it now that he was here. What good would it do, anyway?

There was no beer, so he ordered a Johnny Walker Black on the rocks to calm his nerves. He took it down before he made it five feet from the bar and turned back to order another, the alcohol smoothing out the cocaine high.

The bartender, another aged black man with a neat grey beard, gave Cole an odd look as he ordered the second drink, so

Cole fished a five out from his pocket and dropped it in the tip jar, which was really more of a vase.

As he turned back to the crowd a jazz band comprised of even more elderly black men began to play up on stage.

Women applauded from their tables as the members of the quartet took turns playing solos. The men stood off to the side in clumps, some smoking cigars, others holding glasses of scotch or wine. No doubt they were some of Teller's most elite residents. A hand settled on his right forearm and he turned to find Mandy Ambrose standing next to him.

"Well hey there, Cole. I wasn't sure you'd actually show up," she said.

"Hello Mandy. When you put it like that, I'm not sure if I should thank you for inviting me or run for the exit."

"Oh, come on, now. I'm sure your wife taught you how to conduct yourself like a gentleman in social company, did she not?"

Cole's eyes narrowed. He got the feeling Mandy was having some sort of fun at his expense. "You think that, then I guess you didn't notice my outfit," he said, playing into her suggestion, choosing not to let it bother him.

"I think you look just fine," she said. "I always thought tuxedos made men look like fat little penguins." Mandy smiled at her own joke. "Anyway, I felt like you *deserved* to be here, however you showed up."

"No offense," Cole began, measuring his words as he spoke, "But I'm not sure exactly what I'm doing here, and you don't strike me as the type of girl to invite me out of the goodness of your heart."

She swatted his hand playfully. "Now that's a mean thing to say." She smiled a big, showy smile, the kind intended for other people to see. "I guess I do have a bit of a reputation for enjoying a little drama, so long as it's not at my expense," she said in a low voice. The smile faded now and a tired look came into her eyes. Cole figured that look was the real Mandy, but didn't say it.

Mandy went on. "The truth is, after what happened it seemed like everyone wanted me to shut up and forget about my sister. Keep on smiling, as they say, and not talk about it."

"Including your folks?"

"Especially my parents. I guess that's why I feel like you have more of a right to come here and mourn your wife than anyone else here, social status be dammed."

Cole almost hugged her then. It was the first time he could remember when anyone in Teller had treated him like he'd ever had so much as a right to be in the same room as Kerrie. He said, "Thanks for that. Really. But I doubt Mr. and Mrs. Ferris will feel the same if they see me here."

Mandy pouted her lips a little. "I'm not worried about *them*. They had as much to say about what happened to my sister as anyone in town, or so I hear. Anyway, help yourself to whatever you need tonight, Cole. I'll come back to check on you if I get a chance. Right now, I've got to be the *gracious* hostess."

Her expression straightened to some sort of mock amusement again, and Cole was sure that version of her was an act, not the real girl.

"Don't smile too hard," he said to her back as she disappeared into the crowd.

He sat at a table near the back of the party as if to prepare for a quick exit. He watched the band play as his mind wandered. Something large and square hung behind the stage, covered by a pair of black curtains that had a chain of roses embroidered across the front of them. It looked like a humongous piece of framed artwork, maybe.

Before long he was ignoring the band and doing more people-watching than anything else. He couldn't imagine a world farther from his own. He knew Kerrie had grown up with these kinds of people, going to these kinds of events. She probably would have known every person there. But it baffled him that this could be in the same town he had grown up in.

Most of his friends growing up had shared a small bedroom

in a trailer with one or two of their siblings, worn clothes these people had discarded at the local Goodwill. It seemed unfair, watching these people walking around in outfits that were more expensive than his entire childhood wardrobe.

He finally saw Kerrie's parents seated at the center of a set of long, rectangular tables at the front. The tables appeared to also house this year's Rose Queen and her court. The queen wore an elegant white cocktail dress with woven rose lacing at the neck, while her court all wore similar dresses, except that theirs were pink and had a simple white trim at the neck, rather than the roses.

Only the queen wore a diamond tiara on top of her smooth blonde hair, which had been pulled up into a perfect bun behind her head, using a rose broach made of rubies. Cole snickered at the obnoxious broach; the girl probably had thirty grand stuck to her skull.

He'd about had his head taken off over less not twenty-four hours ago. Chester would have taken hers off for far less. Cole didn't really know what to say about that. She must have been pleased as pie to be up there lording herself above all those other rich folks.

Kerrie's parents, on the other hand, looked gloomy. He'd never allowed himself to consider how they felt after they'd come and taken her body away, hiding behind an army of attorneys so that he never even got to speak to them about it, to plead his case.

He'd known Kerry would rather be buried anywhere than her family's private burial plot, but doing something about it had been another story altogether.

All she'd wanted from her life was to get away from the same socialites who were now attending an event in her honor. It hurt Cole to relive that experience now, and yet one look at the Ferris's faces had him feeling a sympathy for them he hadn't expected to feel.

It was obvious they loved Kerrie the way he had loved her. Her loss had cut them to the bone, the same as him. It made him realize that the last thing he wanted to do was confront them and add to that pain, justified vengeance or not.

It had been a mistake to come here. As he stood up to head for the door he locked eyes with Kerrie's mother, Melinda Ferris. Her face swelled with recognition, and it took a second before she nudged her husband to get his attention, then gestured in Cole's direction.

Anger washed over Tom Ferris's stiff face. Cole calculated how many steps it would take him to get inside the house just as the song on stage ended and a balding man with a rose-red cummerbund stepped up to the microphone.

"Ladies and gentlemen," he said. "I'm pleased to welcome y'all to this year's Festival Benefit Gala, given in honor of Teller's lost daughter, the late Kerrie Ferris. I'm proud to say that all of tonight's proceeds will go to The East Texas Breast Cancer Foundation in her honor. As most of you know, Tom and Melinda Ferris lost Kerrie to breast cancer earlier this year. She was a dear, sweet girl, and when Tom and Melinda approached the Festival Coordination Committee about holding the gala in her honor, we didn't hesitate to accept.

"All that said, as you might imagine, it is my distinct honor as emcee for tonight's gala to announce the unveiling of a piece Tom and Melinda had commissioned in honor of Kerrie."

The emcee, who had not bothered to identify himself because most of the socialites there probably already knew who he was, gestured to the curtains behind him. He nodded to the drummer from the Jazz Quartet.

"Can I get a drumroll please," he said. The drummer obliged. "Ladies and gentlemen," the emcee continued, "I give you, 'Angel of the Pines,' painted by the Italian artist Marcos Floriola, using oil paint on canvas."

When the curtains parted Cole almost fell to his knees. In the enormous painting, Kerrie's face looked more like it had back in high school. She was in full debutant finery, a classy, form-fitting white gown with white, elbow-length gloves and her hair styled big and wavy and blonde, instead of her natural brunette. It was everything her parents had ever wanted her to be, and everything Cole had always known she was not.

The very sight of it sent him into such a rage that he had to choke the anger down in order to be able to take a breath. It felt like having the seams ripped out from the incision on his soul, like someone was trying to cut out her memory and replace it with something gaudy and false and disgusting.

He felt eyes on him and turned to see Mandy Ambrose watching him, taking in his reaction. Her face looked curious, as if she were waiting to see what he would do.

What he did was walk up between the tables toward the painting, intending to rip the goddamn thing into as many pieces as possible, fuck what anyone had to say. Fuck his life, too, if need be. He knew Tom and Melinda Ferris were watching him, but he didn't care. Ten feet in front of the stage he found himself cut off by Melinda Ferris.

"What in God's *name* do you think you're doing here, Cole? You have no business here. You have *no right*."

"I have every right," he found himself shouting. "She was my wife, and I loved her with all of my heart. *You* had no right to take her body away like that. Now you want to immortalize her in that fucking abomination up there, like some snobby shit-heel socialite. You know as well as I do she was nothing like the girl in that goddamn painting. Y'all managed to cut every last inch of her kindness out of her image."

"I know no such thing," she replied. "All I know is that if you'd let *our* doctors treat her here in Teller, she might be here to speak for herself. Instead you kept her away from her family. You started killing her the second you met her, whether you knew it or not. Now she's dead."

Cole snarled. "She wanted nothing to do with this place. Neither of us did. She knew she couldn't accept your help without your control. I'd have given my own life in her place if I could. I'd have done anything, suffered a thousand…" Tears erupted from Cole's eyes without his consent, long, salty trails of regret cutting lines into his face that felt like they would never heal again afterward.

"Melinda, please," Tom Ferris cut in, looking around while attempting to restrain her by her arm. The entire crowd was staring at them, mouths agape.

"I want him out," Melinda Ferris shouted, ignoring her husband. "*Now*. Someone take him out of here—*now*."

Cole backed away from her, realizing how out of control she had become. Her anger had such power that his own evaporated on the spot, and all he wanted to do was get away from her. A gruff hand spun him around by the shoulder and he found himself face-to-face with Jack Gables, who was very much noticing him then.

"You'd best come with me, Mr. Quick," he said. "You won't like how this turns out if I have to force you."

Over Gables' shoulder Cole saw Mandy Ambrose hurrying between the tables. She started talking before she even got close to them.

"What's going on here?" she called out. "Mr. Quick is here at my invitation, to pay respect to his wife. I won't stand for a guest in *my house* being treated so crassly."

Jack Gables just continued on as if he hadn't heard her, leading Cole by force toward the house. "Did you hear me, Mr. Gables?" she added, "This is *my* home, and I want him to *stay*."

"Actually, it's my home," an older man said. It took Cole only a second to realize it was Mandy's father, Tim Ambrose. "And I think it's best if he leaves."

Before Mandy could protest any further her father led her away by the arm in the same manner that Jack Gables led Cole in the opposite direction. Every eye in the crowd followed them until the sheriff made his way back through the French doors and out the front door of the giant house. He stopped on the front porch, once they were alone, and faced Cole.

"You got balls like a bucking bull coming here, *boy*," he

said, all the normal charisma he was known for now replaced with terrifying venom. "You're nothing but a goddam bug in the ass of every single person who comes near you, ain't ya?"

He led Cole by the arm back up the driveway toward the valet, looking around to see if anyone was watching them.

Cole studied his face, saw the way his eyes could shift in a split second from the amicable politician to the cold-blooded killer he was rumored to be.

"You and I have business, Mr. Quick, which I assure you we will attend to shortly. But for now, you'd best get your ass as far from here as you can before I decide to forget all that and drop you in a fuckin' ditch instead. Am I speakin' English well enough for you boy? Nod if it's a yes."

Cole nodded, just wanting to get his keys and drive his truck as far from all of this as possible, damn James Calvert and Jimmy and his debt and anyone else. He'd just run and take his chances with them coming after him. He'd done it once, he could do it again. The valet saw them coming and pulled Cole's truck keys off the board behind him.

"I'll take those," Gables said, snatching them from the valet's hand. "This man is in no condition to drive."

"Come on, man," Cole said, "How am I supposed to get home then?"

"You keep talking and I'll rent you a room at my place, give you a ride over there myself."

Jack Gables had the politician look plastered back across his face again in front of the valet. Cole wasn't getting out of there with his truck, that much was clear. An idea crossed his mind and he acted on it out of impulse.

"Okay, I understand, sheriff. But if you don't mind, would you least walk me up to the truck so that I can get something out of it?"

"What is it?" Gables asked, starting to lose his cool, even in front of the valet.

"I'm staying with a friend while I'm in town. I just want to get the key to his place, then I promise I'm gone."

Gables gave him a look that could have melted a candle, then took notice that the valet was watching to see what he would do. He exhaled a loud breath.

"You'd best live up to your surname, son. You got twenty seconds to get it and get out of my sight."

He followed Cole up to the truck and unlocked the door for him. It was too risky then to try for the coke, so he grabbed the gate opener and key to Jimmy's house, as well as his pack of smokes.

"Sorry about the trouble, Sheriff," he said as the man almost slammed the truck door on his arm.

"Not as sorry as you're gonna be," Gables replied under his breath. Gables glared down on him as Cole wandered off into the darkness in the direction of Jimmy's house, lighting a cigarette against the dark as he moved.

It only took him a couple minutes of walking to get there. No one followed, as far as he could tell. He punched the button on the opener and let himself down the driveway. He had no intention of sleeping in that creepy-ass house but figured it would be too risky to try to get his truck back tonight.

Instead he went out onto the dock, grabbed one of the last two Lone Stars from the fridge and plopped down in the hammock that had hung there for years. Hot tears poured out of his eyes as he replayed the night's events in his mind. He looked up at the stars, wondering if there was a God, and if Kerrie could see him from somewhere up there, the last shambles of his pitiful, wasted life finally coming unglued.

He couldn't decide if she would have been proud or ashamed of the scene he'd made with her mother back at the gala. She'd never been much for conflict, but also had always hated that high-society nonsense. It may well have been she would have felt both, walked away from all of them to a life more worthy of a woman like her.

He'd never understood what she'd seen in him in the first

place. Maybe it was just him letting grief affect his judgment, but whatever it was, the feeling had only gotten darker and more hopeless once she was gone.

He fell asleep with tears still trailing down his face as he pictured little pieces of her memory. Her face when she woke up in the mornings, no makeup, just naturally beautiful. The quick smile she let out when she was self-conscious, or when he teased her. Most of all he missed her touch. Looking back, it was the only thing in his life that had been simple, healing. And now he would never feel it again.

CHAPTER THIRTEEN

Cole didn't know what had hit him at first. One moment he was asleep, the next, face down on the pier. He landed with a heavy thud. Before he could look up to see what dumped him from the hammock, an elephant-skin boot's heel drove down into his chest. He was in a heap of trouble, and he knew it right away.

He rubbed his eyes and saw Jack Gables and Big Zach standing above him. He managed to sit up, still wheezing for breath from where the boot heel had knocked the wind out of him. Jack Gables cracked his knuckles and dropped a right hook to the left side of Cole's face that left him sprawled back on the deck again.

"Son of a bitch," Gables said, shaking his hand from the impact. "Boy, you so goddamned hard-headed it about broke my hand. I ought to drown you right here in the lake, but we've got business to attend to first."

Cole sat back on his haunches again, the left side of his face already swelling from the blow. He still felt buzzed, wondered how long he'd been asleep. He didn't like being down here alone with them like this. It had to be a miracle that he wasn't already dead, the more he thought about the logistics of it.

"My understanding, and correct me if I'm wrong, Mr. Quick, is that a lawyer from Ambrose Oil filed the deed transfer for your daddy's farm with the county yesterday, placing it in your name. I'd say that officially makes you the owner of the farm and the mineral rights. For the moment, anyway." Gables and Big Zach exchanged a look.

"I told you, Cole," Big Zach said, grinning so that his lone silver-capped tooth gleamed in the moonlight.

"Mr. Quick, I'm sure you've figured out that there's a substantial deposit of oil underneath that land. For most folks, that's a blessing. For a guy like you it's a liability. You owe, son, plain and simple. How much would you say your life is worth?"

To emphasize the sheriff's point, Big Zach slammed a giant Wolverine work boot into the center of Cole's chest, knocking all the air out of him again. He wheezed and fought for breath, slumped over onto his side again.

It felt like something had broken inside him, but all he could focus on was getting air. Jack Gables kneeled beside him and pulled his head up by the hair. With his other hand he pinched Cole's nostril shut, further disrupting his efforts to suck in a breath. He was well on the way to suffocating to death when Gables spoke again.

"Nothing goes on in this county without my say-so, Mr. Quick. *Nothing*. Guy like you, who ran off on his debts, he ought to realize his life itself is a gift. That there ain't nothing for him in a place like Teller County. You ran off owing the wrong people money. That alone ought to forfeit your life. But this here's your big break. My understanding is you've already begun to pay your debt. Long as you sign the paperwork being delivered to you at your daddy's place the day after tomorrow and then get your ass out of town after, you get to go on living. You try some smart-ass funny shit like you did back at that gala, well…"

Gables dropped Cole's head to the deck. Cole finally managed to suck in a breath, followed by a violent cough. He struggled to get another, then another. Gables reached into his pocket and came back with Cole's truck keys, as well as the bag of cocaine Cole had stashed in the glove compartment.

"Lot of folks saw your little outburst earlier tonight. And looky, looky what I found in your truck afterward. Back up to your old shit, I don't doubt it. I'd prefer to keep your name out of my jail system, you rotten little son of a bitch. It's just cleaner that way. But you'd be surprised the things that happen in there late at night. People hang themselves all the time. Cut themselves, get beaten to death in the shower for acting queer. You picking up what I'm laying down?"

Cole tried to speak, but his voice wouldn't come at first. Finally, he found his breath.

"I got it," he wheezed. "But what's my guarantee I don't end up dead anyway, I sign the farm over?"

"You don't get one. It's still better than what you've got now. But you cooperate and it's safe to say that so long as you never show your face again in Teller County afterward, you'll manage to keep breathing. I give my word on that. I'm looking for a clean deal here, Mr. Quick. Don't take that to mean I can't handle a messy one."

"Okay," Cole said.

"Okay what?" Gables asked.

"Okay, I'll sign the papers, and get out of town."

"For good?"

"Yes, for good. I never wanted to come back here anyway."

"Glad to hear you've come to your senses, son. Now hear this, too. Don't think I don't know what in the hell you're doing down at the Calvert place, poking your dumb-ass nose around where it don't belong. This unfortunate incident is settled. I know where you got the money to pay Big Boy here what you owed him, too. I was you, I'd forget I ever heard of Jimmy or James Calvert, get the fuck off this property and never even think about it again afterward. I catch you down here again and we're going to do this deal the hardest way possible, am I clear?"

"Yeah, you're clear, Sheriff."

"Good," Gables said, tossing the Silverado's keys at him. Cole scrambled to get them under control and just barely avoided losing them in the lake. Gables and Big Zach snickered.

"Looks like you almost had to walk your ass home," Gables

said. "Now get up and get that raggedy-ass truck out of my sight before I have it impounded and destroyed."

Cole stumbled to his feet and tried to walk a wide circle around Big Zach, but there wasn't enough room. Zach flinched at him as he passed and he almost fell into the water. Just as he passed on, he felt the palm of Zach's hand slam into the side of his head. This time he did go into the water, came up disoriented and unsure which way the shore was.

Somehow, he managed to hold onto his keys, maybe out of survival instinct. Jack Gables and Big Zach erupted in laughter on the pier up above him.

"There's more where that came from, Cole. Keep it in mind," Zach said after he finished laughing. Cole swam his way to shore and stumbled up the path past the house to find his truck parked in the driveway next to a big black King Ranch Edition Ford.

He fired up the engine, shaking and soaking wet. His mind was still so cloudy from Zach's slap that he could hardly figure out how to back the truck up and turn it around. When he finally pulled out onto the road it was all he could do to focus on keeping the tires on the dark country road as the sun rose outside his passenger window.

He needed to think. All the things he'd gotten himself involved in were coagulating into one hell of a mess. He didn't believe Gables would let him live after he signed over the farm. It didn't make sense. He would have arrested Cole if that were the case, used his position at the jail to pressure him into compliance. Gables didn't want Cole anywhere on his professional radar because he knew that most people around town either didn't have any idea who Cole was, or hadn't seen or heard from him in years.

By his own assessment Cole had to admit that there weren't many people who would notice if he disappeared. They had to kill him—no use leaving loose ends like that. That's why they didn't want a record of him in their jail. It would look bad if he died there and had signed the farm over in the days or weeks before. This way they could knock him off after the deal and no one would even remember.

He could only think of two places to go for help. In his gut he trusted Vernon and Millie, knew they would help him if they were able. But he didn't want to get them involved if he didn't have to, and it was hard to deny that being people of color meant they had almost no clout in a place like Teller, where you could damn near tell which side of Fenton Parkway a person lived on by their skin color. He needed to keep Millie and Vernon out of this if possible, protect them the way they'd always protected him.

That left one choice: James Calvert. Gables said he knew where Cole had gotten the money to pay Big Zach. How could that be? He tried to remember if anyone had followed him out there, couldn't. Then it hit him. He'd left Calvert's business card in the moneybag. That woke him right up from his haze. He needed to warn James Calvert. Maybe Calvert would let him stay out at the ranch while they figured it out.

He stopped for gas at a travel station outside of town. He found an old, dirty pair of jeans in the back of the truck and limped around the side of the station into a filthy wood-paneled bathroom to clean himself up. In the cracked mirror his face didn't look much better than the bathroom itself. Swelling down the left side, that eye bloodshot and drooping. That whole side of his face was already turning yellow. Felt like he had busted ribs, too. He couldn't even take full breaths anymore.

He eased up his soaked, bloody shirt to reveal a bruise forming in the shape of Big Zach's boot. He cleaned up what he could, then hobbled back out to his truck and tossed the wet boots and jeans into the bed. He went into the station to pay for the gas barefoot and still soaking wet from the waist up.

A heavy-set woman wearing a Looney Tunes T-shirt two-sizes two big was working the counter. She cocked her head at him and he tried to give her a casual shrug, winced from a pain in his shoulder instead.

"Must have been one hell of a night," the woman said.

"You have no idea," Cole mumbled. He limped to the drink case and picked up a big bottle of water, was headed back to the counter when he noticed a rack of "Don't Mess With Texas" T-shirts. He grabbed a large, tossed it up on the counter with the bottled water.

"Thirty on the far pump out there and a pack of Marlboro Reds," he said. "And some of that Advil over there, please."

The clerk reached above her head and brought down the smokes. She did the same with a travel pack of Advil. "I just love these shirts," she said, scanning the T-shirt. "If I could, I'd wear one every day."

"I don't doubt it," Cole said.

"Fifty-two twenty-eight," she said. "You get in some sort of accident or something?" she added.

"Something like that," Cole said, not wanting to answer any more questions. He exchanged the money with her and went back out to pump the gas. The gas had finished pumping before he managed to pull off his button-down shirt and put on the T-shirt, in absolute misery the whole time. His ribs had to be cracked at a minimum.

He scanned the other cars parked around the adjacent businesses. He didn't know what he should be looking for, but he didn't see anyone or anything suspicious.

At this point he figured Jack Gables knew everything he needed to know about who and what Cole dealt with. Maybe James Calvert knew more than he had let on, too. After all, he'd been a successful part of the Teller community for decades, had even had the connections to get the case file.

Either way, Cole needed to quit fucking around and develop a plan. As he drove off down the highway he remembered something he'd read in a book once. *The only good thing about the worst day of your life is that if you survive it things will never be that bad again.* He couldn't imagine things getting much worse, so he had that going for him, at least.

CHAPTER FOURTEEN

Fresh dust hung over the caliche rock road as Cole drove up toward James Calvert's ranch, meaning someone had just driven down it. Hopefully that meant James was home.

As the house came into sight, flashing lights appeared from multiple vehicles parked in the driveway beyond the white picket fence. Cole's adrenaline spiked as he pulled to a stop.

He squinted his eyes against the sun to make out the vehicles: An ambulance and a State Trooper's car, as well as Calvert's Mercedes and a four-door Toyota Tacoma he didn't recognize.

Something was wrong. He wondered if he should turn around and just get out of there, but pulling off the built-up road down into the pasture would be both difficult and suspicious. The last thing he needed was more trouble from law enforcement, and it might be nothing, or some medical thing. He decided to pull down to the house and see what had happened.

A stump-chested State Trooper met him at the cattle guard between the main driveway and caliche rock road. The man held his palm up to stop Cole from coming any closer. Cole put it in park and got out.

"Afternoon," the trooper called out.

"Howdy," Cole replied, then added, "Everything okay with Mr. Calvert?"

"Are you related to Mr. Calvert?" the officer asked, looking him over with disapproval, which was no surprise given Cole's bare feet and beat up face.

Cole tried to act casual. "Nah. He's a friend of mine. I come out to see him. He sick or something?"

"What's your name, sir?"

"My name's Cole. You?"

"I'm Corporal Dave Marshall with the State Troopers. I'm afraid there's been an accident."

Cole wiped sweat from his forehead and winced from a bruise there. More sweat ran down his back. "Accident?" he asked.

"I'm sorry, but I can't really say anything else about it at this time."

"But is Mr. Calvert okay, can you tell me that, at least?"

"I'm not authorized to speak on it."

"Come on, man, he's my friend. You can't just leave me hanging here."

Trooper Marshall looked around, his eyes shaded by the straw cowboy hat the State Patrol all wore in the hot summer months. He seemed to be struggling with how much to say. "It appears at this time that Mr. Calvert was kicked in the head by one of his horses, and is now deceased from the injury. That's it, I can't say another word, shouldn't have even said that much, but I felt bad on account you know the man. There a reason you were coming down here today? You look like a horse might have kicked you twice."

Cole frowned, aware again of how beat up he must look. "Just to visit. I was in a car accident yesterday, hit my head pretty hard," he lied. "Mr. Calvert and I are old family friends, I guess you could say."

"Old family friends," the trooper repeated. "I see. Well, why don't you hang out for a moment if you don't mind, Mr.—I didn't catch your last name?"

"Quick. Cole Quick," Cole said. He'd wanted to avoid giving his last name, if possible. Trooper Marshall seemed to be a regular cop going about his job, but Cole had no idea who to trust anymore.

"Okay. Well, Mr. Quick, if you don't mind, I'd like for you to stick around for a few minutes, in case the investigating officer has any questions for you. It won't take long. Believe it or not, we get calls like these a couple times a year. Usually the person is okay, but sometimes this happens. Horses are wonderful animals, but they're like women. Sweet until you handle 'em the wrong way, then they'll kick the hell out of you."

"I understand," Cole said, even though he'd only ridden a horse twice in his life. Horses were a way of life to lots of people, and he'd heard them used for every possible metaphor concerning women. "Is there anything I can do in the meantime?"

"Just stay put and don't come past the fence, for now. I'm sure you'd like to make some calls, but I'll ask you not to do that until we're able to notify the next of kin. Maybe you can provide me with some contact information for family members?"

"Honestly, I was friends with his son back in high school. His wife ran off years ago with some attorney or something. I never knew her. His son passed away recently. I'm not really sure of anyone else to call."

"You can't think of anyone?"

"Like I said. At one time his son was like family to me, but we hadn't spoken in many years. Mr. Calvert and I had been getting together recently to just sort of reflect on the loss, I guess you might say. Does that make sense?"

"I reckon so. Anyway, Mr. Quick, if you think of anyone while you're waiting, let me know."

"Will do. I appreciate you being straight with me, I know you didn't have to do that."

"No problem. Just keep it to yourself. You want, I can get the EMT to take a look at your face when he's done."

"Not necessary," Cole said.

"Suit yourself." Trooper Marshall's boots clapped against the concrete as he made his way back over to the ambulance. They had what must be James Calvert's body strapped to a gurney, were lifting it up into the ambulance, probably for transport to the morgue.

Cole was already thinking that no way this could be a coincidence. Jack gables said he knew exactly where Cole had gotten the money for Big Zach, and now the next day the man who provided it turns up dead. Couldn't be clearer, given Calvert's business card was right in the middle of the money.

Gables had also made it clear what would happen if Cole kept looking into Jimmy and Caroline's deaths. Calvert had said he would never stop looking to clear his son's name. Whatever really happened to Jimmy and Caroline, Jack Gables didn't want it coming back up.

At the very least it would be an embarrassment to the department, and might even send the wealthy Bible-thumpers over at Rose Meadows into a fit. No force in Teller County made stronger political competition to the town's old oil money than the Southern Baptists, once they got worked into a moral frenzy. When Cole was a kid they'd picketed several major Hollywood films right out of town. But Cole had a feeling the real reason was far more sinister: Maybe Jack Gables was somehow involved in Jimmy and Caroline's deaths.

He thought about sitting Trooper Marshall down when he came back and telling him everything. About Gables, last night, the extortion, Kerrie, Chester dying. Everything. It would feel good just to get it all out. But for all he knew, Trooper Marshall could be somehow connected to Jack Gables. No telling how far the good ol' boy network stretched across East Texas, especially after having thirty years to thrive.

It took another thirty minutes stuck beneath the scalding sun before anyone so much as acknowledged Cole, other than to give him looks that said, "Stay out of the way."

He tried to do that, all the while feeling the clock ticking on his problems. He would just sign the goddamn farm over to Gables and leave town as planned, except now he didn't believe they would let him live afterwards. He couldn't really figure out why they hadn't just kidnapped him and held him last night. Maybe Gables just figured Cole was too scared to resist.

He needed to stay away from Gables's henchman at all costs from here on out. If he had any sense, he'd just take off driving and not stop until his money ran out, make them take the risks to come and find him.

Except these people might have covered up his friend's murder, maybe also murdered his friend's father. Now they were trying to take away the one thing on earth Cole had a right to, his lone reward for the beatings and neglect and heartache that Chester Quick had filled his life with after his mother died.

Now, more than anything else, he realized that he wanted to beat them, not run from them. If it took his life, he was ready to give it. He felt a piece of Chester's anger clinch its fist inside him and refuse to budge another inch. What did he have to live for either way? Nothing. He was done getting fucked around by rich people, by the law, and most of all by Chester Quick. Live or die, he was done cowing, no turning back.

He hadn't let himself feel anything since Kerrie had died, but last night it had all hit him at once. Now it had lighted a fire in his heart. He would use it to burn the whole county to ashes, if need be. He didn't have a plan and he didn't expect to succeed, but in that moment he vowed to try anyway. He was going to figure out what had happened to Jimmy, or die trying.

A man in dark Wranglers and a straw Stetson came down the driveway toward Cole. As he got closer, he waved, and Cole noticed there was no badge hooked onto his belt.

"Mr. Quick?" the man asked.

"That's me," Cole replied.

"My name is Russ Kirkpatrick. I'm a private investigator. I was working with Mr. Calvert regarding his son's death."

The man extended his hand and Cole shook it.

"Cole Quick," Cole said as they shook hands. "You're the private investigator James was meeting with, former Ranger?"

"I am, yes. You look like someone went upside your head with a crowbar. No offense, just an observation." Kirkpatrick gave a slight grin as if to show Cole he was making friendly, then went on. "I was a Texas Ranger for fifteen years before moving into the private sector. James mentioned you to me, too. I had the unfortunate experience of finding his body this morning. I was supposed to meet him to follow up on some things." Kirkpatrick adjusted his hat and shifted weight from one boot to the other. "Heck of a coincidence, him taking a hoof to the head," he said. "What are you doing out here this morning, did he ask you out?"

Cole wasn't sure how much to say to this man. Calvert had trusted him, but Calvert was dead. For all he knew this man could have killed James Calvert, though his instinct told him Kirkpatrick seemed to be a decent man.

"Nah, I had some troubles poking around over in Teller, wanted to tell James about it. Jimmy was my best friend in high school. We were disconnected for a few years. I came back into town for my Daddy's funeral a couple days ago and heard about what happened. You probably know that James has me poking around. I'm not sure I can be a whole lot of help, I'd imagine anything he said to me he's already said to you, too."

"I see," Kirkpatrick said. "Did he mention to you anything about some new development with his son's situation?"

"To tell you the truth everything he said was new to me," Cole said. "I don't really know much about it except that it's sad, and he didn't trust the Teller County Sheriff's office, which I understand. I saw the case file. I wouldn't have taken Jimmy to do something like that either, but I also hadn't seen him in a decade."

Kirkpatrick's eyes shifted as he studied Cole. He could tell right away the man was sharp.

"Anything you think I need to know about the sheriff's department?" Kirkpatrick asked. "Like, how your face came to look like that, maybe?"

Every bone in Cole's body wanted to tell this man everything that was happening to him, but his mouth simply would not relent to doing it. He got the feeling Kirkpatrick knew more about Jack Gables and company than he was letting on, too.

"Not really. So you found him?" Cole asked, changing the subject instead.

"Yes. Knocked on the door for twenty minutes, saw the barn door was open and figured he must be back there. Went back there and found him unresponsive in a horse stall. Looks like the horse kicked him in the back of the head."

"And they're sure that's what happened? You don't think someone might have whacked him on the head and made it look like that?"

Kirkpatrick straightened up and stood tall when Cole said that. It gave Cole a rush of nerves.

"Their findings aren't final yet, obviously. Why, you know somebody that would want to do something like that?" Kirkpatrick looked Cole straight in the eyes. Again, he wanted to tell the man everything, but resisted.

"Nah," Cole said, measuring his words again. "I can tell you that people don't appreciate me poking around about those murders over in Teller. I guess I don't want to believe something like that can happen out of the blue, but I have no proof anyone would want to harm him. I just saw him yesterday."

"Between you and me," Kirkpatrick said, "he's about got a damn hoof-sized welt on his head. Deputy Marshall said you didn't know much about who to contact. It's all right. He's got a sister out in Abilene, I already checked. I'll look her up and let her know. If you'd like I can have her let you know about funeral services once they figure it out?"

"I wish I had somewhere for her to call me at, to tell you the truth, but I don't." Cole said. He really needed to get a cell phone.

Kirkpatrick reached into his back pocket and brought out a checkbook-sized leather Cowboy wallet. "Tell you what. Here's my card, Mr. Quick. You give me a call tomorrow and I'll relay you the information. I'll have some more questions for you then, if you decide you feel like coming clean. I might could help you if you did." He handed the card to Cole and gave him a look that said he knew Cole wasn't being straight with him.

"Appreciate it, Mr. Kirkpatrick." He put the man's card in his own wallet in case it might be of use later.

"So would I." Kirkpatrick locked eyes with him again. "You decide to come to your senses, pick up the phone. I know a lot of people around this state. And I know Jack Gables is as crooked as a bent stick. Last time I came into contact with him it cost me my job with the Rangers, that's why I'm a private investigator."

"I know you now," Cole said. "You're the ranger from that mess with Bobby Burnell. I saw it on television. You got fired over all the bloodshed."

Kirkpatrick shook his head. "Good, that's true. And now you know that I'm not one of Jack Gables' cronies. I don't mean to pry, but you look like a man who could use a friend. You decide to trust me, give me a call and I'll do what I can to help you."

Cole thanked him, again resisting the urge to tell him everything. He didn't want to make any big decisions in his current state, didn't trust his own judgment. Instead, he went back to his truck, backed down off the road into the pasture to turn around, and drove out of there.

On the highway headed back toward Teller, Cole again felt a fire welling up in him that even Chester would have been proud of. He needed a goddamn drink. Bad. Sweaty palms, shaky hands, the worst nerves he'd ever felt.

He weighed his options, decided to stop over at Vernon's and try to eat, maybe give him a rounded version of the problem and see if Vern had any advice. He didn't figure Vernon would recommend trusting a cop, former or otherwise, but it was worth feeling out. If he decided to, he could call Kirkpatrick back after, tell him everything. At this point he had no one else to turn to. He was done running, he knew that much.

He wanted to talk to Mandy Ambrose again, too. He had the feeling she might know more about what her sister and Jimmy were up to than they'd had a chance to discuss. It was a dangerous conversation to try and have, but he was running out of time. No way was he going to sign the goddamn farm over to Gables now. If they killed him, they'd do it without his signature on the deed. He'd do everything in his power to make sure Gables never saw a dime of whatever black gold was stored beneath the farm.

Which meant he needed one hell of a plan, and he needed it now.

As he drove he started to formulate one. Before the week was out they might bury him in Teller County, but he wasn't going to go without a fight.

He pulled up to Chester's farm and left the engine running while he went inside and changed into some clean jeans and a plain grey T-shirt. He cleaned his face up as best he could again, put on some socks and tennis shoes, and gathered up all his stuff. He took the pistol and the last baggy of cocaine out of the cupboard, too, tossed everything in his duffle bag and took it out to his truck.

He had no intention of stepping foot back inside that hellhole ever again as long as he lived, however long that turned out to be.

The parking lot at Vernon's was empty when he pulled up, too early for happy hour and past the lunch rush. He parked around the back of the building and went inside. Vernon looked up from a plate full of ribs and wiped his mouth with a napkin.

"Whadaya say, Cole?" Vernon had to swallow before he could continue talking. "Caught me getting my lunch. Only time I get to sit still and get some nourishment." He stood up, wiped his hand on the front of his apron again and shook Cole's hand. He looked tired.

"Hey Vernon," Cole said. "Please, don't let me disturb your meal."

"I done ate so many of these ribs I can't taste 'em no more anyhow. What the hell happened to your face?" Vernon asked, shock showing on his own.

Cole paused, unsure of what answer to give, knowing that every word he was about to say might put Vernon and Millie in danger, but unable to stop himself. He needed to tell someone about what had happened, about everything that was about to happen.

Vernon must have sensed his hesitation. "Let me get Millie to fix you something to eat and you can tell me about it," he said. "You want a beer? I think I might have one myself."

"Finish eating first, I can wait till you're done," Cole said.

"Hell naw, Cole. Be right back. Pull up a chair and set with me."

Cole sat in the chair across from Vernon's. Vernon stuck his head through the kitchen door and asked Millie for "a Hunger Hanger for Cole."

"Cole out there?" Millie said. "Good. I whip one up and come take a break."

Vernon poured a pitcher of Shiner Bock and brought three pint glasses with it to the table. "Now tell me what happened," he said.

"It's kind of a long story," Cole began, measuring the words in his head. "I'm in some trouble. Stuff from the past, reason I left. Chester wasn't the only thing I ran off from. I owed some money and I skipped on it, but they caught up with me soon as I got back into town."

"Huh," Vernon said, taking it in. "I knowed you ain't run off solely on account of Chester, I guess."

"There's more. Chester left me his farm, and there's apparently some oil underneath it. Problem is, the guy I ran off on wants me to sign the farm over to his boss. And his boss is Jack Gables."

"What's that I hear about Jack Gables?" Millie said, coming out of the kitchen with Cole's sandwich. "That man the crookedest creature to ever walk around on two legs. His cronies 'bout beat Lousie's boy Jerome to death for nothing, put some nonsense robbery charge on him, and he been up at Huntsville three years on it now."

"I've been seeing him in that light lately myself," Cole said, turning back to Vernon. "You remember my friend I brought in the other day, James Calvert?"

"I felt bad 'bout the way I come straight out with that business about his son."

"Well, he didn't think his son could have done what they say he did. In fact, he was so sure of it that he paid my debt off to these guys in exchange for me looking into it, seeing if I could figure out if Jimmy owed a big drug debt to anyone who might have killed him for it, since I used to run in those circles some. That's where things have gotten messy. After I paid them off yesterday, they said it wasn't enough, I still had to sign over the farm. Last night Jack Gables himself beat the tar out of me and threatened my life if I don't sign Chester's farm over tomorrow. Said he'd frame me up for a bunch of stuff or maybe just drown me in the lake if I refused.

"He also told me he knew I was poking around about Jimmy and Caroline Ambrose's deaths, and he knew who put me up to it. He said if I wanted to stay in one piece I better sign and disappear. I'm worried I'll disappear either way."

Cole paused. Vernon nodded his head to show he understood so far. Millie shook her head no, the way someone might do after dropping something expensive and made of glass.

"Jack Gables the one beat you up like that?" she said.

"Yeah. Early this morning. Suffice it to say, my nerves are redlining. So I drove to James Calvert's ranch down near Crockett this morning to warn him about what happened. Seems James got kicked in the head by a horse this morning, and now he's dead."

"And you think Jack Gables involved in that, too, somehow, huh?" Millie asked. Vernon still just sat and listened.

"I do. It's too much of a coincidence. But that's got me thinking. These two messes I'm caught up in, maybe they're the same mess. Maybe the same people looking to kill me were looking to kill Jimmy, maybe even for similar reasons. His father seemed to think he and Caroline Ambrose might have run up a big drug debt with someone, and I'm thinking it could be the same someone I owed. What I can't figure out is, how did Jack Gables know about the oil on Chester's farm? I only found out by stumbling across a file stashed under Chester's mattress."

"This place a tangled web, Cole, listen to me now when I say that," Millie said. "And Jack Gables, he the spider going around wrapping up the flies. But it ain't his web, he just the enforcer. They's a group of white folks round here own whatever they like, do whatever they like, and ain't nothing nobody can say about it."

"Now Millie," Vernon broke in, "Don't go filling this boy's head with no ghetto conspiracy nonsense. He in trouble."

Millie's face contorted as she hunched her shoulders. "Vernon, shut your mouth and let me talk, I know what the hell I'm saying. He need to hear this." She turned to Cole, her eyes serious. "Cole, I done had a lot of friends that cleaned house for them rich white folks through the years. Them Ambroses, Coopers, Brownwoods, and Colstons. All the big-money families you can think of 'round these parts. Every single one of 'em has told me stories 'bout the nonsense them folks involved in. Sex, blackmail, white collar crimes. No offense, you understand, but it's like white folks forget a nigger even in the room so long as she dustin' the china."

"What kind of stuff did they say?"

"Just double-talk, shady business stuff, social gossip centered around that damn Rose Festival they be havin' every year. All kinds of adultery and backstabbing. Sound to me like you stepped up in the middle of some of they schemes. I was you, I'd sign them papers and then run back off to where you been hiding, forget you ever heard of this place. I hate to see you go again, but that's just the truth."

"You in deep, that's for sure," Vernon said. "I hate to see you lose what's coming to you from Chester, but Millie's right when she say them folks do as they please, can't nobody stop it."

Cole leaned away from his plate, took a big drink of beer before he replied. "Up until last night I was planning on signing the farm over and getting the hell out of town. But I've got no guarantee they won't kill me even if I do. Anyway, I'm tired of running. I've been running half my life from this thing. I've decided to stay here and fight this out, defend what's mine."

Vernon rubbed his chin. "I understand that sentiment, Cole, really I do. Anyone put in your place gonna feel like that for a minute. But think, son. What's your life worth? Ain't nothing fair in this world, sometimes all we can do is take the ass whoopin' and move on to the next one. Ain't none of this worth dying for."

"Maybe not to you. Yesterday not to me either. Today is different. These people aren't gonna absorb my life just because they feel entitled to it."

"You'd best think on it hard, Colton," Millie said. "I don't wanna read about you in that damn paper like I done read about your friend. Sound to me like even white folk ain't safe from this. Ought not to matter, but that just the way it is in East Texas."

"I appreciate your concern," Cole replied. "And you're right, this place is a racist shit hole most of the time. But I can't just keep running from things the rest of my life. Besides, I don't feel like I've got anything left to lose."

Vernon put a hand on his shoulder. "If there was some way we could help you, Cole, Millie and I would, wouldn't we, Millie?"

Millie nodded. "We sho would."

"But we got a business, Cole. It ain't been easy, Reggie locked up. Cost of everything always on the rise. I get up at four a.m. to wrap brisket tacos and work sixteen-hour days just so we don't have to pay someone else to do the extra work part of the week."

"I'm sorry to bring this trouble to your door at all, Vern," Cole said. "I appreciate you letting me talk it over with you, at least. I think I just needed to hear myself say some of these things out loud. Makes them real. I wanted y'all to at least know that if I disappeared again, it wasn't because I ran off this time, it's because I was murdered. I don't want to go to my grave with everyone who ever remembered me thinking I'm too much of a coward to face up to my problems. Even Chester was better than that."

Millie put her hand on top of Vernon's. "You ain't got to prove nothing to us, Cole. Listen. We here for you. Always. You don't never have to go to bed hungry or alone, long as that's true. Whatever you gonna do, you gonna do. Just use your head."

"I will, Millie. Thank you."

"Ain't nothing. Like I always said. The Good Lord says to look out for our brothers and sisters, and that's just what me and Vernon do."

"I know it is."

"We be seein' you again soon, then?"

"I'm going to do everything in my power."

"Fair enough. You want me to wrap that sandwich up to go? Ain't barely touched it."

"I'll get it down."

"All right then," she said. Millie leaned down and gave him an awkward hug. It felt good to have someone show him affection, something he hadn't really had much since Kerrie died.

"I got to get back to work too, Cole," Vernon said. "This one on the house though. You got bigger fish to fry."

"Not necessary."

"Maybe not, but I insist."

"Well, thank you then. Hey, one last thing, Vernon?"

"Sure."

"You know any attorneys, someone who maybe handles estate planning and contracts, but doesn't work with the corrupt people around town?"

"Matter of fact I do, Cole. My old buddy Cecil Johnson. He helped Millie and me lots of times. He hard-nosed, but he a good man."

"Do you trust him? I mean, do you think he might be in any way connected to any shady people like the ones I'm tangled up with?"

"He hate the fucking sheriff, if that's what you askin'. He ain't big on white folks in general, tell the truth. It be hard for any black lawyer 'round here not to feel that way. They got a courtside seat to how we be treated."

"You think he'd do some work for me?" Cole asked.

Vernon scratched his head like he was thinking about it. "Like I said, he honest. And if I vouch for you won't be no problem, he treat you just like you was me, he just bitch about it the whole time is all."

Would you trust him with your life?"

"Why you ask me that, Cole?"

"Because I might be trusting him with mine, and I want to be sure he'll do what I ask him to do."

"Yes, I do. I'll give him a call. Stop back by this evening and I let you know what he say. Millie'll be itchin' to see you still all right, or you still whatever this is now, anyway." Vernon gestured at Cole's appearance with his hands. "You know she be acting tough, but she gon' worry herself sick about you now that you done told her all that mess."

"I'm sorry for that, Vernon. Thanks for listening. I promise, if I get out of this I'll make it up to you for everything you've done for me."

"Not necessary, Cole. Just be careful and stay above ground, that's enough. I see you tonight."

Cole nodded and they shook hands, then Vernon followed Millie back into the kitchen. Cole took a few more bites of his sandwich and washed them down with a full pint of beer. He opened the barn-style front door and walked out into daylight like a man awakened from a coma.

In the truck, he opened Chester's file and found the name and business address of the landman Chester had worked with on the exploration, Bobby Hendon. He lit up a smoke and headed across town to the man's office.

CHAPTER FIFTEEN

Bobby Hendon's office was located in one of the old false-façade buildings just across the street from the courthouse down on the square. Cole pulled open the glass front door and came into a small room with two navy-blue upholstered chairs against the front wall and some sort of Dallas Cowboys homage framed behind them.

"Hello?" a voice called from the open office door to the far side of the waiting room. "Come on back to the office."

Cole stepped through the doorframe to find a plump, balding man in a navy-blue Dallas Cowboys polo shirt, sitting behind a desk with a laptop open in front of him.

"Can I help you with something?" the man asked, clearly disturbed by Cole's beat-up appearance.

"I'm hoping so. Are you Mr. Hendon?"

"Please. My stubborn-ass daddy was Mr. Hendon. Call me Bobby. And you are?" Hendon extended his hand across the desk. Cole stepped up and shook it.

"My name is Cole Quick. I think you might have done some work for my late father a few months back regarding a potential oil lease for Ambrose Oil. Do you recall any of that, by chance?"

"I do, as a matter of fact. You said late. So stubborn old Chester passed on then?"

"He did."

"I'm sorry to hear it."

"Thanks, but I doubt that's true."

"You got me there. It's a shame, though, man dying sittin' on all that money."

"That's what I came to speak to you about. He left the farm to me. I only just found out about the potential lease. I was hoping maybe you could tell me, assuming you even know, why my father sat on this instead of allowing it to be developed?"

"I don't want to shoot my mouth off too much, but I can tell you *exactly* why. He just didn't understand how the percentages of these kinds of deals work. I came into contact with him because Ambrose Oil contacted me. They'd done some drilling and exploration in the area and believed his land was worth drilling on. I determined he was the mineral rights owner and I contacted him with an offer from Ambrose. I did my best, but he was hard to manage.

"Companies like Ambrose invest a truck-load of resources into developing a well. They expect a return on their investment, just as anyone would. Your father had other ideas. Where he got them, I don't know. He was asking nearly double the industry-standard percentages on the lease, said Ambrose owed him that on account of years of service to them. Kept threatening to go to the competition. Finally, I called off the project and had to tell Ambrose I couldn't get the deal done. You might imagine that doesn't happen to them often. That's a *substantial* well you're sitting on there, son, but there wasn't a company on earth gonna give him a dollar more than Ambrose had already offered. Does that surprise you?"

"I'd be more surprised if a rattlesnake bit me for grabbing a hand full of rattle," Cole said.

"So that's your spread, now, huh?"

"For the moment."

Bobby whistled. "I don't know what your finances look like now, but that's a solid score to fall on top of. Hard to believe nobody ever discovered that pocket before now, really. Man's cut of that could make him a millionaire, given time."

"That was the impression I got from reading the paperwork from the exploration, or what I understood of it, anyway."

"Was the land sentimental to your father or something, maybe some other reason to hold out?"

"Chester was as sentimental as I look pretty. Just hardheaded and mean, and he liked other people to know it. I'd say he was being a son-of-a-bitch on account that's all he knew how to be."

"You and your father weren't close, I take it?"

"You take it correct," Cole said.

"Well then, I'll have to conclude that you're a much more reasonable man than your father. Mind if I ask you something?"

"Shoot."

"What the hell happened to your face?"

"Car accident."

"Must have been a hell of an accident. So tell me, are you going to take Ambrose Oil's deal?"

"Would you, in my position?"

"Were I in your position, they'd have torn half my land up six months ago, and I'd be on a beach in Hawaii with some strange in my face."

"I'll take that as a yes."

"You're taking me correct, too, then. I can't fathom why you're still standing here talking to me when you could be over there working on a check?"

"If you can't, then neither can I," Cole said. "Thank you for chatting with me, you've been informative."

"Glad I can help. Enjoy your new good fortune, Mr. Quick. Sorry about your father. Might want to have a doctor look at that face and stay away from whoever really did that to you, though."

"I'll let you know how that goes," Cole said, already on his way out the door again.

Next, he drove over to the motor bank where Randall worked. He parked next to the BMW they'd done bumps in the night before, dug up the check for four-thousand dollars from Chester's insurance policy, and took it inside with him.

"Good afternoon," the lone female teller inside the tiny lobby said, looking at him as if he were a bum coming in off the street. "Is there something I can help you out with, sir?" She wrinkled her nose as she said sir like it hurt her to say it, but she had to anyway.

"Yeah, hey there. I'm here to see Randall."

"You mean Mr. Harrington, the Branch Manager?" Her tone said she couldn't fathom Randall knowing someone who would ever end up in Cole's condition. Typical socialite Teller woman, looking down on everyone so much it was a wonder she didn't hit her head on the floor.

"Yeah, Mr. Harrington, the *Branch Manager*," Cole said, imitating her tone. "He's an old buddy of mine. He around?"

"Um...yes sir, he's back in his office. Let me just go tell him you're here. Your name, please?"

"My name's Cole Quick."

"Great, Mr. *Quick*. I'll be right back."

"Don't get lost," Cole said. He was tired of being treated like trash by everyone in this sorry-ass town.

She rolled her eyes and scurried off down a hallway out of sight. Cole poured himself a coffee from the stand in the bank's tiny waiting area, was about to sit on one of the couches when Randall came out of the back with the snotty teller on his heels. He looked nervous.

"Well, heck, hey there Cole," Randall called out as he approached. He stopped when he noticed the bruises and cuts on Cole's face. "What in the hell happened to your face?"

"Long story. Maybe I can tell it to you over a beer sometime."

"Maybe," Randall said. "To what do I owe the pleasure?"

"I mentioned last night that I needed to open an account."

Randall's face loosened up a little. He must have thought Cole was coming by to ask him for money or drugs, given his condition. "Oh yeah, sure. Come on back to my office and we'll get you set up."

Randall turned and headed off down the hall. Cole pushed past the teller and followed him, coffee and check in hand. The teller took up her spot back behind the counter and folded her hands in front of her like she was putting a wall up between them. The look she exchanged with Randall made Cole think there was something beyond professional about their relationship.

Randall's office was tidy with an oak desk and a boar's head baring its teeth from the wall behind his brown leather office chair. The glass-topped desk had a computer and a few neat stacks of paperwork, a set of matching armchairs in front of it and a filing cabinet behind.

"So, tell me, Cole," Randall said, sitting down behind his desk, "What type of account are you looking to open?"

"I need a checking and savings account. I've got a life insurance check to deposit."

"Not a problem. Can I just see the check, and your ID?"

Cole handed him the check and his license.

"You want me to use this Colorado address?"

"Nah. You can use my daddy's farm for the address, for now. You got something for me to write on?"

"Sure," Randall said, pushing a bank letterhead notepad across the desk and setting a pen on top of it. "Go ahead and jot down your Social, too, I'll shred this when we're done."

Cole wrote down the address to Chester's farm and his Social Security number and passed it back. Randall punched it into the computer.

"Just out of curiosity," Cole asked, "When will these funds be available for withdrawal? I got a few bills I need to pay here pretty quick."

"Well, normally we put a hold on the funds for forty-eight hours on a new account, but since we know each other and this is practically a cashier's check, I'll go ahead and clear it. I'll issue you a temporary debit card, as well. The real card will come in the mail in seven to ten business days. There's a drive-thru ATM in the last lane out back."

"Thanks, Randall, I appreciate it. Let me ask: you think I can pull, say, three-thousand out now?"

Randall raised his eyebrows, then shook off the look. "I guess that would be okay. By the way, since we're back here in the office, what happened to your face?"

Cole tried to fake something akin to a grin. "Not much to tell, really. Ran into some other old acquaintances last night, too. They weren't all that happy to see me, I guess."

Randall folded his hands on the desk and leaned in. "Old drug debt or something?"

"Something. Anyway, it's over now."

Randall stood and picked up the papers off the printer. He pulled a blank credit card out of his desk and swiped it on the computer's card scanner.

"Just sign the bottom of the last page there, then go ahead and punch in your desired pin in that pad right there."

Cole signed and entered Chester's birth year for the pin, 1950.

"I'll fill out a withdrawal form and be right back with the cash."

"Perfect, Cole said, leaning back in his chair. Randall was gone two minutes and came back with a stack of bills, counted them out on top of the paperwork.

You're all set, Cole," he said. "Welcome to Bank of Teller."

They shook hands and Cole walked back down the hallway past the teller, who watched him go out the front door into the sunshine.

He stopped at a Cricket phone store in a dilapidated shopping mall on the north side of town and picked up a cell phone, had the dreadlocked female clerk put two hundred minutes on it. Though he didn't know exactly what he intended to do yet, he was starting to get a good idea. It might be handy to have a phone around.

He dug Russ Kirkpatrick's card out of his pocket and called the number on it. He let it ring until it went to voicemail, debated leaving a message, hung up instead. What he had to say would be hard enough to say over the phone at all, and impossible via voicemail.

He'd try back later and see what he could come up with. For now, he drove back to Vernon's as the late afternoon sun made its way below the horizon.

CHAPTER SIXTEEN

The parking lot at Vernon's was full when Cole pulled in. As soon as he opened the door he heard Sheldon back by the pool tables talking shit to someone, meaning Vernon must have gotten over the other night. When Vernon saw Cole, he stopped in the middle of taking someone's order and came out from behind the counter.

"I got you all set up," he said. "My man Cecil were skeptical, but I told him you probably the only person hate rich white folks more than him in all of Teller County. He like that. He still skeptical, but he comin' up here in about a half hour, when he get through workin'."

Cole clapped him on the back. "Thank you, Vernon. Really, you've got no idea how much this means to me."

"I got some idea, Cole. It mean life or death. But he gon' want some money, right up front."

"That's how I figured it already. I brought cash enough for a retainer, at least."

"Good. I best get back behind the counter. I sit down and talk with y'all, I get the chance. Go have a seat and I'll have Millie's cousin's daughter Kiesha bring you over a pitcher. She work on Thursday through Sunday, when we get busier. I can't afford her, but family's family, and they be needing the money. Be needing she stay out of trouble, too. This way she get both."

"I get it."

"She ain't suppose to serve booze but ain't nobody said nothin' yet. She be right with you."

Vernon jogged over to the counter and got back to work. Cole found an empty table and took a seat. He watched Sheldon trying to hustle a couple of guys at the pool table until Sheldon noticed him watching, nodded, and gave him a shit-eating grin. Cole nodded back just as a young girl who looked a little like Millie with braids came over with a pitcher of Shiner Bock and two glasses.

"Vernon told me to bring this over to you," she said, gesturing with her head toward Vernon.

"Thank you," Cole replied. The girl disappeared toward the kitchen before he had a chance to say anything else. He poured a glass and drained half of it, took a breath and drained the rest. The beer calmed his nerves some. The plan he was about to set into motion might get him killed, but it was either this or sign the farm over to Jack Gables and probably get murdered anyway. He could run, but he was done running from his problems now.

Dropping Jack Gables in the grease would be tough, though. He needed to talk to Mandy Ambrose again. He figured to tell her that he thought her sister had been murdered by someone else, over drugs maybe, and see what she said.

Maybe she knew more than she'd told him the first time. He wasn't sure whether he could trust her, but the way she hadn't wanted him thrown out of her party told him that she wanted something from him that she hadn't gotten around to saying yet. He wished he'd gotten a phone number from her.

Half an hour later a middle-aged black man in a peach-colored suit came through the front door. Vernon came out from behind the counter to greet him. It had to be his guy. Vernon led him over to the table and Cole stood up.

"Cole, this my good friend Cecil Johnson. He the man gonna help you out."

"Good to meet you, Cecil," Cole said, extending his hand.

"Ain't no good I can see," Cecil replied, not reaching out to shake Cole's hand. "This business. And it sound like shady business. Which mean it gonna cost you. I ain't never not even once had a white client, I want you to know that. 'Round this town ain't no white folks gonna hire a nigger lawyer for no legal work. I went to Thurgood Marshall School of Law down in Houston, graduated top of my class and worked every goddamn night as the house nigga at a catfish restaurant while I done it. I got back here and realized I might as well have gone to The African University of Nigerdy Niggas instead, all the good it did to work that hard. I tell you all this so you know I don't plan on taking no shit from you."

Vernon said, "He cool, Cecil, like I told you. Boy grew up poor, white or not, them folks ain't treated him no better."

"You know that's bullshit, Vern. Poor white boy still blend in in ways a nigga never could."

"Mr. Johnson," Cole said, taking a more formal tone now. "I promise that you're speaking my language. I'm not here to measure pain or trauma, nor do I think I'd measure up if I did. But far as I'm concerned, fuck all those people. I don't need anything shady from you, either. I have one unorthodox request, but I'll pay what it takes for you to do it."

"You damn right you'll pay. Up front, in cash. That's if I decide to do it. I ain't trying to get my ass shot off helping no white boy who in some bullshit fuckup of his own creation."

"Just pull up a chair and listen to what I have to say, that's all I ask. I'll buy you as many beers as you want while you listen."

"I don't drink beer. I take a bourbon and Coke, and keep 'em coming. I run out of drink, you out of time. Got it?"

"Fair enough," Cole said. As much as he didn't like the disrespect, he understood it. He needed someone he could trust because their anger matched his own. Cecil struck him as the kind of man who wouldn't back down out of fear, regardless of whether he liked Cole. Cole wasn't planning on asking him for anything but discretion and to file some documents anyway.

"Can you get that bourbon and Coke, Vern, or should I come

to the counter and wait in line?" Cole asked.

"I get it. Cole. Y'all just get to talking."

"Thanks, Vern."

"It ain't nothin'," Vernon said, moving off to get the drink. The girl, Millie's niece, had taken to ringing up customers in his absence. Cole felt for her. He'd spent many nights in this place when he was her age, but still it seemed like she was too young to be here. Vernon probably kept a sharp eye on her, at least. Cole leaned his elbows on the table as Cecil finally sat down across from him.

"Don't expect me to fall the fuck out just 'cause you willing to wait in line. So what you want, *Cole*?" Cecil asked.

"I need you to draw me up a last will and testament."

"What for? To hear Vernon tell it, you ain't got nothing to leave nobody. He think that make you like us. I think it don't mean shit."

Cole stayed calm, took the aggression in stride. "Let's just say I have reasons to believe I could die, I've come into possession of some things of value, and I want to have my affairs in order before I act on those things."

"First you gonna tell me why all this secretive bullshit. Before I decide."

"Again, let's just say I'd like to get my affairs in order without certain circles of people knowing what I'm up to. People around Teller like to gossip, and that kind of gossip could go very poorly for me."

"So you needed you a nigga, but you don't wanna tell him what he getting involved in. I knew it would be some shit like that."

"What I need is a legal ally. I've got some paperwork that's an offer for a substantial amount of money to develop a well on some land I recently inherited. Powerful people have their eyes on it, and they're trying to pressure me into signing the land over to them. I want to sign a lease, but with Chromatic Oil over in Dallas, not Ambrose. There's two offers in the file. I'd like you to handle that deal."

"Uh-huh. Boy, you in some kind of drug bullshit, that's what this is. You ain't foolin' me even for a second."

Cecil was sharp.

"Maybe so," Cole said. "What makes you say that?"

"Believe it or not, black folks 'round here be lucky to even have these kinds of problems in the first place, but they do. I seen a bunch of 'em get in with the wrong people and end up signin' what little they have over. In Teller it always about drugs, period. You askin' me to draw up a will just make it that much more obvious."

"Vernon said you were smart. And you're right about most everything you've said so far. But you might think different of me when you know what I want you to write in that will."

"Yeah? I doubt it. What you want me to write?"

"I want you to arrange it so that if I die, Vernon and Millie inherit my property, including the mineral rights."

Cecil sat back and scratched his chin. "All right, I can do all that," he said after a moment, "if it's what you want. First white boy I ever met was itchin' to give his shit over to niggas, though. Anything else?"

"Yeah. I'd like you to draw me up a signed, sworn affidavit outlining the circumstances surrounding my current extortion problem with certain powerful people here in town, in case I get killed. I want it sent to the FBI, State Troopers, and a former Texas Ranger turned private investigator named Russ Kirkpatrick. I've got his work address and phone number for you to use."

Cecil sat back, crossed his arms over his chest and shook his head no. "Now that gonna be a problem, Cole. Sound to me like this the point where I get in some shit don't concern me with people already like to see me dead as it is. I come through a ton in my time working 'round here. I ain't about to get shot over this bullshit."

"I'm willing to make it worth your while. How about this. I'll cut you in ten percent on the mineral rights to the farm. You can draw it up yourself in the paperwork. That way if something happens to me and the affidavit gets sent out, you'll get paid for taking the heat. I've got paperwork in the truck that shows what the well is worth. Ten percent would be tens of thousands of dollars, potentially."

Cecil took a sip of his drink, which Vernon's niece had brought over. He cocked his head and looked serious, didn't say anything for a moment.

Finally, he leaned forward. "Tell you what, Cole Quick. Go get that paperwork out yo truck. I wanna see it for myself before I say anything else."

"Cole stood up. "I'll be right back," he said. He lit a cigarette and puffed it on the way out to the truck. He dug through his growing pile of paperwork until he found the exploration documents, tucked them under his arm and headed back into the restaurant. Vernon was standing above Cecil shaking his head when Cole came back.

"What's all this about a will, Cole?" he asked as Cole approached.

"Just a precaution, Vern, that's all."

"But what it got to do with me and Millie? We don't want no trouble, Cole."

"You won't get any. Y'all are the closest thing to family I got left. No way I'm going to let Jack Gables take what's mine, and I've got no one else to leave it to if I get killed."

Vernon's eyes looked wild. Cecil held out his hand and Cole handed him the paperwork for the exploration.

"What if I says no, Cole?" Vernon said.

Cole sat back down across from Cecil. "If you want to relinquish your rights to it, you can. Maybe Cecil here can set you up a blind trust or something, so nobody can see who got the money. Hell, give it to charity, or your church, whatever you want to do with it. I just want to be sure there's someone with the legal right to distribute it to anyone except Jack Gables."

Cecil folded the lease over and looked up when Cole said

Jack Gables's name. "What Jack Gables got to do with this?" he asked. "And tell me the truth now, boy."

"He's the one trying to get me to sign over the farm."

"I knew it. Drug shit. Yo ass done fallen into the oldest trap in Teller County."

"What?" Cole asked.

"They been runnin' this scam on black folks for decades. Catch somebody's grandkids selling crack, trade grandma the boy's freedom in exchange for they mineral rights, sometimes rights to land they ain't even know they own before it come up. Feel like a get-out-of-jail-free card 'less you come to see what it actually cost."

"What if I could deliver you proof of that type of extortion at work?" Cole asked, leaning close so as not to be heard. "What would it take, and who would need to have it, to get something done?"

"Let me tell you something, white boy. This what I mean by we ain't the same. You think you can just jump in and stop corruption older than you are. I got none such illusions. This some serious shit here. I know you in it, but I ain't in nothing yet, neither is Vernon or Millie. You talkin' 'bout taking down forces been at work since Teller County come into existence, acting like it ain't nothin' but a matter of 'file this document here, send a letter to these folks over there.' I was you, I'd probably just sign this shit over and get out of town, but it look like you ain't got no sense."

"I don't think they'd let me live even if I did that. They know I've got no one who gives a damn if I disappear, and I know too much about what they do. Even if that weren't the case, I'm not going to do it. I'm prepared to see this through."

"Typical honkey, think he too good to get killed. That don't mean I do. Don't mean Vernon and Millie do, neither."

"We here for you, Cole," Vernon broke in, "but this serious. Ain't nothin' worth gettin' killed for, son."

Cole looked Vernon in the eyes. "I have to do this, Vernon. I can't do anything but ask you for your support. If I die, I want y'all to have that money, however that has to work. I know you don't believe I owe you anything, but I do. Y'all have treated me better than anyone in my life that I can remember, other than my wife. Please, if something happens to me, take this money. Then you won't have to work so hard all the time. Y'all can leave here, go somewhere better, maybe."

"This work ain't just what I do, Cole. It's who I am. You might not understand, but I like it. These recipes, they been passed down in my family for generations. It ain't much, smoking meat day and night, but I like it. *We* like it. There ain't no other place for me and Millie. You go on and do what you gotta do, if you really feel like you got to. Just admit it ain't because you owe us nothin', or doing nothin' for us. It's because you need our help, not the other way 'round. We don't need nothin' from no one."

"You're right, you don't need me. I do need you. You've been there when I needed someone more than you might realize."

"Vernon, I don't know why you even thinking about touching this bullshit," Cecil said.

Vernon smiled, odd for the energy at the table. "Cole like a long lost son to us, Cecil. He need my help, I gon' help him, same as I would your boy."

Cecil sighed, massaged his temples with his hands as he examined the lease document again. "Well, fuck it then, I guess."

"What's that mean?" Cole asked.

"That means if Vern want to help you then we gon' help you. I'll do the work. But I want some up-front money."

How much?" Cole asked.

"I want two thousand to start, just to do the will and create the affidavit. I expect more than that on the other end once the work done, too."

"Done," Cole said. "I've got some of the cash for you out in the truck right now."

"Well take your white ass back out to get it then. Come back with the cash and I'll get all the information from you. One more thing, though."

"What's that?"

"I want Vern and Millie to have ten percent mineral rights, up front, regardless of outcome. They takin' the risk of you pointing that money in they direction, they ought to get paid no matter what happen. I can make up a blind trust that provides some protection, but it ain't absolute."

"You're probably right," Cole said. "Done."

"Good. I have this shit all done up by tomorrow mornin'." Cecil turned to Vernon now. "Make sure you ready for this shit, Vern. This here gonna change your life, one way or another. I'll do what I can to keep the money from being linked to you directly, but it ain't impossible to find."

Vernon nodded as Cole scooted back from the table and headed out to the truck to get Cecil's money.

When he got back inside the restaurant, Cole finished up the details with Cecil and paid him all the cash he had, beyond what was left of the five hundred James Calvert had given him. He wrote down Russ Kirkpatrick's phone number, email and address, as well, for the affidavit. They agreed to meet at Cecil's office the next morning at ten, and Cecil walked out without saying goodbye. Vernon got up and headed back to work, too.

Cole took a long drink of his beer and was planning his next move when Sheldon slid in across from him.

"Wassup Little Chester? You 'bout ready to come up off some money on some cards? You look like someone already took some out of yo ass."

"Considering that the majority of my money just walked out the door, you're right. That in mind, I'll pass on the cards."

"You just scared what you got left gon' walk out, too. You look like someone done beat the brakes off you anyway."

"They did. But forget about that. I'll buy you a drink if you'll sit and chat with me about Chester a little more."

"Yo ass got daddy issues, Little Chester. Mothefucker weren't worth saying his name when he alive, now you can't shut the fuck up about him."

"Try this on. Chester did have a big payout coming, he wasn't lying about that."

"No shit? Where Chester Quick was gonna come up on some money?"

"The farm's got oil beneath it. Only Chester was too stubborn to sign the lease on it and catch a check."

"Huh. Well, that sound about right. Old dumb-ass Chester were as stupid as he were stubborn."

"Maybe they're the same thing. I was hoping you might tell me more specifics about his accident. Ambrose's spokesman would hardly tell me anything over the phone other than he drove off the road and hit a tree in the company truck, died at the scene."

"They ain't like to come up off them details. Too many folks be suing them if they do that. Way I heard it around here, Chester hit a tree going about eighty-five, didn't even touch the brakes."

"Where'd you hear that?"

"I got a homeboy who worked with him. He say a lot of them think he done it on purpose, though don't nobody at the company say that. Everybody know to walk a wide circle around that shit."

"You think he was drunk?"

"Hell, nah. Chester ain't never drink at work. He always goin' on 'bout drinking being a nighttime game."

"Any chance you think someone staged his death? Like, maybe someone wanted to kill him off for unpaid gambling debts or something?"

"Now you sound as crazy as his dumb ass. Errbody I know wanna knock his dumb ass the fuck out at one time or 'nother. But ain't nobody gon' kill him. What be the upside in killing him for debt? Ain't no payoff."

"I don't know, Sheldon. All I know is forces, whether intentional or just bad luck, have conspired to bring me back here to Teller and keep me here, and everything about it seems to revolve around Chester's death."

"Go ahead and shut the fuck up now, Cole. Whatever pot you boilin' in, I ain't fixing to jump in with you. I don't wanna know none of that shit you about to talk."

Cole sipped his beer instead of responding. Sheldon seemed to be thinking about what he'd said.

"Anyway, I need something else from you, Sheldon."

"You want more of that yack, huh?"

"That too, maybe. But I have a proposition for you. You can say no, it doesn't really matter."

"Tell me and I see," Sheldon said.

"I need a car. It can be stolen, but not if the tags will come back hot within the next couple of days."

"You serious? What the fuck I look like? Like I be out there stealing cars for Chester Quick's dumb-ass son? Hell, nah. You act like every nigga you run into just automatically know where to get a stolen car. That shit fucked up, Cole. What happened to yo truck, anyway?"

"It's out in the parking lot. You don't have to steal the car, just set it up for me. And I know you know where to get it, Sheldon, don't bullshit me on that. It ain't because you're black, it's because you hustle. That's the life you're in. Tell me I'm wrong."

"What the fuck you trying to say, Cole? That black people all know somebody can steal a fucking car? Racist white motherfucker." Sheldon smiled, then added, "Why don't you just go rent a car then?"

"I need something that can't be traced back to me, if possible. I'll make you a deal. You get me a car like that, I'll sign my truck over to you and give you five hundred dollars for the car. I've got the title to my truck out there in the glove box right now. All I need is a car that won't show up hot for a couple of days until I can get back out of town."

"Why the fuck would you give me yo truck for some ragged-out drug car?"

"I got people looking for me who know that truck. I sell it to you, you can go register it yourself, get new tags so it doesn't even have my plates anymore. Then it's your truck, nobody to fuck with you about it, no more sitting around waiting for rides all the time."

"And all I got to do is get you a car won't come up stolen for a few days?"

"That's it."

Sheldon tapped his fingertips on the table like a drummer while he thought. "All right, I do it. I know someone might have something for me. I got to drive my aunty in her car to the doctor 'round noon tomorrow, so it have to be after that. You best come with title and cash in hand though, no bullshit."

"Can I meet you at your house then, say around two?"

"Hell, nah, you can't meet me at my house. How I'm gon' bring a hot ride to my auntie's crib? We meet somewhere else."

Cole thought about it for a minute. "What about the Rose City Motel, say around two. Can you make that happen?"

"I can probably do that, yeah. If I ain't there on time, fucking wait, I guess. It might take me a minute to make it happen."

"I can live with that," Cole said.

"Good, we set then. Now I got to get back to hustling, Cole. I only got a couple g's left of that shit you picked up the other night. How much you want?"

Cole had to think about it. He still had about half a bag left from the three grams he'd bought before. Still, he was headed back up to Jackson's next to pump Randall for more information on Jimmy, and a little cocaine to spread around might help him get some more answers.

"I'll take two of 'em, I guess," he said.

"See? No money, my ass," Sheldon said. "White people full of shit. Meet me in the bathroom and we do the exchange. Good?"

"Sound's good," Cole said, finishing his beer. "I got to get on the road anyway."

CHAPTER SEVENTEEN

Jackson's was much more crowded than the last time he'd been in. Dolled-up couples and groups of businessmen were seated for dinner in the dining room to the left of the front entrance. Several people waited for drinks at the bar, mostly men in Texas tuxedos with their ties undone.

Cole ordered a Lone Star and a shot to balance out the coke he'd snorted in the truck before coming inside. His throat felt numb and his ears were hot. He surveyed the room, trying not to grind his teeth, realized people were staring at him because of his beat-up face, not his grinding teeth.

Though it probably didn't help. He shrugged it off and headed out onto the back porch with his beer. He spotted Randall and three other men huddled around several empty Margarita glasses on the same table he'd seen them at last time he'd been here.

One of them said something and the others whooped it up. Randall spotted Cole as he approached and scrunched up his face, stood as if to greet him.

"Damn Cole, you following me around or something?" he said. The other three men at the table stopped laughing and gave Cole guarded looks. "Fellas, this here's Cole Quick, an old acquaintance. Cole, this is John Rawlins. That's Tucker Colston, and the fat fuck on the end there is Jerry Lang, but we just call him Fat Jerry."

"Nice to meet y'all," Cole said, shaking each man's hand, though none of them seemed to care much about it.

"I know you," Fat Jerry said in a raspy, almost hoarse voice when Cole reached for his hand.

"How's that?" Cole asked.

"You was at the gala the other night, made that big scene."

"Hell, you saw that?" Cole tried to sound casual, but the memory stung.

"The whole town saw it. Least everyone who matters. You weren't all beat up like this though. What happened?"

Cole sighed and sat down. "Kerrie Ferris is my wife. Was, rather, before she passed."

"No shit?" Tucker broke in. "I knew she run off with some—someone, against her folk's wishes. Probably made her daddy sicker than a coon dog on trash day."

"Still does, I guess." Cole already didn't like this guy.

"So, what happened to your face, then?" Jerry asked.

"Let's just say my night didn't get any better from there. I'd had too much to drink and got myself into a jam shortly after," Cole said, hoping to squash the talk about his face and relax everyone a little.

"Well then, that explains the scene you made. Hope it was worth the whipping."

"I'd say you should see the other guy, but he looks just fine," Cole joked.

Jerry said, "Shit. I never been much for all that Rose Festival mess anyway, but I never miss a good party. Cole, how do you and Randall know each other?"

Cole could feel Tucker studying him. He ignored it. As he started to answer, Randall cut him off.

"I knew Cole through Jimmy Calvert way back when. He and Jimmy was running buddies. Cole here used to supply the party favors, if y'all take my drift."

"You ran with Jimmy, huh?" Tucker asked. Must have been a bona-fide party animal. I went to a few parties over at his place last year and things got loose. Even more so once he got Miss Loosey-Goosey on his jock full-time."

"Cole still got a little of that wildness in him," Randall cut in, as if managing the conversation. He leaned in toward Cole. "You got any more of that business from the other night? I'd be happy to pay, as would these boys."

"Matter of fact I do," he said, still trying to come as off casual, realizing he probably looked ridiculous with his face all beat to hell.

Randall winked at Tucker and grinned. There was something about it that made Cole a little uncomfortable.

"You wanna sell any of it?" Tucker asked. "We been sitting here pining for a gagger for the last two rounds of margaritas."

Cole gave his own grin, his eyes too jacked up to wink, thanks to the bruises. "I don't want to sell it, but I'm happy to share. I got a little more than a teener, we just need somewhere to do it."

"That'll hunt," Tucker said.

"It's good blow, too," Randall added, his voice quieter now. "I can vouch. Gave me a few key bumps the other night and I damn well couldn't sleep when I got home."

"So where can we get this party going?" Cole asked. "I ain't crazy about taking turns going to the bathroom here all night. Besides, Randall said he doesn't roll that way anymore."

"None of us roll that way anymore," Tucker said. "Town's too damn small. This is my uncle's place. He'd lose his goddamn mind if I got spotted doing some shit like that in his bathroom. I tell you what, though. We can have us a party over at my place, y'all want."

Randall grinned again. "Tucker's got himself a regular pussy palace over on Strongbow. Pool table, swimming pool, the works."

"A full fridge of beer and a stocked liquor cabinet, too,' Tucker added. "Hell, I might even call my man Chantree and invite a few skinnies I know to come over."

"How's that sound, Cole?" Randall asked.

"Sounds like I can't figure why we're still huddled around this table," he said.

"Now that's exactly what I like to *hear* right there," Fat Jerry said, scooting his chair back to stand up. "We gonna put ourselves together a hell of a party. Tucker, get on the horn and see if you can get some of that poontang headed our direction, too. I'll call off on my missus."

"Hell boys, I can't make it, unfortunately," John Rawlins, who hadn't said much up to that point, broke in. The disappointment was clear in his voice. "Sherry's been on my ass about staying out after work. I have to get home and deal with her and the boy tonight."

"Sherry's been on your ass because you got caught with your straw in the cookie jar," Tucker said, whipping him with an imaginary bullwhip. He turned to Cole. "John here came up on some go-go juice himself a couple months back. Waited until his wife Sherry put the little one down and went to bed, decided to have himself a little party right there on the coffee table." Rawlins shot Tucker a look that ought to have shut him up, but he continued anyway. "She come downstairs and caught him sucking up a gator tail right off the coffee table. Picture that, preacher's daughter, never even seen a drug, come downstairs and there her husband is, nose to straw on the three-thousand-dollar marble coffee table."

Rawlins looked like he might get angry, but when he spoke his voice was even. "Thanks for bringing that up, Tuck, I appreciate you airing my business to strangers."

"Easy John, I'm just busting your balls. Besides, the whole damn town knows anyway. That's the way it works. Come hang out, surely she's over that bullshit by now."

"My ass she is. I'm still going to marriage counseling once a week with that loudmouth motherfucker Roach over at Rose Meadows. Besides, it's easy for you to act tough with your wife out of town. I saw you ducking for cover with Tracy the other day. Getting caught by the wife is one hell of a job hazard."

"What's the job description?" Cole asked.

"Father. Husband. Socially presentable man at Rose Meadows on Sunday. The usual. You were married, right? So you know." Rawlins shrugged as if to say *What else can you do?*

Cole shook his head. "I was married, that's true. Wasn't like that, though."

"What was it like?" Tucker said in a sarcastic tone.

Cole hesitated, part of him wanting to grab the smartass by the neck and shake him. "It was, just…calm, I guess. I never even wanted to party anymore, once I got out of Teller. Started to even believe a normal, quiet life might be just the thing."

The collective group snickered at that.

"Where'd y'all run off to, anyway?" Randall asked.

"Colorado. But y'all don't need to hear any more sob stories from me. We making the trip to Tucker's, or what?" Cole said, changing the subject.

"Ready when y'all are," Tucker said.

They tossed back their remaining drinks all at the same time. Randall dropped a hundred-dollar bill on the table. Fat Jerry made a lot of noise as he stood up, like it was killing him. The band on stage was singing "Fool Hearted Memory," which struck Cole as a little ironic. Some of these boys sounded like they'd be living it in short order.

"I'll see y'all later then," John said. "Don't have too much fun without me. Nice to meet you, Cole," he added, extending his hand.

Cole shook it mechanically. "Nice to meet you, too."

"Let's do this," Randall said. I'm itchin' for some booger sugar. Cole, pull around back and you can just follow my car."

"Will do," Cole said. "See y'all there." He turned and made his way back past the throng of socialites to his truck.

A few minutes later Cole pulled the Silverado around the back of Jackson's to find Randall's black BMW idling there with a silver Jaguar idling next to it. He flashed his lights and they took off together in a caravan, the Jaguar in front.

They drove across town and then turned south, out toward Lake Strongbow. Eventually they turned into a neighborhood, maybe two coves over from Jimmy's place.

Cole kept an eye on his rearview mirror but didn't notice anyone following him. He was still confused as to how Gables was able to keep such good tabs on him when he never felt like he was being followed. Maybe they were just that professional. Maybe they weren't watching as closely as he assumed. He didn't even know what to look for in a tail, anyway.

They wound down into the neighborhood past painted brick houses and odd contemporary-style teardown-rebuilds, pulled into a driveway that led to a multi-level house. The Jaguar led the way down the driveway and pulled into a three-car garage.

Randall pulled the BMW up in the circle drive across from a red front door and parked. Cole parked his truck behind the BMW, then watched back up toward the road in his rearview to see if any headlights passed, but none did. He stubbed out his cigarette in the ashtray and put it in the bottle of butts, got out of the truck and followed the others into the garage.

"Nice place," he said as Tucker worked his key in the lock. "Does everybody in Teller live on Lake Strongbow these days?"

"Everybody worth mentioning," Tucker said. Cole frowned. "I'm fucking with you, Cole," he added, smiling. "You know how it is around here. The place to be is the place to be, and anybody with money is gonna be there."

"I get it," Cole said, thinking he didn't even remotely begin to understand these people or their motivations.

Randall clapped him on the back, which made his bruised ribs ache. "Glad you made it out, Cole. My nose itches, let's get on in there and scratch it."

"Tell you the truth, I hate cocaine," Fat Jerry said.

"Is that right?" Cole asked.

"Yeah," Fat Jerry said, grinning, "but I love the way it smells."

Randall and Tucker cackled in unison. Cole forced a smile,

having heard the joke too many times to make it funny anymore.

That's just the kind of people these were, all rehashed jokes and thoughts so unoriginal that even the people they got them from had copied them from somewhere else.

The house had an open floor plan with steps between three levels, brown-stained concrete floors that matched the stained wood trim along the ceilings and down the corners of the walls. Two big square windows looked out on Lake Strongbow. The lake wouldn't have been visible at night if not for the moonlight that reflected off the surface.

Cole followed the three men through the house to a big, open room off the back that had a pool table, full bar, including stools, and big French doors that led out onto a patio with a swimming pool. The pool's water level came right up to the edge of the patio, appearing to drop off down the hill toward the lake at its farthest point.

Infinity pool, that's what Kerrie had called the style the only time he'd ever been in her parents' house.

He used the new temporary debit card to break out one-inch lines on a mirror Tucker had taken down off the wall. Tucker fixed them all Crown and ginger ales while they listened to generic music and shot a few rounds of 8-ball, stopping occasionally to hit a few more bumps. The conversation was fast and loose, but mostly just small talk.

At one point Tucker broke out four Cohibas and they sat around a custom stone firepit on the back porch, dipping the tips in Courvoisier while they smoked them. Tucker liked expensive things, that was obvious. Cole couldn't argue that the cigars were nice, even with the uncontrollable urge to grind his teeth into the butt.

"How do you get these from Cuba?" Cole asked. "I thought they were illegal?"

"They are," Tucker said. I get 'em shipped through a service overseas. They tax 'em pretty good, but it's worth it. What's the point in having it if you don't plan on spending it, right?"

"No argument," Cole said, puffing on his cigar, having no idea what that would be like. He'd never had it, so he couldn't say.

"Jimmy was the same way," he said, finally directing the conversation where he'd been wanting it to go for the last hour. "He sure liked nice shit."

"Jimmy liked that right there," Fat Jerry said, gesturing to the mirror with the coke on it. "He was one wild-ass partier. I love me some fun, but he had a way of taking it too far, like that was the only place he knew how to get to."

"He liked to turn it up," Cole said. "That's absolutely right."

Tucker had a look on his face like something smelled bad. "I never took much count of Jimmy," he said. "In fact, I thought he was a prick. He did like to turn shit up, though, y'all are right about that much. I like to turn shit up myself. Matter of fact, I'm gonna make some more calls and see if we can't get us a couple senoritas over here to turn them up a little."

Tucker stood up and pulled out his cell phone. "If I can get Chantree on the line maybe he'll pick up some more blow and bring it over. You know Chantree, Cole?"

"Don't think so," Cole said. "Chantree who?"

Randall and Tucker exchanged a look and a grin.

"Chantree Gables," Tucker said. "His grandfather been the sheriff here for about two-thousand years?"

Cole tried not to let his shock register on his face. Tucker laughed. "Don't worry, he's cool. Likes a good time about as much as anyone I ever knew. Always got a load of women in tow, too. Kind of girls I wouldn't let in my house in the daylight, but they sure are fun at night."

Tucker went inside to make the phone call. Cole had too much of a buzz to feel the proper level of panic. Jack Gables himself hadn't seemed to recognize Cole until the trouble with Kerrie's parents. This kid Chantree might not even know what kind of shit his grandfather was really into, but you never knew.

He wondered if Chantree and Jimmy had ever run around together, if there might be some sort of connection there.

"Jack Gables, huh?" he said to Randall and Fat Jerry. "Kind of ironic, guy with the drug connection being the sheriff's grandson. Bet that makes for some fun Thanksgiving dinners."

Randall smirked. "Hell, he ain't all that connected anyway. More of a party boy than anything else. Like Jimmy."

Cole sat back, took a sip of his cocktail and draped his arm across the back of the couch, trying to seem casual. "Like Jimmy, huh? You think they partied together?"

"Chantree didn't like Jimmy any more than I did," Tucker cut in, coming back in the room. "I kinda feel like we had him pretty well pegged, seeing how he turned out."

Randall started to look uncomfortable, cut Tucker off before he could say more. "Cole and Jimmy were friends, Tucker. Keep it in mind," he said.

"Nah, it's all good," Cole said. "I hadn't seen him in thirteen years when I found out he'd passed. I'm actually really interested to know what y'all thought about Jimmy. What happened confused the hell out of me, but like I said, I hadn't seen him in a decade. Did y'all see that level of craziness coming?"

"Shit, not that," Fat Jerry said. "Something bad, for sure. But I never took him for the violent type. That shocked me. He was pretty twisted off on the booger sugar, so you never know. But I'd have taken him for too much of a coward to kill anyone. Shows what I know."

"Like I said, guy was wild, and kind of a showoff," Tucker said, his phone at his ear again now. "You ask me, everyone knew something was gonna happen to that whore he was running around with, either way. She was out of her mind long before the drugs, cut anyone who came near her."

"Tucker isn't a fan of the Ambrose sisters, either," Randall said.

"Couple snotty bitches who think their daddy hung the moon. Wasn't nothing to like about Caroline other than her backside. Girl had an incredible ass. Her older sister's nose is so stuck up high that you can't hardly see what color her eyes are." Tucker laughed at his own joke, dialing another number on his phone with the cigar butt sticking out of his mouth.

"Any of y'all ever think maybe somebody killed those two, set 'em up to look like a murder-suicide?" Cole asked. The question sort of hung in the air until he wished he'd waited, phrased it differently or something. Everyone was looking at him now.

"Not me," Tucker finally said. "In the papers the police were positive about what happened. You ask me, that skank was asking for it and he finally gave it to her. They was known to fight out in public. Bet her daddy loved that. I'm kinda surprised he put up with her as long as he did. Jimmy, too. Girl liked to sleep around, use people for drugs, that kind of thing. Probably lots of people who wanted to do something bad to her. My guess is Jimmy got tired of getting cucked, got high and went too far."

"Most people in my circles tried to scoop that mess under the carpet almost as soon as they heard about it," Fat Jerry added. "It looks bad when one of the wealthiest families in town has a daughter turn into a crackhead. People like to gossip about it behind the scenes, but won't nobody talk about it in proper company."

Cole nodded. "I'm not trying to suggest anything, you understand. I'm just curious. Let me ask y'all this. You ever hear of a big ol' country boy named Zach Ellis, guy who about sells his weight in cocaine every year?"

"Doesn't ring a bell," Tucker said. "That who you got this blow from?"

Nah, got this from a friend. But I heard he and Jimmy were acquainted, thought maybe that might be where he was getting his stash. Jimmy's dad said that both he and Caroline had been cut off from their trust funds for months, and Randall here confirmed that. Seems like they might have racked up a drug debt worth killing over, is all. I'm just throwing wild theories out there because I'm high, honestly," Cole forced a laugh. "I guess he was just my friend and I don't want to remember him as some guy who mangled his girl and shot himself."

Randall looked uncomfortable at having his name mentioned on the peripheral of Jimmy's tale, like always.

"Understandable," Fat Jerry said. "You know, actually, I do happen to know that the guy he used to score from was a big cowboy-looking motherfucker, kind of like you're saying. I saw him drop off a package once at one of Jimmy's parties. I just thought he was a weird guy to be a dealer, you know. Normally it's some thug nigger doing that kind of shit."

"How's about we fluff up the subject a bit, boys," Randall said. "All this Jimmy talk is killing my buzz."

"I agree," Tucker added. "Let's hit another gagger and see if we can't cheer everyone up. It's bad enough that every goddamn piece of ass I know ain't picking up the line. Fucking Chantree, either. Least we could do is talk about something interesting."

"Hell, Tucker," Cole said, "It's your house, man. All you gotta do is say the word."

Asking any more questions would be weird, so Cole let it drop. The more he asked around, the more connections between people he discovered beneath the surface of this town. He needed to get Russ Kirkpatrick on the line first thing in the morning. He'd pretty well exhausted his personal investigative abilities at this point.

Time was running out and he wasn't making the kind of progress that would save him from much of anything at this point. He chopped out a fresh set of lines and sucked one up.

For the first time in his life it felt like he couldn't even feel the high from the cocaine. All he could think about was how sad it would have made Kerrie if she could see him now.

CHAPTER EIGHTEEN

Cole woke up early on the couch in the big living room of Tucker's obnoxious house, stiff and sickly with a pounding headache. He sat up and checked the time on the cable box. Eight-thirty. They'd been up until almost six. He'd snuck off into the living room and hit the couch, had a vague memory of Randall lighting out sometime after the sun came up. He hadn't been able to sleep, was unaware of when he'd dozed off.

He gathered his things, slipped his boots on and stumbled out the front door into mind-numbing flat daylight. It was overcast, but the moisture from the clouds just increased the stickiness. At least it would keep the temperature low, maybe even below the nineties. He almost lit a cigarette, but thought better of it. He had to lean on the hood of the truck and vomit into the grass alongside it a few times before he could straighten himself out to drive.

He fired up the engine, shut the radio off, and drove slowly down the quiet country roads that connected the coves on Lake Strongbow.

For all the damage he'd done to himself last night, he hadn't come up with any sort of useful information, no leads on how to go about getting to the bottom of Jimmy's murder, if it *was* murder. Cole had the feeling that if he could just put that together, he might solve all his own problems, too.

As he was trying to figure out what else he might do, he drove past a woman in tight pink-and-grey workout spats, walking a chubby black lab. He only realized it was Mandy Ambrose after he'd already passed her. He pulled off into the ditch and busted a U-turn, slowed, and rolled the window down as he came up alongside her.

"Seems like everyone in Teller owns some sort of retriever," he called out the window. Mandy stopped walking to turn and face the truck. She raised her eyebrows but kept her face neutral when she recognized him.

"You out here following me around, Cole Quick? Poor Winston and I never can get any alone time."

His head was throbbing, but he managed to smile anyway. "I didn't mean to disrupt y'all. Just passing by, coming from a friend's place, and saw you walking."

"Well, I guess I'll take that as a compliment, dressed this way. Can't say I can return it, though. You look like someone hit you with a bus."

"That's about how I feel, too. And I think you look just fine in what you're wearing."

"My mother taught me that a lady never leaves the house unless she's dressed for success. She'd never be caught dead out here with no makeup on, walking the dog. Caroline was the same way. But I'm my own woman, apparently. What happened to you?"

"Long story. I'm glad I ran across you, actually. I was gonna stop by your house today and see if I could catch you on account of I wanted to apologize for making that scene at your gala. I didn't realize I was going to react that way. I appreciate you sticking up for me, though."

"Yes, you did. It's alright, I understand. I'd be lying if I didn't admit I invited you there at least a little in hopes you'd make a scene. Those things can be so stuck-up and boring. I'm sorry about what that creep Jack Gables did, dragging you out like that. It embarrassed the hell out of me to be disobeyed in my own home. I haven't spoken to my father since. Please tell me Gables isn't the one who did that to your face?"

Cole didn't answer that yet, wasn't sure how to approach it. "I get it, tough situation," he said instead. "I didn't do myself any favors with my behavior. You said that stuff bores you, but you're thick in the middle of it far as I can tell. Why do it if you don't like it?"

Mandy leaned into the window frame and rested her arm on it, draped the dog's leash over the rearview mirror. Winston sat down next to the truck and panted.

"I never really wanted to be in it. I mean, I guess for a time I sort of did. For sure all the girls in my class thought I'd be the Rose Queen. But there's a lot that goes into the selection process, social status, who's cozying up with whom that year. Most of all who's willing to pony up the most money for the honor. Cindy Fuller had me beat somewhere in there. My mother cried. Daddy was furious. When it came time for Caroline's class to fill the court, he made sure she didn't miss out." She frowned, and Cole caught a glimpse of some hurt in there. "She was daddy's favorite," Mandy continued. "She had that same crush-all-dissent mindset he has. Part of me was happy to watch Caroline crash and burn, until…well, you know."

Cole shook off a wave of nausea and composed himself. "I get it. Hey, listen. I got to get moving if I'm going to make an appointment on time. But I'd really like to talk with you some more. Would it be too forward of me to ask if we could have coffee or tea or whatever you're into, maybe this afternoon? I been trying to get some closure on this thing, but it hasn't been working out."

Mandy straightened as if she had to think about an odd request. It took her a while to reply.

"I'm not sure…actually, you know what? That would be fine. It kind of feels good to talk about it. My whole family spends about half their time doing whatever it takes to pretend like all this never happened, and the other half ignoring it completely.

Maybe you could stop by my place around three o'clock? Is that too early?"

"That works fine," Cole said. "I'll stop by and see you then."

"All right. One more thing?"

"Shoot."

"While we're at it, you have to tell me who turned you into a punching bag. You know I love to gossip. Stay out of trouble in the meantime."

"That ain't been going all that great, but I'll try," Cole said, He waved his hand and drove off, dropping the smile from his face as soon as she was out of the window frame.

He had a hangover pulsing through every cell in his body. He needed to straighten up before he met with Cecil. He picked up a coffee and some Advil from the gas station, as well as a chocolate milk and some powdered donuts, same as always. He wished he had snagged some pot from Sheldon the other day. It would dull his hangover and make eating a lot easier now.

He tried Russ Kirkpatrick and got the voicemail again. He didn't have anywhere to go yet, so he drove circles around town and noted all the things that had changed.

Colvin Street had widened to four lanes from two. They had installed a median down the center of the main loop that surrounded town, which seemed to have created more traffic than it helped free up. The movie theater his mother had taken him to as a child was boarded up and anchored a now-dilapidated, decaying shopping center.

The rush south away from colored folks had rendered the middle-class neighborhoods of his childhood to rental housing. This was probably the best he could ever have hoped for if he'd stayed, and snobby people had abandoned it like a plague. He sure couldn't have hoped to keep Kerrie in a place like this.

New, fancier shopping centers had been built south of town to replace those he'd known as a kid, too. They housed all manner of corporate chains that would have been unthinkable back when he'd left. Progress had a way of touching every place, he supposed. Even Teller County.

He drove out Midday Road toward the two-track dirt road they'd driven down for pasture parties in high school, only to find it had become a neighborhood of red brick houses with matching manicured lawns. Even when Teller changed, it stayed exactly the same in most of the ways that mattered.

He was on his way back into town when the Cricket phone rang and what looked to be Kirkpatrick's number flashed on the screen.

"Hello?" he said into the receiver.

"Yeah, I missed a call from this number, this is Russ Kirkpatrick?"

Cole pulled off into a grocery store parking lot and parked so he could talk.

There was an awkward silence before he said, "Yeah, hey there Mr. Kirkpatrick, this is Cole Quick. We met the other day out at James Calvert's ranch?"

"Family friend, I remember. What can I do for you, Mr. Quick?"

"Well, to be honest, I'd like to sit down and talk with you about what happened to Mr. Calvert." Cole paused, not sure he was ready to say what he needed to say next.

"Go on," Kirkpatrick said.

"So… As you know, James was sort of paying me to poke around in the local underbelly here in Teller. I'm not a detective like you are, and I've been getting into it a little over my head. Honestly, I'm a little concerned with the timing of Mr. Calvert's death."

"Are you saying you think somebody killed him?"

"I don't know what I'm saying, exactly. But maybe. I was just hoping I might be able to sit down with you and talk about it, get your thoughts. Looking into the thing has gotten a little dangerous for me, and I could use some professional advice. Any chance you have plans to be in Teller County in the next day or two?"

Kirkpatrick's breathing came through the phone for a few seconds before he replied. "I'm actually headed down to Llano now for a couple days, but I could be up there after that? Or we could handle it now by phone."

"The thing is, I've got some stuff going on here that's pretty hard to explain over the phone. Maybe I can have my attorney fax some stuff over to you where you're staying, so you can look it over tonight? I think it might help you with what you were working on with Mr. Calvert. Please understand, it's a pretty bad situation I'm in, and without some sort of help it could go terminal for me."

"I gotta be honest, Mr. Quick. I've had some experience out there in Teller. Every damn tree in the county grows crooked, just about. That's just a fact. But there was nothing in particular about what James Calvert sent me regarding his son that convinced me of anything. Any chance you've got more than he did for me?"

"All I've really got for you is a sworn statement about my experience, and a bunch of circumstantial connections between people who may be involved. I know there's got to be something foul going on, but I can't prove it any more than Mr. Calvert could. But it could be helpful to at least add to your file, no? I'm figuring that as an ex-Ranger, you've got some connections, and I could use some outside help. Everybody official in this county is more of the problem than the solution."

"Send it and I'll see. I know what you mean about the officials being part of the problem. I've got my own bones to pick on that, independent of James Calvert. Tell you what. I'll be at the Llano Best Western. I'm driving or I'd give you their info. You can look them up online and fax what you have over to them. We can go from there. Sound good?"

"It'll have to do, I guess. I'll just be glad to get it to someone outside of this county in case something happens to me, I suppose."

Kirkpatrick was quiet for a moment. Finally, he sighed and spoke again. "I'll tell you what, Mr. Quick. I'll call you back after I read what you've got. If I can help, I will. Best I can say before I see what you have."

"Understood," Cole said. "I'll send it over this afternoon. You hear what I have to say about Sheriff Jack Gables, it might change your mind."

"Jack Gables," Kirkpatrick said, his voice changing again at the mention of the name. "Send over your information, I'll see what I can do, and I'll call you either way."

They said goodbye and hung up.

Now what, Cole thought. He'd hoped to persuade Kirkpatrick to come see him today, though he'd known it was a long shot. If he could enlist the man's help, it might be that Gables was less likely to kill an ex-Ranger. Or not.

He tossed the phone across the bench seat and pulled onto The Loop back toward the north end of town, where Cecil's office was located. He pulled up to what had once been a prestigious group of two-story office condos with tall, narrow windows stacked on top of each other, separated by strips of beige concrete.

He tried the glass front door but it wouldn't budge, so he cupped his hands around his eyes and looked inside to see a middle-aged, dark-skinned secretary with super-short hair, sitting at an old desk, staring back at him.

He motioned to the door, but she didn't move, so he knocked. She looked annoyed as she took her time scooting her chair back to hit a buzzer on the wall. The door gave an electronic click and he pulled it open to the smell of must and cheap cleaning supplies.

"I help you?" The secretary asked, professional but not friendly, more just humoring him.

"I'm here to see Cecil, he's drawing up some paperwork for me?"

"Oh yeah? And who're you then?"

"My name's Cole Quick, I met with him yesterday evening."

"You did, huh? I don't know what in the world is going on around this place anymore, apparently. I'll pop my head in and let him know you here."

"Much obliged."

"Is my job."

The secretary poked her head into the office behind her and said something to what Cole assumed was Cecil, who said something back that Cole didn't catch either. She shut the door and sat back down at the desk.

"He say have a seat right over there, he be with you in a minute."

"Thanks, Cole said. He sat down in a small waiting area of folding chairs with Jet and Ebony magazines dating back to the late nineties on the end tables. He'd thumbed through two or three of them before Cecil finally stuck his head out of the office.

"Come on back," he said, no emotion in his voice. Cole stood and walked slowly into his office. If Cecil could take his time with things, so could Cole. Except that was a lie, he was the one running out of time. He was too hung over and too cornered to put up with any of that white-boy bullshit today, either way.

"Shut the door," Cecil said as he sat behind the desk. The office had various degrees and a couple of awards for civic leadership on the wall behind Cecil's desk.

Cecil squared off to him and watched him take in the room.

"I done up the affidavit, like you asked," he began. "Took me a bit to track down all the loose ends. I got a man in the State Patrol out of Houston been good to me in past dealings, so I set it up to send your affidavit to him. Jack Gables be known and feared in the law enforcement community statewide, so I got a feeling everybody who see this gonna laugh and toss that shit in the trash. Probably think I just another crazy nigga with a vendetta. They ain't wrong, but that just make it more far-fetched that they help."

Cole put his hands on his knees. "I don't need you to like me, Cecil, I just need you to cover my back in exchange for money," Cole said. After you send this stuff out, no matter what happens to me, you and Vern and Millie will be set."

"More like set up. Probably can't never step foot in Teller

County again, none of us."

"Once those affidavits go out, I think there will be too much heat for Gables to come after you directly. And if you handle the trust right, chances are he will never know who Vern and Millie are."

"That's one big-ass assumption. You be surprised the kind of influence he got. He find out I done the legal work, no telling how hard that man will lean to find out the rest."

"You think I'm dumping my problem on y'all, that it?"

"Nah. I just think we all seeing dollar signs and you like the devil walking us out the frying pan and into the fire."

"But you'll send the affidavit, and file my will and the lease, correct?"

"Motherfucker, you think I sat here drawing 'em up so I could just toss 'em in the garbage? Believe it or not, black folk value they time, too."

"Relax, I just wanted to make sure. You seem like you might be getting cold feet a little bit."

"I relax when this over and you up out my life again. I don't know why Vernon got such a shine for you, but you best be glad he do. I'm helping you because he ask, not because I think any of us should be involved in this mess."

"Let me ask you this, Cecil. You think there might be some sort of conspiracy here in Teller, kind of a reverse Robin-Hood thing where they rob the poor to feed the rich?"

"You really asking me that bullshit?"

"I really am. Why?"

"Any black man within a hundred miles who don't know something like that going on have to be deaf, dumb and blind. These people be up at the country club playing golf together on Sunday, prosecutor and judge on Monday. Judge shoot a bad round, you might as well kiss your black ass goodbye, you 'bout to get that time. They kids be marrying each other, and the same families be getting richer every single year, generation after generation, while everyone else get poorer. Hell, yeah, I heard all kind of theories on the subject."

Cole shrugged, didn't have the energy to take the question any further. "So what do I need to sign to make this all official?"

Cecil passed all the necessary documents across the table to him, showed him all the places he would need to sign. After he'd signed them Cecil called the secretary from the front room in to act as notary.

"So you'll file the new lease paperwork with Chromatic Oil—when?" Cole asked.

"I touched base with someone over there this morning, sent them copies of everything. They expectin' it by late this afternoon. You get out of whatever the fuck you done stepped in, you gonna be just one more rich white motherfucker. You understand I don't tell you good luck then, right?"

"I do," Cole said, then took his copy of the documents off the desk and walked out of the office without looking back.

CHAPTER NINETEEN

He pulled up to the Rose City Motel at around one, parked the Silverado in the back where it wouldn't be visible from the road and made his way into the office toward the front. He rented a room from a twenty-something clerk with thick braids and a nametag that said her name was Yolanda.

"You want a half day or all night?" she asked. The question made Cole hesitate at the thought of sleeping in the bed. He took it for two nights and she pushed him a key with an oval plastic tag that said "212" hanging off of it.

She didn't mention his poor state of appearance, but he figured any clerk at a place like this had learned to keep her mouth shut a long time ago. He made his way up the stairs to 212 and unlocked the door to reveal yellowed walls, a queen-sized bed with frayed multi-color spread, two flat pillows, and a small table with two ancient chairs pushed up beneath the front window. Smoking rooms were the only kind they'd ever had at the Rose City Motel.

He unloaded the truck's entire contents into the room, then cracked the shades and kicked back in the chair. He had to get up and go throw up his breakfast in the toilet, wanted to lie down afterward, but couldn't chance missing Sheldon if and when he showed up.

Instead, he lit up a smoke and sat in one of the chairs while he waited. He didn't know what kind of car Sheldon might show up in, but from this vantage point he could see everything that pulled into the lot. Once he'd gotten rid of the truck he would feel like doing what he was about to do. The hunted was about to become the hunter, and he didn't want them to see him coming.

It was another hour and a half before Sheldon showed up in a rusting blue Pontiac Sunbird. Cole spotted him behind the wheel, noted that the windows weren't even slightly tinted. It would have to do either way.

Cole snuffed out his cigarette and went outside. He needed to meet Mandy Ambrose at three. Sheldon parked in front of the building a few spots down from Cole's room.

"Hey, Sheldon," Cole called from the balcony. "I'm up here, room two-twelve."

"Alright, I'm comin' up," Sheldon said. He came up the stairs, two at a time, then walked slowly and casually until he reached Cole.

"I know you ain't staying here in this skank-ass place," Sheldon said. "Where I live everybody know this spot put the 'ho' in hotel."

"I noticed," Cole said, leading him inside and shutting the door behind them.

"You look like dog shit, even for a young-ass Chester Quick," Sheldon said.

"I feel about like Chester right now."

"Yo ass stayed up all night on that cocaine, huh?"

"Is it that obvious?"

"Is all white people racist?" Sheldon laughed. "Hell, yeah, it obvious. Plus, most folks don't be buying four grams of coke in three days 'less they usin' it. You best watch yo ass, Cole. Shit will sneak up and take a bite out of it."

"It'll have to get in line, there might not be many bites left soon. Anyway, I think I got all that shit back out of my system finally. I need to keep my head straight."

"Good fucking luck with that. So let's do this. I'm tired as a motherfucker, was up late myself. It ain't got no title or nothing, but ain't nobody gonna be looking for it, either."

"Perfect."

"Thing is, it been getting passed around by crackheads for a while now, so the inside all fucked up. One of 'em scored it off a cracked-out used-car-lot owner, dude so strung out he renting out cars for crack. Best I could do on short notice."

"It'll work. I filled out the title to the truck and signed it, already got all my shit out of it."

"I see that. This all your shit, really?"

"It is now. I had a bunch of stuff in storage up in Colorado, but I let the bill lapse. I'm sure they've auctioned it off by now."

"Who gives a fuck, Little Chester? You got a sob story don't be dropping it on me, I got plenty of problems all my own."

"You know what, Sheldon?"

"What's that, Cole?"

"I don't think you're half the heartless piece of shit you pretend to be."

"I ain't sure how to take some bullshit like that, Cole."

"Take it as a compliment."

"Don't nobody need yo backhanded honkey compliments."

Cole almost laughed. "Here's the signed title and the truck keys. That car got keys or am I starting it with a flat head?"

"See? Fucking racist-ass honkeys. Hell, yeah, it got a key, Cole. It in the ignition."

"I'm assuming it won't leave me stranded on the side of the road?"

"Assume whatever the fuck you want. It's yours till it turns up hot or stops working, whether tomorrow or next year. I was you I'd only drive it for a few days, then ditch it. Might want to wipe down the door handles and steering wheel, too."

"Point taken. Anything else I need to do?"

"Try not to get yo ass fucked up, I guess." Sheldon turned and opened the door to leave.

"Hey Sheldon," Cole said. Sheldon looked back over his shoulder.

"Yeah?"

"Thanks."

"Bet," Sheldon said, then walked out and closed the door behind him. Cole sat back down and lit up a smoke. The Silverado had been such a big part of his adult life that its loss felt like a friend had just died. He felt more remorse losing that truck than he ever could have over Chester dying.

He snuffed out the smoke after a few drags and headed down to see what kind of shit-pile car he'd be driving around for the next day or two. Maybe the last couple of days of his life.

He felt embarrassed about driving it over to Mandy's place, but there was nothing he could do about that. If she didn't like it, fuck it. He wanted to see if he could get her to open up about her sister some more. He got the impression she didn't have any love for Jack Gables, either.

Maybe he could persuade her to help him somehow. At this point he didn't care who knew what Gables was trying to do to him, or whether they believed him or not. There wasn't much else he could do but try to pile up as much dirt as he could on Gables, maybe link him with some kind of hard evidence to either extortion or drug sales, or Jimmy and Caroline's deaths.

He took a shower and shaved, brushed his hair and put on a clean pearl-snap and jeans. He wandered out into a now sunny, hot afternoon. The clouds had broken and been sucked up into a series of enormous thunderheads that pocked the sky. It would rain later, might even rain out the last hours of his life. Nothing he could do about a thing like that.

CHAPTER TWENTY

Mandy opened the door in a sunflower dress that exposed the tanned curve of her shape without losing the proper, classy vibe she carried herself with.

"You're looking a little better than this morning," she said.

"Little too much nighttime last night. I tried to get myself back into presentable condition. Nothing I can do about my face, though."

"Trust me when I say I want to hear all about it." She smiled, but Cole couldn't tell if she was serious or just ribbing him. "Come on out onto the back patio, I've got us set up with some margaritas."

"That sounds awful, but I'll try my best to have one," Cole said. He didn't want to be rude, even though the thought of tequila made him want to start puking again.

"I figured that. This is actually my hangover cure. After a few sips you'll be good as new. My father says it's the electrolytes in the salt on the rim."

"He does, huh? Well a man in his position knows what he knows, I guess."

She frowned. "What's that supposed to mean?"

"I just meant he probably has a few tricks up his sleeve to get to the station he's risen to in life."

"He's done well for himself, but I don't know about risen.

He carried on the family business. He'd like for me to do the same since he never had a boy, but I'd just rather live off my trust, which I think confuses him. He'd never be content to have a lot of money if it was possible to have all of it. He's been trying to marry me into this bunch or that since I was twenty-two or twenty-three. The only thing positive that came out of Caroline's murder is that he doesn't seem to have the heart for it anymore."

"I figure a pretty girl like you can pick out whatever man she wants. I don't see that you'd need his help for that."

"Not his help, just his approval. If I like them he doesn't approve. If he approves, I don't like them. It's a cycle, you might say."

"So you just hole up in this big ol' house all by yourself and drink Margaritas all day, that it?"

"Not exactly. I'm pretty involved with the Junior League, and I do an awful lot of charity stuff. I'm not all that interested in the festival, but my father would have a heart attack if I didn't host the charity event each year through our foundation. Teller is all about appearances, after all."

"You ever thought of just picking up your money and leaving?"

"Leave Teller?"

"From the looks of it you don't have a shock collar that'll zap you if you go past the city limits," Cole said.

"Oh, I travel, but this is my home. I know it's hard to explain to a man like yourself."

"How's that?" Cole asked.

"I mean, a person who hasn't had all the advantages, who has probably wanted to get as far from here as you could since the day you learned to walk."

"That's about right, sure."

"My family and friends are here. They might be more in my business than I'd like, but that doesn't mean I want to shut them out of my life."

"These days it would be easy enough to stay in touch from somewhere else, no?"

"That's not the same. I want to be a part of their daily lives. I always thought that even if I didn't have children, I would be here to experience my nieces' and nephews' lives. I guess that's shot now anyway."

"I get it. For some folks there's no place like home. Had my daddy not been whipping my ass twice a day I might have felt the same way."

"What about your wife, Kerrie? I didn't know her really. How'd she feel about home?"

"She loved her folks, I can tell you that. I hated them for a long time, but she eventually convinced me that they were good people, just confused. She didn't want their fancy, socialite life. She was quiet. She liked to read and go on hikes and just have experiences. She never wanted to step foot in this town again, if given the choice. Now she's buried here."

"Her parents cut off her trust after you left, huh?"

"How'd you know that?"

"Just a guess. Around here the way you control your adult children is with money."

"So I've noticed. Not to change the subject, but I'd like to ask you a kind of hard question. I don't want to upset you or have you think I mean anything by it, though. Is that all right?"

"I'm a very straightforward girl, Cole, in case you haven't noticed. Take your best shot, I'll manage."

"Have you ever considered that maybe someone Caroline and Jimmy owed money to might have killed them and made it look like a murder-suicide instead? You said yourself your parents cut her off, and Jimmy's dad done the same thing to him. Myself, I've been wondering where they got the money to buy all those drugs?"

"My understanding was that the police were absolutely certain Jimmy murdered her. Why, did you hear something different?"

Cole sat back, tried to be casual, but serious. "I'm just going to level with you on some things because I've got nothing to lose at this point. You might not like what I have to say, I don't know. But I feel like I've gotta say it, just in case you maybe know something, maybe even something you don't yet realize is something."

"I'm all ears," Mandy said, her body language tense now.

"When I came back here to Teller for my daddy's funeral, some stuff from my past caught back up with me. I owed a chunk of money to a local drug dealer named Zach Ellis when I left. It's a big part of *why* I left, but not all of it. You ever heard of Zach?"

Mandy exhaled, looked apprehensive. "Can't say that I have, and I'm not sure what this has to do with Caroline's murder."

"Maybe everything, maybe nothing. I just want to provide a little context, so hang in there. This will also explain how my face came to look like a rotten banana."

"Got it. Please continue."

"Well, first thing after the funeral, I get pulled over by a sheriff's deputy, Deputy Desmond Charles. Guy drags me out of the truck and roughs me up, cuffs me and tosses me in the back of his cruiser. Turns out Zach Ellis is sitting in the front seat, and he starts pressuring me about signing my father's farm over to his associates as payment for my debt, which was around seventeen grand. The farm's worth more than that, but that's just how extortion goes. Anyway, the guy, Zach, he says his associate is none other than Jack Gables himself."

"Wait, wait, slow down," Mandy interrupted. "Are you suggesting that Jack Gables is a drug dealer?"

"I'm not suggesting anything. I'm outright saying it's a fact that Jack Gables runs *all* the drug dealers in Teller County. Always has. I used to think it was some sort of urban legend, but I've since seen it with my own eyes. Anyway, so right after that I run into Jimmy's dad, James, and we go get some lunch to talk about what happened. This is the part you're probably not gonna like, and I don't blame you. But I need to say it, and I hope you'll keep an open mind, because you might be able to help me."

"I'll try, but no promises," Mandy said, apprehension radiating off her now.

"James Calvert didn't think Jimmy could have done that to your sister, and not because he thought Jimmy was too good of a guy or anything. He thought Jimmy was too much of a coward to do it. Given that both your sister and Jimmy had been cut off from their trust funds, James suggested that someone had been bankrolling their drug habit and might have decided to collect without success. Either way, he gave me the money to pay off my debt in exchange for poking around town trying to find out."

"Wait, he gave you seventeen thousand dollars to look into a case the police have already solved?"

"That's just it. James felt that Jack Gables might have swept this thing under the rug for some reason or other. Maybe to protect one of his drug dealers or something, I don't know. Anyway, even after I paid Big Zach Ellis the money James gave me, he still said I owed the farm. And worse, he said I was gonna have to sign it over to Jack Gables himself. I've since found out that my daddy had an exploration done on the farm, using your father's company. It's siting on a substantial deposit of oil, as it turns out. Somehow everybody involved already knew about that, except for me." Cole watched Mandy's face close, probing for her reaction, but she seemed careful not to give it away.

She exhaled and said, "This sounds pretty far-fetched so far, Cole. In the first place I don't really see how your situation, if it's even real, is linked at all to what happened to my sister. I mean, *assuming* there was a drug debt, killing them wouldn't get the money back, would it? There's a reason they haven't killed you yet, according to your own story, no? Between the two of them, Jimmy and Caroline had access to quite a bit of money, potentially. And I still don't even remotely see anything credible in what you're saying about Jack Gables. You've got a hunch, at best, as far as I can tell."

"We can both agree the bruises and cuts on my face are real, right? And everything you said is fair. You may even be right. However, Jimmy's house was tossed, no way he just did all that in a rage. There were other things you didn't see, too, horrible things." Cole paused, not sure how to approach what he needed to say next.

"Well?" Mandy asked, when it was clear he wasn't going to continue right away.

"James Calvert gave me a file of the crime-scene pictures. His lawyer finagled them somehow. In the pictures, the gun Jimmy allegedly used to shoot himself is in his right hand."

"So? What does that mean?"

"Jimmy was left-handed, Mandy."

"Oh." Mandy seemed to be working hard to maintain her demeanor and keep from tearing up. "Well, that is strange."

"It gets stranger. After that gala at your house, when Gables threw me out, he took my truck keys and sent me off on foot. Not having anywhere else to go, I went to Jimmy's and slept on the hammock out on the boathouse deck. Gables and Big Zach woke me up a little while later to an ass-whipping; told me I would either be signing my family farm over to Gables himself, or else they'd kill me. That's how I came to look like this. But he also came down hard on me for being at his crime scene, seemed to know his way around it pretty good. He said he knew where I'd gotten the money to pay off Zach, and why. He backed me off, told me next time he found me sniffing around that place he'd deposit me at the bottom of Lake Strongbow."

"Jesus God."

"When I went to tell James Calvert about what happened to me, I found out he'd just had an accident. According to the guy I spoke to there, he got kicked in the head by a horse out in his stable, and now he's dead, too. Personally, I find that a mighty big coincidence, considering."

"Maybe. But tell me this, Cole. How do I know you're telling me the truth? I barely know you."

"I can't verify everything to you, Mandy. But I do have some proof, the potential lease, as well as the file of the crime scene photos from your sister's murder all out in the car."

Mandy sat back and took a deep breath. Neither of them had touched their margaritas. "Can I *see* them?" she finally asked.

"Do you really want to?"

She hesitated. "I—I'm not sure. I guess I never expected to be given the chance. Honestly, I think it's wildly inappropriate that you have them. I hate the idea that just anybody could be looking at her body in that state."

"I know. I can understand that. I thought maybe you might feel that way. The most comfort I can provide is to tell you I haven't been showing them around. But think about it like this. What if someone else did kill them, and that person is out walking the streets right now?"

"Then I would want that person to be brought to justice."

"And what if that person had unreasonable access to preventing justice? How would you handle that?"

"I don't know. Never thought about it, really. I'm the only person in my family who seems to want to think of Caroline at all. Don't get me wrong. She infuriated me. She was ornery, always ready to pick a fight or put someone in their place. She had a habit of never thinking consequences through. You want to know something kind of gross? I think my parents were relieved that if she had to go off and get strung out on drugs, at least she did it with a boy from a wealthy family."

"I know you might not want to hear it, but Jimmy was a pretty good guy, at least the Jimmy I knew. He just had that wild hair. Like your sister, I guess."

"I liked Jimmy before all this happened. He knew how to have fun and didn't seem to care what other people thought. That's a rare thing around this town. I can't help worrying about what others think. It's why I stay involved with all this social nonsense. I don't want people to think poorly of my mother and father. Especially now that Caroline is dead."

"Did you ever get the impression that Caroline was scared,

like scared of Jiimmy, maybe, or maybe even something or somebody else?"

"Not really. I can tell you that she was always a party girl. After she was the Rose Queen she really stepped it up. Something about that experience was traumatic for her, but she was too proud to admit it. My parents would never even harbor the possibility that anything negative might have come out of it beyond her embarrassing us all with her behavior on the float."

"She never said anything about it to you?"

"She made some cryptic comments here and there when she was drunk, but usually I tried to steer clear of her when she acted like that. I only let her stay here when she was trying to get sober. I can tell you this much: Afterward, she refused to have anything to do with anyone who was involved with the festival."

Mandy picked up her sweaty margarita glass and took a big sip. Cole did the same, almost wretched as the tart liquid went down his throat, then took another big swallow.

"So?" Mandy said.

"So what?"

"So are you going to go get those pictures, or what?"

"If that's what you really want. Are you saying you believe me now?"

"I'm saying I want to see the damn pictures," Mandy said, her controlled voice displaying just a hint of anger.

"Not a problem." Cole stood up and walked back through the house and out through the heat to the car, brought the file back in and set it in front of her.

"Before you open that," he said, his hand still resting on top, "I just want to warn you. The pictures are graphic as hell. They were hard for me to stomach, and she's not even my sister."

"You might be surprised what I can stomach, Cole Quick. My father taught me and Caroline to hunt when we were little girls. I've gutted more deer than half the men in this county. I can handle a little blood. I can shoot better than most men I know, whether pistol or rifle. And no matter how bad they are,

I'd rather see the truth than the images that come up in my head when I think about it."

"All right then," Cole said, taking his hand off the file.

She opened it and immediately put her hand over her mouth, used the other to flip slowly through the images inside. She stayed on the image of her sister's mutilated body for what felt like hours. Cole didn't want to put her through this, but he needed more information, and making an ally out of her was the best shot he had at getting that. They sat in silence as she flipped through the pictures again and again. Finally, she looked up.

"How dare you," Mandy said, standing up, showing her anger now. "How dare you go around showing *pictures* of my dead sister's body! I'm trying to be proper, Cole, but your having these is ten miles past out of line. I find it shocking that anyone would think it's okay for you to have them. Especially James Calvert."

"Mandy, I apologize if I've upset you. I haven't shown them to anyone but you, I swear. I'm just trying to figure out what it is I've got myself caught up in."

"Yeah? Well maybe it's exactly what it looks like. Maybe Mr. Calvert got kicked in the head by a horse. Maybe Jack Gables is taking down some side money in the drug business, I don't know. Maybe you ran off on some money you shouldn't have, and now you have to pay. None of it means anything happened to my sister besides your psycho friend cutting her up like an animal."

"I'm sorry, Mandy, really. I'm not saying any of those things. I'm not trying to sling mud on anyone, and I'm not trying to rip the scab off fresh wounds. I don't believe that Jimmy did this thing. I want to find the truth, that's all. I owe it to him. He was a good friend and I just ran off and left him without a word. Most of all I'm trying to dig my own ass out of a hole before I get buried in it. I've been honest with you about everything that's happened to me. I'm looking for an ally, I just figured you were my best shot."

Tears streamed down Mandy's face. She looked wrung-out now, and Cole realized she'd been hiding that behind a brave face for a long time.

"You don't know what you're asking, Cole," she said. "Now I think you'd better be on your way. I don't feel like talking about this anymore. I must have been out of my mind to let you bring another potential scandal to my doorstep."

Cole stood up. "I really am sorry, Mandy. I don't want to embarrass you or cause your family trouble." He tore a corner off the file folder, wrote down his new cell phone number on it. "If you decide you know anything that you think might help me, or if you just want to talk some more, you can call me at this number. But otherwise we probably won't meet again. If we do, I hope it's on better, friendlier terms. You seem like a nice person."

"I'm glad to hear you think that, Cole. Now hit the road. Oh, and leave the file. You have no right to have it. You have no idea the kind of social hornet's nest even saying these kinds of things out loud can stir up in this town. I won't be part of breaking my father's heart all over again. Caroline made her choices, and she paid with her life. There's no way to fix that for my family. I hate to tell you, but there's no way to change Jimmy's fate, either."

Cole took one last gulp from the Margarita, which was making him feel a little better, then picked up the file before Mandy could stop him. "I'm sorry," he said. "But I need this. It could save my life." He turned to move toward the living room, ready to dodge her if she attempted to get it back, but she didn't. Instead, she put her hands to her face and mumbled something to him. "I'm sorry?" Cole said, not understanding her.

She moved her hands and spoke again. "I said take it then, and get out. Don't ever come back."

As he walked back up the driveway to the Sunbird, Cole found himself sweating as much from the heat radiating off his face as from the hot afternoon sun.

CHAPTER TWENTY-ONE

He drove back to the motel a little angry at himself for how he'd mucked up the conversation with Mandy Ambrose. He locked the door, put on the rape chain and dug Chester's pistol out of his bag. He popped the clip into it and racked a round into the chamber. He wasn't going down without a fight. The next time Big Zach or Jack Gables or Deputy Asshole put their hands on him, he intended to kill or be killed. He wanted to live, but he was willing to die if that's what it took to keep those scoundrels off his throat.

He stretched out on top of the bed with the pistol laid across his chest. He fell asleep out of sheer exhaustion. When he woke up again, it was dark outside. Headlights streamed across the outside of the dark room's curtains.

He felt sick, unable to grasp his whereabouts for a moment. He sat up and rubbed the sleep from his eyes, checked the ancient clock-radio on the nightstand. Just after eight. He'd been asleep for four hours, maybe more.

He was hungry and wanted to go to Vernon's, but couldn't take the risk of showing up anywhere that whoever had been following him might have seen him. His time was up, and if Gables knew where to find him to deliver the paperwork, he was done for. He decided it would be best to keep digging, do what he could to figure out what exactly had happened with

Jimmy and Caroline.

Except he was out of places to ask around. It was time to be a little more persuasive with his questions.

He tucked the pistol into a small gym bag that had been in his truck for years before he cleaned it out, made his way outside and down to the Sunbird, staying in the shadows beneath the awning while he scanned the lot to see if anyone noticed him.

There were four other cars in the lot. None of them appeared to have any people in them. He checked the parking lot of the Whataburger next door, also didn't see anyone. He decided to pull in their drive-through and grab a burger, then drive out toward Outlaws, a strip club the Burnell family had operated since he was a kid.

As a teenager it had been thrilling going in the place to pick up his stash. Now he was worried it was the kind of place he might get killed. He'd never dealt with any of them but Zach. But if they were keeping tabs on him, maybe it was time for him to keep tabs on them, too.

It wasn't too late to run, but he was past that now. He was going to take Jack Gables down for good or die trying. He needed evidence that would tie Gables to corruption. He planned to deliver it to Russ Kirkpatrick and let the man run it through his law enforcement contacts as necessary. Maybe Cole could prove Gables had covered up the truth about how Jimmy died, get him on obstruction of justice or something like that. Except that was all still speculation.

Outlaws was ten miles out from the eastern edge of town. The thumpers at Rose Meadows Baptist had been trying to shut it down for decades without success. Cole pulled into the back of the parking lot and backed the Sunbird into a spot where he could see the front door.

He had no idea if Big Zach still posted up there as his headquarters, but he also had no idea of anywhere else to look for the man.

Just as he lit up his fourth cigarette a sheriff's cruiser pulled into the lot and around to the back of the building. It looked like Desmond Charles, but he couldn't tell for sure in the dim parking lot.

He tucked the pistol in the back of his waistband, got out of the car, and made his way down the line of pine trees on the edge of the lot, then down the side of the building, where it backed up to more pine trees and some brush. At the back corner he stopped and pressed himself up against the building, peeked around the corner, careful not to stick his head out.

Sure enough, Big Zach was leaning on the cruiser's passenger window, filthy jeans tucked into big obnoxious patterned cowboy boots, white V-neck T-shirt half soaked through with sweat. Zach said something Cole couldn't hear, then gave two bumps on the top of the cruiser and stepped back.

Charles backed the cruiser out the way he'd come. Cole had to duck back behind the wall's corner to keep the headlights from shining on him when Charles swung the front end around to drive out the other direction. As soon as his car pulled away Cole took the pistol out from his back waistband.

Big Zach was focused on finding the right key on his key ring to open the back door as Cole made a wide, quiet circle so that he was behind the gargantuan man. Just as the Zach inserted his key into the lock, Cole hammered the butt of the gun down hard above the wrinkles that connected his fat neck with his head. Zach grunted but didn't go down, swung his right arm wild behind him and knocked Cole backwards. As Zach spun around Cole pointed the pistol at his face.

"Move another inch and there will be one less fat asshole selling cocaine in Teller County," Cole said.

Big Zach put his palms out in front of him and laughed. "Now I know you've done lost your mind, Cole."

"Maybe so. Looks to me like I'm the one holding the pistol, though."

"For the moment, anyway. You ain't a killer, and we both know it. Man who had killing inside him wouldn't have run off like you done. You ain't got it in you."

"Make a move and we'll find out what color your blood is. I'm guessing green. If not, turn your big ass around and walk."

Zach grinned, not totally taking him seriously, but not stupid enough to make a move. He started to walk toward the parking-lot side of the building.

"Not that way, big 'un," Cole said. "The other side, by the trees and such."

"You best have one hell of a plan, Cole. This here gonna cost you more than just your life. I'm talking major pain."

"Who says you're gonna get away? Now walk."

Zach did as Cole instructed and Cole followed five feet behind him, the pistol pointed at his back.

"Where am I walking to, Cole, or did you forget to think that through?"

"Blue car back in the corner over there. Try anything funny and I'll blast a couple holes in you and drive out of here alone. If you wanna live, you'll climb your fat ass in the driver's seat instead."

"How the fuck am I supposed to fit in that little worm burner?"

"I don't give a damn how you fit in it, long as you do. Scoot the seat back as far as it will go, I don't care. Suffer. It's better than the alternative, I'd imagine."

Cole held the gun close to his hip as they came around the car under the parking lot's dim light. He climbed into the back seat as Zach scooted the driver's seat back as far as it would go and tilted the steering wheel up so he could sit down. The keys were still in the ignition.

"Fire it up and make a left out of the parking lot," Cole said.

"Where am I headed?" Zach asked.

"Drive over to my boy Jimmy's place. You know where it is. Last time you were there you kicked the shit out of me and I got a hunch that the time before that you probably killed Jimmy and Caroline Ambrose."

"That what you think, Cole?" He could almost hear Zach smile. "You one dumb son of a bitch, I'll tell you that. You've got no idea what you're in the middle of."

"Keep the opinions to yourself and drive, I'm having a hard enough time not shooting you as it is. Try anything funny and we'll see if I can't get a bullet into your head before we crash."

"Okay, I got the message, relax bubba. Jimmy Calvert's place it is. But just so you know, I may have sold him a bunch of cocaine, but I didn't kill him. I didn't have a goddamn thing to do with it."

"Who did, then?" Cole asked.

"I don't know," Zach replied. "But you're stepping in things a hell of a lot bigger than you or me."

"I'll be the judge of that," Cole said.

Cole closed the front gate behind them after they pulled in, was surprised the gate opener still worked after having gone in the lake with him. They pulled down to the house and he told Zach to park the car on the grass beyond the end of the driveway, where it wouldn't be visible from the road. Zach shut off the engine and Cole got out of the car on the passenger side, kept the gun trained on him through the window.

"Get out, and bring the keys," Cole said. It took Big Zach a bit of work to free himself from the vehicle, but he did it and shut the door.

"Now what?"

"Inside, through the back door," Cole said. He followed Zach just like before, five feet behind, gun pointed at the center of his back. "The key's on the ring," he added when they got to the French doors on the back of the house. "Unlock it and go on in."

Zach did as Cole said, opened the door and started to enter. Just as Cole stepped across the threshold the door swung back into him hard. He fired blindly through the window, shattering one of the panes in the door. Zach grunted as he stumbled backward onto his ass. Cole lurched to his feet, kicked the door open with a front kick to find Zach moaning in the wrecked living room, a hole in his right calf from the bullet.

"What'd I tell you?" Cole said, wondering if anyone could have heard the shot. The houses on this part of the lake were spaced far enough from one another that the neighbors might not know where the shot had come from. They probably wouldn't expect it to be Jimmy's house, considering Jimmy was dead.

It was a lot of faith to put in chance, but Cole didn't have any other options. He needed to get the information he came for.

"You sum-bitch," Zach said as he rolled around in a growing pool of his own blood, "I'll fucking kill you for this, I swear."

"Bubba," Cole said, parroting Zach's own terminology, "It looks to me right now like you the one in danger of ending up dead. He backed his way toward the kitchen, found a towel on the floor.

"Press this to your wound, fat boy. In fact, I'll tell you what. You answer some questions for me and I'll call you an ambulance. If not, you can lay there however long it takes to bleed out. Maybe some estate planner might find your body next week or something. Still a better option than you gave Jimmy."

Zach winced, still gripping his calf. "Goddamn it, Cole, I ain't had nothing to do with that, I told you."

"Then tell me who did, and I'll make sure you don't bleed out."

"I don't know who, exactly, but I know you don't want to tangle with them. It didn't go so well for your friend, did it?"

"Try me. I want to know what you know, otherwise you can rot your fat ass here just like my friend had to."

"Like I told you, Cole, I don't know who. I sold Jimmy a fuck-ton of coke, that's true. But he always paid. Rich folks ain't got the same problems as people like you, Cole. They know it's easier to stay and pay than to run and owe."

"He and Caroline were both cut off from their trust funds, I know that for a fact. Where in the hell did he get the money to keep up his habit?"

"You think I ask 'em where the money comes from? I just

drop off a couple ounces and they give me the money. That's it."

"You know of anybody else he would have gotten his cocaine from?"

Zach growled, gripped at his leg with both hands, squirmed around in his blood some more. "Hell no, Cole. I'd have run any other motherfucker off, the kind of money they was spending. Those two were practically a pair of cash cows."

"Then why would someone want to kill them? I know someone murdered them, and I'm pretty sure your boy Jack Gables swept the whole thing under the rug."

"Why do you think that?"

"Don't worry why, worry about how you're going to convince me you don't know who it was."

"There's forces at work here, Cole, like I said. Even above Jack Gables. I couldn't begin to tell you who they are except to say they are not people you want to fuck around with."

"Last chance, Zach. Tell me who killed Jimmy or lay here and bleed out."

"Cole, I. Don't. Know. Go ahead and shoot me again if you want. I ain't got nothing else to say about it."

Cole pointed the pistol at Zach's head, felt an urge he could only associate with Chester to pull the trigger and end this man's life. An unbridled rage, maybe his birthright. But Zach was right. Cole wasn't a killer. In fact, this was the first time he'd ever even pointed a gun at someone, much less shot them. He took a deep breath, tried to get his head straight.

"I'll tell you what, Zach. I'll drop a call to nine-one-one on my way back out. Feel free to explain to them how you got here if you want, I really don't care at this point. I ought to kill you, but if I did it would make me just like you. But do me a favor, huh?"

"What's that? Zach asked, his face still tight with anguish.

"Tell your boy Jack Gables I'm coming for him, and he'll never see a dime of my inheritance no matter what he does to me."

Cole slammed the butt of the pistol into the side of Zach's

head and the big redneck crumbled to his side in the blood. Cole dialed nine-one-one on his Cricket and reported an intruder at Jimmy's address. He left the gate open as he drove away down the otherwise quiet country roads.

CHAPTER TWENTY-TWO

Cole was almost back to town when the Cricket phone rang. His adrenaline was still pumping as he dug the phone out of his pocket and swiped it to life.

"Mandy?"

"How did you know it was me?" Mandy replied.

"Nobody else with a Teller area code has this number, that I know of."

"Oh." Mandy paused, as if considering what to say next.

Cole filled the silence. "Listen, I want to apologize since I've got you on the line. I didn't mean to offend or upset you. I can't imagine what you're going through with your sister's death. It was selfish of me to drop all that on you."

"Listen Cole, forget it. I did some thinking after you left, and it led to something I think you'll find important."

"Yeah?" Cole pulled to the side of the road to talk.

"Yeah. I mentioned earlier that I used to let Caroline stay here in one of my spare bedrooms occasionally. Mostly when her and Jimmy were fighting, but only when she said she wanted to get sober. Nobody knew she stayed here. My father would have had a conniption fit after they cut her off if he'd known I was supporting her some of the time."

"It's your house though, no?"

"Cole, when your money comes from a trust, nothing is ever

really yours. There's strings attached to everything, both financial and emotional."

"I knew that, just wasn't looking at it that way."

"Anyway, after we spoke earlier it occurred to me that I haven't been back in that room since she died. It was just too much, and to tell you the truth I think I've been avoiding it."

"Why's that?"

"She left some of her stuff here. Listen, are you busy right now?"

"Not at all."

"Would you be willing to stop over and talk with me again? I want to show you something."

"Sure," Cole said, already hitting the u-turn. "Only thing is, my situation has, uh, *progressed* since we spoke this afternoon. I kind of need to get my vehicle off the street."

"Progressed?"

"Sometimes you've got to hit back."

"Oh. Well come over, it's important. You can pull the car down inside the gates so nobody can see it. This place was practically designed to be a fortress, so I don't think you'll have any trouble here."

"Sound's good, we can work all that out. I'll be there in ten minutes or so."

"Good, I'll open the gate and close it behind you."

Mandy answered the door in a flowing white robe with satin nightgown underneath. Everything Cole had seen the girl wear suited her, but she had bags under her puffy eyes, and she looked stressed out.

"Come in, I already shut the gate," Mandy said.

"Thanks."

She led him into the big living room and they sat on opposite white leather couches that had a long oak coffee table between them. The table was empty except for a fancy pink-striped notebook.

"So, what's up?" Cole finally asked.

"Well, as I explained on the phone, I got to thinking after you left, and went upstairs to look through the room Caroline stayed in. She kept some clothing and things like that in the dresser up there. As I was going through it all and just sort of remembering her smell, as weird as that sounds, I found this." Mandy picked up the notebook and passed it over to Cole.

"What is it?" Cole asked as he took it from her.

"You can look through it for yourself, but that's Caroline's journal."

Cole raised his eyebrow at her as he opened the journal to a page that had been earmarked. The page was full, front and back, with loopy, almost formal handwriting.

"She kept a journal?" he said, almost incredulous.

"She was sentimental when she thought no one was looking. But read what's inside. She was *gang raped*. At her coronation party, by her date and another man. They must have drugged her. I think she never said anything to anyone because she and Jimmy were blackmailing them, or at least one of them."

"You're saying she and Jimmy were blackmailing the guys who raped her?" Cole said, barely able to contain his shock.

"Just one of them. But the other one refused to pay. I *know* one of them really well. He's from a respected family. But it's the other one that I think you'll find most interesting."

"So spit it out then," Cole said.

"The one I know well is Tucker Colston. His uncle's the mayor, actually."

Cole stood up off the sofa, ran a hand through his hair. "Holy shit," he said. "Really? Tucker Colston?"

"You know him too?"

"You're gonna find this as hard to believe as I do just now, but I stayed over at his place last night. Never met him before that. Who was the other one?"

"It was his little running buddy, Chantree Gables. I'm assuming you know him, too, then."

Cole felt sweat start to develop on his back, even though it must have been sixty-five degrees in that house with the AC going full-blast. He composed himself, took it all in along with a deep breath.

"I was out with Tucker and Randall Harrington trying to pump them for information about your sister and Jimmy, met them at the bar. He was trying to call Chantree all night to round up some women. You know what? Tucker never even blinked when I asked him about your sister, but he had some nasty stuff to say about her. I stayed up half the night with them but didn't even get a hint they might be involved in any of this."

"Tucker is half sociopath, and all coward. I never liked him or his older brother, Trey. They're both sweet and polite when people are around, but two of the nastiest people I've ever met when nobody's looking."

Cole sat back down now, leaned his elbows on his knees and said, "Guess I didn't see that side of him. He did keep going on about getting girls over there. That's not how he put it, but you get the idea."

"Screw him," Mandy said.

"So how would you weigh this in with your sister and Jimmy's death, now?" Cole asked. "I think it's clear, don't you? In the journal, Tucker was paying, but it seemed like she and Jimmy were trying unsuccessfully to lean on Chantree. To me that says Jack Gables and company might have had motive to kill them."

"So you don't think it was a murder-suicide now?"

"I don't know what I think. But your story makes a lot more sense to me than it did. It can't be coincidence, the name Gables coming up in this and him telling you to keep your nose out of it, like you said."

"For sure it looks like that's where Jimmy and Caroline were getting their money, by blackmailing Tucker. I bet when Chantree refused to pay they got stuck on whether to keep getting money from Tucker or expose them both, since Chantree wouldn't pay.

That's an awful lot of motive for murder, if you ask me."

"I'm sorry, I think I'm going to be sick again. Excuse me." Mandy's bare feet padded softly against the travertine floor as she ran out of the room. Cole sat back and tried to put it all together some more. Gables had to be involved in this. But they still needed more proof to connect him fully. The journal would be a start, but not enough to take Gables down. They needed to maybe lean on Tucker to get more information. After a few minutes Mandy came back in and re-took her seat.

"I'm sorry about that."

Don't be," Cole said. "I was in your shoes I'd be sick. too, I suppose."

"It's just too much. I think I'd rather be in your shoes than mine right now, Cole. That's how awful I feel."

"Hearing all this, I can't say I blame you. If this is what money buys, then maybe money's not worth having. So anyway, look. I appreciate you showing me all of this stuff. But I can't help wondering, why? Earlier you said you would never expose your father to another scandal. This looks like a pretty big scandal we've got brewing here."

"Scandal is one thing. But she was raped, and at a festival that is supposed to demonstrate just how civilized and charitable we all are. Besides, blackmail won't even make the board of embarrassing things Caroline did. I want justice for what happened to her now. That's why I'm going to help you. You mentioned you've arranged to have an affidavit sent out. I think you should add in copies of what I have here in the journal."

"I appreciate it. It doesn't mean squat for my problems with Jack Gables at the moment, but I do. It will take more than this to take him down. I think he knew this wasn't a murder-suicide, but there's no hard evidence here that he killed them, or even covered it up. All we have here is a deceased person's journal. It might implicate some people in an assault, but there's no evidence of murder. All this will do is cause a scandal and drag some people through the dirt. If we want something done for your sister, we need to figure out a way to implicate her killer. Once we have that, maybe we can prove that Jack Gables was involved in some sort of coverup, or maybe he even killed them himself. That would take care of my problems with him, too."

"You said yourself you were running out of time, Cole. Besides, I'm not scared of these people—I'm the one they ought to fear now."

"I can get behind that. In fact, I wish we'd had this conversation a few hours ago, because I kidnapped and shot a man tonight, one of the guys who's been following me around and whipping my ass. After I spoke to you earlier I was desperate, didn't see any other way out. I got Big Zach to admit that he was the one selling Jimmy and Caroline the cocaine, but I don't think he was involved in their murder. He said they always paid up front, so we know the blackmail must have been working for a while. I still can't believe I shot him. I was questioning him at gunpoint and he went for the gun, so I fired. They'll be looking for me hard now. I need to lay low."

"You don't have to so much as leave this house until we figure out what to do, if you don't want to," Mandy said.

"I appreciate that. But all my stuff is over at the Rose City Motel, so I'll need to go get that at some point. You got a scanner?"

"I've got a printer and scanner upstairs."

"Good. I'll scan the pages and email them to my attorney, and that former Texas Ranger I mentioned. Hopefully this along with the affidavit will be enough to at least get him down here and on our side. But we still need to get more evidence. I have a good idea of where we can get it."

"Tucker."

"Exactly."

"Far as I'm concerned, we can just go shoot that son of a bitch and be done with it," Mandy said. Her stress seemed to have faded and been replaced with anger now.

"Let's just cool off and think before we hit him up. We need to do our best to keep emotion out of it and just try to get some information to connect these things together. I think all roads lead through Tucker."

"I know him. I think he's too weak to have killed my sister and Jimmy. He's a pretty boy."

"I agree. I think we ought to pay Tucker a little visit and put some pressure on him, though. But first if you don't mind, I'd like to go pick up my stuff."

"Those are the keys to my Escalade there in the bowl on the table." Mandy indicated a set of keys in a shiny golden glass bowl with her forehead. "There's a gate opener on the visor. Go get your stuff and we can figure out what to do about Tucker after. The windows are so tinted that no one will see who's driving anyway, but be careful."

"I'll gather my stuff and come right back," Cole said as he picked up the keys and headed for the door.

He backed the Escalade into a spot in front of the motel, went inside and told the clerk he was checking out, then came out and popped the hatch. It took twenty minutes to load all his stuff into the back of the Escalade.

He was just about to shut the truck's back hatch when he noticed a Sheriff's cruiser turn into the motel's parking lot through the front windshield. His adrenaline spiked as he jumped up into the Escalade and pulled the hatch shut behind him.

The cruiser pulled in a few cars down and Deputy Charles got out looking around as if he owned the place. Satisfied that he might, he strutted over to the front office. Cole climbed over the bench into the driver's seat, fired up the engine and threw it into drive. As he passed the front office, he saw Deputy Charles leaning on the counter, waiting for the clerk to come out from the back. Cole pulled out of the parking lot and headed toward the lake. He didn't know if Charles had seen him, but the clerk would know he just checked out, might tell Charles what Cole had been driving, if she saw. He needed to get back to Mandy's.

He felt panicked all the way until he was parked back in Mandy's garage with the gates shut behind him. Even then he had to sit still and take some deep breaths. He couldn't afford to take any more risks like that now that he'd shot Zach. No question they'd be looking for blood now.

Mandy wasn't around when he came back into the house. He called her name as he came up the stairs and heard her muffled reply from somewhere down the hall.

He found her in some sort of dressing room, which had mirrors on each wall as well as a chaise lounge and a few special racks for hanging potential outfits on.

"Did it all go okay?" She asked.

"Sort of. When I was loading up the truck at the hotel, one of the deputies that's been following me pulled into the parking lot. I don't know how they even knew I'd been there because I ditched my truck not long after I checked in."

Mandy sucked in her breath. "Did he see you?"

"I don't think so, but I had to climb through the back hatch and up to the driver's seat to get out of there."

"Did you get all your stuff?"

"Barely. A difference in thirty seconds and they'd probably be pulling my teeth out with pliers right now."

"Jesus. That really what you're looking at?"

"You saw what happened to your sister and Jimmy. I have no doubt these guys are involved. Look at my face. Hard to deny what they're capable of. Either way, I think it's official that Gables and his boys are on the hunt for me. It's too dangerous for me to be seen in that Escalade again, in case the clerk gave Gables' man a description. Can we take a different car?"

"That's probably a good idea. But where are we going?"

"I'm thinking I'll have you drop me over at Jackson's, I'll see if Tucker is up there. I got the impression the other night that he's damn near always there. I'll see if I can lure him back to his place somehow. I might need to pick up some party favors to lure him with, though."

"You mean drugs? What kind?"

"Cocaine, that seems to be his deal. A guy I know might still have some, but I have to be careful going to find him."

"All right then, if that's what you think will work. I keep a bottle of Xanax upstairs, for when I can't sleep. Maybe that would be useful?"

"It's possible."

"What happens if you see a sheriff's deputy while you're in there?"

Cole showed her the pistol stuffed into the back of his pants. "I bite back."

"I really hope it doesn't come to all that, Cole."

"I hope so too. But if it does I don't plan to be on the wrong end of the stick anymore."

CHAPTER TWENTY-THREE

Mandy dropped Cole behind Vernon's. They drove her Mercedes in case the Escalade had been spotted.

"Wait out here, I'll be right back," Cole said.

"Sound's good," she said. "Be careful."

He peeked around the building and studied the parking lot, didn't see any police cruisers. The Silverado wasn't there as far as he could tell from his limited vantage point. He said fuck it and jogged past the smokehouse to the back kitchen door, which was open, save for the screen. He stepped inside to stainless steel prep tables with whole briskets lined out on them, along with racks of ribs. A resting pit toward the back exhaled a thin stream of smoke. The door into the restaurant swung open and Vernon looked startled to see Cole standing there.

"Jesus, Cole," he said, "you about scared the mess out of me. What you doin' back here in my kitchen?"

"Sorry for startling you, Vern. I've got folks lookin' for me so I'm keeping a low profile."

"They more than looking for you, Cole, they huntin'," Vernon said.

"What's that mean?"

"Sheldon dead, Cole. Couple teenagers found him shot to death a few hours ago off the Spur, down some of them power line access roads. Maybe you wanna tell me how he come to end up that way in the back of yo truck? Deputy who come in here lookin' for you said they seekin' you for questioning in connection with the murder."

Adrenaline made him shudder. "Sheldon's dead?" he asked, still shocked.

"What I said. Strange you don't know it, given the circumstance. But you ain't answer my question. Why he be in yo truck?"

"I traded him my truck earlier today for a ghetto rental. Signed the title over to him and everything. They knew my truck, and I wanted to separate myself from the guys who were following me."

Vernon's face twisted into a scowl. "So what you saying is, you used the boy as a decoy?" he asked.

Cole felt tears coming on suddenly. He choked them back and straightened himself up. "It wasn't like that," he said. "At least, I didn't mean for it to be. I'm a little out of my league and I didn't think it through. I figured worst case scenario he'd tell them I sold it to him and that would be that. Goddammit, I should've known better. I bet they had a tracker on it from the first time they pulled me over, that must be how they've been keeping tabs on me."

Vernon stood with his hands on his hips for a moment, then picked up a metal tray of potato salad and launched it across the kitchen, almost hitting Cole. "Should've known better?" Vernon spit. "Yeah, I'd say so. Police be knowin' Sheldon, guess that ain't occur to you either. They already calling it a drug deal gone bad. My guess, they cut his ass up tryin' to find out where you be. Sheriff's Department gonna say it was you who killed him, too, watch."

Cole stepped around the potato salad as if to approach Vernon, but the big man waved him off. "No more sympathy here, Cole. I ain't about to be the next nigga you throw under the bus running from yo problems."

A sense of shock overcame Cole, then anger. "Goddamn it,

Vernon," he said, his voice shaking. "I'm telling you it wasn't like that. I fucked up, as usual. Gables and his cronies are the ones who probably killed Sheldon, though. Not me. I'm sick to my stomach about it, I really am. I never wanted anyone to get hurt, I just wanted some cover to hit them back for a change."

"It's a damn shame yo cover be yet another man's life. A black man, as usual. Ain't nothing ever change around this place, not even you." Vernon wiped his forehead with the sleeve of his chef's coat, looked as if he might dab at his eyes, too, but didn't. "Now maybe you want to tell me why you up here sneakin' around looking for him. Is you back on drugs again, too?"

"Not exactly. When I took him home a few nights ago, I did get some coke from him, that's true. I was feeling low, hadn't touched it in thirteen years. But I got all that bullshit out of my system yesterday and wised back up this morning, ready to turn over a new leaf. You have to believe me that I didn't know this would happen. I feel like a son of a bitch rolled up in an idiot's skin."

Vernon's voice was softer now. "Son, people like Jack Gables looking to either kill you or frame you up for murder, and they gon' kill anyone get in the way. What's done is done now, I ain't like it, but it is what it is. My advice, forget that bullshit, grab what you got left and hightail it out of town. Cecil say he took care of you. He say you crazy and gon' get us all killed. I'm starting to see his point. Millie scared out her mind we all gonna end up just like Sheldon now."

Cole felt like he could puke. "I hope not, Vernon. I'm so sorry I got y'all into this. I knew it was a mistake and I did it anyway out of some dumbass sense of payback."

"You done said that, Cole. But you keep showing back up with more trouble to spread around. Now listen, I got to get back out here and run the restaurant. Watch your ass, son, and don't come back no more. We strugglin' enough as it is without more bodies to think about."

Cole nodded, stuck his hand out to shake with Vernon. "I'm

sorry I ever came back in here at all, y'all don't deserve this," he said.

"Aw hell, Cole," Vernon said, and reached past the hand, pulled him into a hug. "Whatever you up to, I hope it works out. But for now, you got to go."

"Thanks Vernon," Cole said. "If it doesn't, I want you to know y'all are the best damn people I ever met."

"Ain't no way that's true. Now get gone, son. We see you again, I hope it's on better terms."

Cole pulled away and stepped back out the back door, made his way to the Mercedes and got back inside.

"How'd it go?" Mandy asked.

Cole sighed. "It didn't. In fact, I got one of my friends killed today."

"How so?" Mandy gave him a confused look.

"I'll tell you about it some other time, I'm not sure I can talk about it anymore at the moment without falling apart. For now, I need to focus. Cops are all over the place looking for me, saying I killed my friend. You said earlier that you kept some Xanax around the house?"

"Yeah, why?"

"Change of plan. I've got an idea of how we might get Tucker to talk, and those pills are a big part of it."

They drove back by Mandy's house and picked up her Xanax. Cole waited in the car with the window down while she went inside to get them. The humidity outside had dropped, but the air still felt thick, a mixture of summer's oppression and fall's eventual relief.

He and Kerrie had spent many such nights driving down country roads together with the windows down and the same kind of air filling the cab as they talked about what the future might hold. Now Sheldon had been murdered in that truck, and Cole was positive neither of them ever could have imagined a future that looked like this.

A loneliness came over him again, the kind that made a person want to lay down and just stop breathing. Then his anger pushed the feeling out again, and he could feel hatred's electricity in his veins.

Sheldon was dead. Everyone who came near him seemed to end up that way. He wondered if he ought to just get out of the car and walk off into the night before it happened to Mandy, too. Her family name might protect her, but that hadn't worked out so well for her sister. He didn't have time to consider it much before she was climbing back into the driver's seat with a prescription bottle of pills in her hand.

"Sorry," she said, "I couldn't find them at first. They were way at the back of my cabinet. You okay?"

"I'm fine," Cole replied. "Why?"

"Well, besides the fact that you just said another one of your friends was murdered, you've got this look in your eyes like you're about to either fall over dead or cause somebody else to."

"It might be both. Now let's go see if we can figure out who in the hell keeps killing people around here."

Mandy turned the Mercedes around in the driveway and punched the accelerator so hard it kicked up rocks as she pulled between the iron gates and out onto the country roads.

CHAPTER TWENTY-FOUR

Cole directed Mandy to pull up to the back of Jackson's, where Randall usually parked. Randall's BMW wasn't around.

"You can either come inside, hang here, or just take off and I'll text you. It's up to you," Cole said. "Might be better if I go in alone, though."

"How do you know if he's even here?"

"That's the Jaguar he was driving last night parked right over there." Cole pointed at Tucker's car, parked in the same spot it had been the night before.

"I'm not sure I could be in his presence without trying to claw his eyes out, even if I thought I could help," Mandy said. "Should I just wait here?"

"That'll work. I'm gonna see if I can lure him back to his house with the promise of a party. You know where Tucker's place is, just in case?"

"Of course. Two coves over from mine."

"Good. I'll see you in a little bit, then. But if I come out with Tucker and get in his car, you just drive over and meet me at his house, don't feel like you need to follow us directly."

"Got it," Mandy said, unbuckling her seatbelt.

Cole entered through the back door and waited in the corner just outside the restroom while he scanned the room for anyone who might be looking for him. The band must have been between sets, because the only music was an old Ronnie Millsap tune crooning from the jukebox. Cole bellied up to the bar and ordered a Shiner, then took it out to the back porch. The porch was mostly empty since the band was on set break, but Tucker was at the same table as the day before, along with John Rawlins.

Good. Maybe Rawlins would have to duck out after his wife again like the other night, leave Cole and Tucker alone at some point. Tucker spotted him but only nodded. Cole made his way over to their table anyway.

"What's shakin', boys?" he said.

"Cole," Tucker said. Rawlins nodded and kept sipping his margarita. "I'd say it's good to see you, but my head still aches from the last time I saw you."

"Mine, too. Mind if I pull up a chair?"

"Have at it," Tucker said. He took a big pull off the pint glass of beer in front of him.

"What kind of trouble y'all out getting' into?" Cole asked.

"Just having some drinks to kill the hangover," Tucker replied.

"Your wife try to skin you alive last night after you made the only responsible decision at the table, John?" Cole asked, trying to be casual.

"Not really. She threw a fit for a minute, but she always does until she remembers whose money bought her a Lexus and a five-thousand-square-foot house."

Cole forced a smile. "Showed her who's boss, did ya?"

"A good-looking woman from a good family is a lot like a thoroughbred," Rawlins said. "You ain't gotta ride her hard, just show her the whip and let her remember where the feed comes from, she'll run the race herself from there."

"I see your point."

"That's if you like to bet on only one horse," Tucker said. "I prefer a variety of options."

"We can't all be playboy bachelors," Rawlins said, standing up. "And on that note, I'm off to the stable to get groomed."

"I might call it an early night, too," Tucker said. "There

ain't an ounce of pussy to be had in this place, and I've got an incredible hangover."

Cole said, "Well, you boys sure know how to make a friend feel welcome. Don't show her too much whip, John, she might not fear it if she gets familiar with it."

"The only thing Sherry is familiar with is her lifestyle. There's not a whip big enough on the planet to split her from it. You all take care. Nice to see you again, Cole."

"Nice to see you, too, John." Cole turned back to Tucker. "What about you, Tucker, I know you don't have a wife callin' you home. Stay for another drink with me?"

Tucker nodded. "I'll finish this beer with you, best I can promise. But first I gotta hit the head. I'll walk you out on the way, John."

John nodded as Tucker stood up. They walked in a line inside the doors and were gone from sight. Cole got the feeling that Tucker might not come back, but there was nothing he could do about that.

Instead he held Mandy's pill bottle in his lap and shook out three pills into his palm, then put the bottle back in his pocket. He used two quarters between his thumb and index finger to smash them into his other palm, checked to see if anyone was watching, then dumped them into Tucker's beer.

The powder looked like it might sit on top of the beer at first, then disappeared into the golden liquid. Cole used his finger to stir it the rest of the way in and sat back just as Tucker was coming back onto the porch.

Up on stage, the band was just picking up their instruments again. A few clumps of people came out of the door behind Tucker and walked past the table as he sat back down. The band settled into an old George Strait tune that Cole couldn't remember the name to, something about putting out old flames.

The music seemed to loosen Tucker up a bit, or maybe John Rawlins leaving had done that. Cole tried not to look like he was watching as Tucker took a big gulp off his beer. He didn't seem to notice anything wrong with it. They sat and watched the band for a while. Tucker finished his beer just as Cole finished his own, but made no move to get up to leave.

"I'm gonna grab another one," Cole said. "Can I buy you a drink?"

Tucker hesitated, then relaxed back into his chair. "You know what? Why not. I'm starting to feel a little better, and these boys up on stage sound pretty good."

"What are you having?" Cole asked.

"These Lone Stars are treating me right. Can you have 'em throw a splash of tomato juice in my next one though?"

"Got it," Cole said as he stood up. Inside he went to the bathroom, rather than the bar, crushed up a couple more pills and cuffed them in his hand. After the bartender filled his order he dropped a ten on the bar and told her to keep it, put his hand on top of Tucker's drink to pick it up, and let the Xanax fall into it as he did.

He carried the two drinks outside and set them down on the table. Tucker's entire vibe had changed in the time Cole had been gone. He had a calm smile on his face now, was bobbing his head to the music. Cole sat down and did the same, figuring it was good to let him get in the spirit rather than try to talk his ear off. They clanked glasses and both took a big pull off their beers.

Between songs Tucker turned to him and asked, "What time did you get gone this morning? I slept half the damn day."

"Early, unfortunately. Had a meeting to get to."

"I would have canceled that shit quick-fast, if it had been me."

"Didn't really have much choice. But I hear you. I wouldn't mind getting into a little more monkey business tonight, actually, now that I'm feeling better. I feel like I still need to blow off some steam, maybe find some girls. What about you?"

Tucker slurred his words now a little. "Maybe I could do with a little action. You got any particular ladies in mind?"

Cole gave him a wink for effect. "Matter of fact, I do. And I got a buddy who can probably score us some more of that good blow. Interested?"

"Am I interested? If there's some snatch involved, I'm always interested."

"I'd say let's take this party to my place, but it wouldn't hold a candle to yours."

"We can do it at my place, no problem."

"All right, tell you what. I need to go holler at my boy and pick up the ladies. How bout we meet up over at your place in say, forty-five minutes or so?"

"What girls, who are they?"

"Let's keep it a surprise," Cole said. "Trust me, you won't be disappointed. I'll have 'em bring suits and we can hot-tub it."

"Now you're talking. I'll tell you, older I get, there just ain't a lot of places to get any action around this town anymore."

Cole stood up. "No doubt. So I'll see you at your place within the hour?"

"Hell, yes," Tucker slurred, obviously intoxicated now. "I'll have four margaritas waiting."

He stood and slapped Tucker on the back for effect. See you in a few."

Cole slid back into the passenger side of the Mercedes and slammed the door shut.

"So?" Mandy asked, turning to face him.

"He's in. Go ahead and pull on out of here before he comes out and sees us. I told him I needed to go pick up some coke and some women and I'd meet him at his place."

Mandy raised her eyebrows. "Women?" she said.

Cole shrugged. "He was looking rough so I sweetened the deal. Plus, last time I was at his place he kept jawing about calling up some 'snatch.'" Mandy shot him a look, so he added, "His words, not mine. I figured I'd head him off and keep him from calling anyone else over. I managed to get several crushed up pills into his drink, so he ought to be nice and primed by the time we get there."

"Good. Let's see how he likes getting drugged and taken advantage of. Should we go there now?"

"Let's take the long route, give him a chance to get there first." Cole took the pistol out from under the seat where he'd stashed it, checked to be sure it was still loaded. Mandy's eyes tracked the pistol as she drove.

"You're going to shoot him, right?" she said.

"I don't intend to, no. I might rough him up, though. But I figure no way a predatory guy like him doesn't have some guns stashed around the house, so I want to be sure mine's ready, if it comes down to that."

"Makes sense. But what if he calls the cops?"

"He goes for the phone, he gets the one-eyed stare."

"I meant after we find out what we're looking for. *If* we find out what we're looking for."

"He ain't calling nobody."

"Why not?"

"I mean, would you? Guy raped a girl from a prominent family, then paid the hush money when she came back hollering about it. People who pay for silence don't usually turn around and break it on their own account. If anything, he'll call Chantree Gables and ask for help. That might bring this whole thing to a head. Let's just see what we can get him to own up to and figure out how to play it from there. He doesn't strike me as the type to kill, but he might know who did it."

"You just don't know his type the way I do," Mandy said.

"What type is that?"

"Rich. Spoiled. Entitled to whatever he pleases. There's no one more ruthless than an entitled trust-fund kid, trust me. I'm one of them. No telling what strings he'll pull once he's scared."

"I get that. But if I was him I wouldn't have paid if I was gonna just turn around and tell everybody in town. Would you?"

"I guess not."

"First thing's first; let's put him on the spot," Cole said, tucking the gun into his back waistband. He hoped he wasn't about to shoot a second person in the same day he'd shot the first.

CHAPTER TWENTY-FIVE

They pulled up to Tucker's house to find him leaned over the front of his Jaguar looking at the front bumper, which was hanging almost to the ground beneath a bowed hood. Cole told her to wait just a minute in the car before getting out, so as not to spook him yet.

"Whadaya say there, Tucker?" Cole called out as he approached.

"Hell," Tucker slurred, "Looked down on the way home and ran this goddamn piece of shit into a street sign. Fucking goddamn pieces of trash fold up like an accordion if you blow on them wrong."

Tucker laughed, but it came off drunk and ornery instead of funny. He looked beyond Cole to Mandy's car, still idling twenty feet behind him. "I see you've got classy friends, Cole. Tell 'em they don't have to be shy, come on out."

"They're prettying themselves up. Goddamn, how'd you manage to take out a street sign? You ain't drunk, are you?" Cole gave him a real grin this time.

"Hell no," Tucker said. "I'm just getting started. You get that booger sugar, or what?"

"I've got exactly what you need. Let's head inside and get a head start on these ol' prissy gals."

"Best idea I heard all night." Tucker staggered off in the direction of his front door. Cole nodded to Mandy and she killed the engine. He watched as her outline stepped out into the darkness left by her headlights. He motioned her to follow him inside, then followed Tucker to the front door, which Tucker struggled to get open in his drugged state.

"Goddamn keys always stick," Tucker said. "Best fucking locks money can buy, and you just about can't get them to open with their own key."

He finally struggled the key into the lock and turned it, walked inside and had to fumble with the alarm system's keypad for twenty seconds before he managed to punch the code in. By then Mandy had followed them inside and was standing right behind Cole, who was standing right behind Tucker.

"Now, how's about we get this party started with some go-go juice."

Tucker turned and started to say something else, but his eyes flared out as he noticed Mandy's shape beyond Cole's shoulder. "Who's your friend?" he asked, but even as he asked, his eyes widened with recognition. "What the hell is she doing here? I thought we were gonna have a good time, not hang out with some snotty bitches who think their snatch laid the golden egg."

"Kinda like the fun you had with my sister on coronation night?" Mandy snapped before Cole could stop her.

Tucker ignored her and looked at Cole instead. "What the fuck is this bitch babbling on about?"

"Maybe you could tell me. You forked so much cash over to her sister and Jimmy that I have a hard time believing you don't know."

Tucker tried to stand taller but only succeeded in looking more intoxicated. "What the hell is going on right now?" he said again, stumbling through the words.

"As if you don't know," Mandy said. "I mean, really."

Cole held up his hand to silence her. "Relax," he said. "I got this." He turned back to Tucker. "This here's what my daddy would have called a 'Come to Jesus' talk. What happens now is you get to unburden yourself of the secret you were paying Caroline Ambrose to keep to herself, and if you're lucky, avoid going to jail for a double murder. Now tell us about how you and Chantree Gables drugged and raped Caroline the night of her Rose Queen coronation. You might even feel better after, assuming you have feelings."

Tucker opened his mouth to speak, but Cole shushed him before he could. "I've been poking my nose around trying to figure out what happened to Jimmy. I made a new friend over the course of my search, and I'll be damned if she didn't find a little interesting reading material when she decided to go through her sister's things at her house. Information about rape, blackmail, the works. I guess what I'm trying to say is, we know what you did, and now you're gonna tell us who killed Caroline and Jimmy to keep them quiet."

The rosy alcohol-induced color drained out of Tucker's face. "That's some story there, Cole. I have a feeling the sheriff might not see it the same way you do. Now how about you get the fuck out of my house before I call him?"

Cole shrugged. "I was worried you might say that," he said. He pulled Chester's pistol out of his back waistband. Tucker's eyes widened more as Cole slapped him across his right cheek with the pistol's barrel, not hard enough to knock him out, but hard enough to let him know he meant business.

Tucker took the blow and bent over at the waist holding his cheek. Blood seeped between his fingers and dripped on the floor in front of him. "I tried to be nice, but we can do it like this, too," Cole said. "I've got nothing to lose at this point."

Cole smacked him across the ear this time with the pistol, then kicked him over with the heel of his boot. Mandy watched with a look on her face that showed she was trying without much success to act as though she didn't enjoy the violence a little. Cole pointed the pistol at Tucker's head.

"Okay! Shit, Cole, take it easy, don't shoot," he said, writhing on the concrete floor like a toddler throwing a fit as he said it.

"It was all consensual, I swear. She wanted it, girl was a *freak*. We was all just having some fun and then she turned on us later." Cole motioned to him with the gun to remind him of the situation. Tucker raised his arms and shook his head.

"Some fun?" Mandy's voice had acid in it. "You get a girl blacked-out drunk and pass her between you and your loser friend and that's what you call consensual fun?"

"Please," Tucker said. "That's how it was, I swear. Don't shoot me."

"Apparently Caroline didn't agree with you that it was fun or consensual."

Cole was sweating now, had to wipe his forehead with the back of his hand that held the pistol. "Now let's talk about who knocked her and Jimmy off to keep them quiet. I doubt you had it in you, but I'm keeping an open mind."

Tucker dry-heaved twice. The third time a puddle of thick, tomato-colored bile spilled out onto the floor in front of him. He was shaking and pale, sweating hard now. "I didn't have nothing to do with killing her," he mumbled. "I swear on my life."

"Your life doesn't buy much credibility right now." Cole leaned in and put the barrel against Tucker's clammy head.

"I paid. I'm telling y'all it was consensual, but when she threatened to go public with it anyway, I paid. I fucking paid, Cole. Seriously."

"Why would you pay if you weren't guilty?" Mandy asked.

"I didn't want to. It was my uncle Kevin, he made me."

"As in the mayor, Kevin Colston?" Mandy snapped.

"He forced me to. This was all right in the middle of the last mayoral election, and he didn't want the scandal. I would never kill anyone."

Cole cut him off. "I'm only going to say this one more time, Tucker. Who killed Caroline and Jimmy? Last chance to do the right thing."

"It had to be Chantree and them. His grandfather is into all kinds of shit. My uncle tried to get him to pay too, but he wouldn't. He said that's not the way they handled things in his family."

Cole and Mandy locked eyes. "Did Jack Gables have them killed?" Cole asked.

"Far as I know that was a murder-suicide, just like they said. I won't deny it was beneficial to me, but nobody told me anything about it if they did."

Mandy stepped forward and soccer kicked Tucker in the chin, which caused him to collapse face-first into the puddle of vomit in front of him. "That's for my sister, you predatory piece of trash," she said. She hobbled backward as if the kick might have done more damage to her foot than his face.

Cole stepped between them before she could do anything else. "Easy," he said, "Take it easy."

"I'm sorry," Tucker mumbled, bleeding from his nose now, too, the blood mixing in with the puke on his face. "Really, I'm sorry. But I didn't kill them. I paid. I fucking *paid*, and that's all I know. If Chantree or Sheriff Gables or whoever else killed them, that's on them. I wouldn't kill anyone. I paid."

Cole and Mandy exchanged looks.

"What the hell would Jack Gables' grandson be doing at an event like that in the first place?" Cole asked her.

"He's been trying to pass Chantree off in Teller high society for most of Chantree's life. Far as I know, Tucker here is the only one who ever wanted to be friends with him. Chantree is a screw up. He's also an arrogant little sociopath just like his grandfather."

Cole shifted his focus back to Tucker again. "Listen up, Tucker. I'm not a violent person, but don't push me. In a few seconds, Mandy and I are gonna turn around and walk out of this place. If we're all three lucky, you won't ever have to see or hear from the two of us again. If you're thinking about calling the sheriff or maybe your uncle or whoever usually cleans up your messes, I'd think again. If I have to come back over here it will be for blood, period, and this thing is already set up to move into hands outside of this county, so you'll only make things worse for yourself."

Tucker hung his head, defeated. "So how much do you want to keep it quiet?" he asked.

Cole had to pull Mandy back before she could kick him again. "You think I need your money?" she snarled. "You think that's what this is about? That's all anyone around here cares about, money. Save it for your lawyer."

They turned and walked out the front door, got into Mandy's Mercedes and drove away as if nothing had happened at all.

CHAPTER TWENTY-SIX

"What do we do now?" Mandy asked once they were sitting on her couch, locked behind the gates to her home. "You think it was Jack Gables who killed Caroline and Jimmy?"

"Don't you?" Cole replied. "To me that just makes good sense. I don't think it was him, exactly, but one of his henchmen. I've got one in particular in mind. As to your first question, I'm gonna try to give that P.I. Kirkpatrick a call and see if I can talk him into driving up here tonight."

Mandy took a deep breath. "My head is spinning. I feel like someone locked me in a washing machine and turned it on."

"I know what you mean."

"I want to apologize again to you, Cole. For the way I acted when you first came to me with all this. I've been a bit crazy since Caroline died. It felt like my whole family died with her. It almost killed my father, I think, but he's too proud to show it. I really hate to call him with this, but honestly, I'm scared, and he could protect us. He knows powerful people in the state Legislature and beyond."

Cole stood up and took out his phone. "Don't call him yet," he said, redialing Kirkpatrick's number from the call history. "Let me see what I can set up with Mr. Kirkpatrick first. He said he's still got high profile law-enforcement connections." The line rang four times and Cole was preparing to leave a voicemail when

Kirkpatrick answered.

"This is Kirkpatrick."

"Mr. Kirkpatrick, this is Cole Quick again."

"Mr. Quick, how are you? I just got the information you sent, was about to look it all over. Can I call you back after?"

"Unfortunately, that might be too late. I'm in a pretty dangerous situation, and I need your help."

"How's that?"

"I've got some more evidence you need to see regarding everything my attorney sent you. I've got some evidence that Teller County Sheriff Jack Gables is involved in extortion, drug sales, and possibly three murders." Cole let that hang on the line, waited for a response.

After a moment Kirkpatrick said, "Go on."

"It's not airtight by any means, but I'd be willing to testify to what I know in court, assuming I live long enough. Gables and his men are looking for me, and if they find me this will be our last conversation. Right now, I'm hiding out. I was hoping you might come up here and use your connections to get a non-corrupt agency with jurisdiction involved, maybe the Rangers or FBI."

The other end of the line remained silent, so Cole went on. "Right now, I'm just really worried that the next time I step outside, someone is going to put a bullet in me. In fact, Jack Gables already told me he'd do as much."

"You came to the right place," Kirkpatrick said. "In fact, I may be one of the only people in the state who would believe a story like that. I've had some personal experience with Jack Gables, as I mentioned before. The problem is, I'm down in Llano. It will take me seven or eight hours to get there even if I leave this minute. Which I will do. It will be mid-morning tomorrow, at the earliest, before I can get there; can you hide out until then?"

"They could be digging my body out of the lake by then, but I'll do my best.

"Stay put where you are and lay low, I'll be there as soon as

I possibly can. But understand up front, you're leveling some heavy accusations against one of the longest-running sheriffs in Texas. There have always been rumors about Jack Gables, but that works against you because people will think this is just more of that. Once I get there we can get you somewhere safer and figure out who to bring everything to."

"The documents I sent you earlier are personal diary entries from the girl who James Calvert's son supposedly killed. She was raped, and she was blackmailing her attackers for a while after. One was the mayor's nephew, the other was Jack Gables' grandson. We think Jack might be involved in killing both Caroline and Jimmy to take care of the problem. Tucker Colston was paying the blackmail, according to the diary, but Jack's grandson refused. Given that both Jimmy and Caroline were involved in the blackmail, according to her diary, there was plenty of motive to kill them both. The video should at least warrant some outside attention. With me testifying to his attempts to extort me, surely we can put something together that will stick?"

Kirkpatrick exhaled into the phone's receiver. "I'll start thinking of who to send this all to while I drive. No promises, though, just so we're clear. I'm not as popular as I once was. A big part of that is because of Jack Gables, and that's exactly what most of them will point out. I'll let you know when I'm close to town, for now stay inside and don't tell anyone where you are. I mean that, not a soul. I'll get there as fast as I can."

Kirkpatrick hung up.

"So, what do we do now?" Mandy asked Cole.

"Now we wait. He says he's driving up from Llano now, so it's gonna be a bit before he arrives. He said to hunker down and lay low."

"That's the best he can do? I'm scared, Cole. Tucker knows I'm involved in this too now, and he knows where I live. What if Tucker calls Jack Gables tonight and they come looking for us?"

Cole frowned. "I see your point. If they killed your sister, why not you? But my gut says that he might call his uncle, but probably not anyone else. You said yourself this place is practically a fortress anyway, so ain't nobody coming in here unless we open the gates or it's the swat team. I doubt they're going to bring more people into the mess, so hopefully we can wait things out until morning and get out of town."

That didn't seem to calm Mandy any more than it was comforting Cole.

"I know you asked me not to," she said, "but I think I should call my father and let him know what's going on. He's powerful, and people respect him. No one is walking up in here and killing him without consequence."

Cole chose his words carefully, not wanting to upset her, but needing to persuade her to hold off until morning. "I get it, Mandy, really I do. But you said yourself he won't be happy if more scandal comes up, and no offense, but I saw the way he dismissed your wishes at your party. He may not agree that the diary is evidence of anything other than why your sister's behavior became so outlandish. That might put Chantree and Tucker on the hot seat, but it won't take down Gables. As it is, none of this is enough to take him down. My goal is just to make enough noise that he can't kill me without putting himself in danger. I think it's best to keep your father out of this until Russ Kirkpatrick arrives and brings in some outside help."

Mandy sighed. "You're right that my father doesn't listen to me. But he's my father, and I trust him. He loves me. If I were in danger, even if he didn't believe me, I know he'd protect me. I think it makes sense to ask him for help."

"I'm in no position to tell you no, nor would I want to. I'm thankful for your help and your hospitality. But keep in mind that in the event he doesn't believe you he could toss me back out on the street just like before, and then my chances of survival are almost zero. At least wait until in the morning when Kirkpatrick is already on his way. Can you do that for me?"

Mandy didn't respond for a moment. "I have no idea how

I'm going to sleep feeling like this."

Cole stood up, grabbed his phone off the table. "Me either, but we need to try. To be honest, I'm running on fumes, and after the adrenaline dump earlier at Tucker's, I'm not sure I can function much longer without some real rest."

"I understand. You can take the room upstairs at the end of the hall. I'll stay awake for a while to make sure no one shows up."

Cole thanked her and made his way up the rounded staircase and looked back down at Mandy sitting with her legs crossed, one foot shaking back and forth, on the couch.

In the guest room he unbuttoned his shirt but left his jeans on, set his boots next to the bed, and put the pistol under his pillow. He couldn't sleep at first.

When he finally drifted off into a shallow sleep, he dreamed he was back in the hospital with Kerrie, her head bald and eyes sunken the way they were in those last months before she passed. That old, helpless feeling of watching someone you love slip away probably would have awakened him if someone's big, gruff hand wrapped around his throat hadn't done it first.

CHAPTER TWENTY-SEVEN

"Boy, what'd I tell you was gonna happen?"

Cole opened his eyes to find himself face-to-face with Jack Gables, the man's meaty hand holding him by the throat, that cowboy pistol he carried as a service revolver poked into Cole's face with the other. "Don't answer that. You and I got business. Now get yer ass up out of that goddamn bed."

Gables yanked him to his feet. Cole wrapped his hands around Gables's wrist as if that would make him let go. It didn't. Gables thumped him on the temple with the gun's butt, leaving him woozy.

"Let's us go on downstairs and have a little pow-wow, whadaya think?" Gables said.

Cole didn't respond.

Gables released his hold on Cole's neck and told him to move, pointed the pistol at his back as he walked down the half-circle staircase into the living room. Mandy Ambrose was sitting next to her father on the couch with her hands folded in her lap. Deputy Charles stood across from them blocking the front door.

Charles scowled and sucked his teeth, then gave Cole a sinister grin that said pure sociopath. Cole had him figured as the one who gutted Caroline Ambrose, but no proof. Not that it mattered now, either way. He shifted his eyes to Mandy.

"Cole, I didn't know, I swear," she blurted out.

"Sweetheart, you just sit there and keep quiet," Tim Ambrose said.

"Good idea," Deputy Charles piped in.

"You best keep your mouth shut, too, deputy," Gables said from behind Cole. Charles nodded and didn't say anything else. Mandy looked away, tears spilling now from the corners of her eyes. Cole could see she was scared. She'd called her father for help. Maybe he called Jack Gables out of concern for his daughter, or maybe he had other reasons. Which one hardly mattered at this point.

"Have a seat, Mr. Quick," Tim Ambrose said. Cole obeyed the man, not having much choice. "Now, I understand that you've been filling my daughter's head with a whole lot of nonsense. That is, when you're not out making a scene all over town."

"It's not nonsense, Daddy," Mandy said. "We've got…"

"Sweetheart, I asked you to keep quiet. I'm talking to Mr. Quick. As far as I'm concerned you're through talking to him or anyone else on this matter."

Mandy's face went pale, but she didn't attempt to speak again. Tim Ambrose went on. "Everything else aside, I have a more important question for you, Mr. Quick. Are you ready to sign the papers Sheriff Gables went to so much trouble to have drawn up for you?"

Cole relaxed back into his seat and let out a big breath. "I can't believe I didn't figure this out before, given the track record of this town," he said after a moment.

Tim Amrose said, "Come again? I hardly find that to be any kind of answer."

Jack Gables, who was standing behind the couch, poked Cole in the back of the head with his pistol as a warning.

"You boys always get your money, don't you?" Cole said. "Except Chester, he never was much for being shoved around. Y'all probably knocked him off, thinking you could lean on me and make me give up the farm, right? This whole goddamn thing was one big railroad, wasn't it?"

Gables slapped him behind the ear with the pistol's barrel. "One more try, Cole, you best get the answer right this time, or the next one's really going to hurt."

"That won't be necessary, Sheriff," Tim Ambrose broke in. "Mr. Quick, the paperwork is all laid out here on the table. I had my own title company draw it all up. Are you prepared to sign?"

Mandy opened her mouth, but nothing came out. Charles smirked, but kept his thoughts to himself.

Cole leaned forward, said, "See, that's gonna be a problem. I already signed a deal with Chromatic Oil on that lease, the paperwork was filed today. Or yesterday, depending on the time. You can check for yourself first thing in the morning, if it makes you feel better. I also had my attorney send the FBI and a whole truckload of other law enforcement a signed affidavit explaining everything that's been happening to me since I got back to town. Y'all can do whatever the hell you want to me, but one thing you'll never have is the lease to my daddy's land. You might fade all this heat, but you won't take that lease."

Gables hit him hard this time with the gun, so hard he saw reality vibrate. He felt warm blood pouring down the back of his head now, was struggling to stay conscious.

"Get a towel, for Christ's sake," Tim Ambrose said. "I don't want him bleeding all over my couches. In that bathroom behind you, above the toilet." He motioned for Charles to retrieve it. The big man got up and cop-walked over, came back with a towel and tossed it at Cole.

"Cover your head with that, Fuckhead," he said. Cole made no motion to pick it up, so Charles shoved it to the back of his head, snatched Cole's right hand up and made him hold it there.

"I'm afraid you've made a grave mistake, Mr. Quick," Tim Ambrose said. "That farm was the only thing keeping you on two legs. I'm disappointed, to tell you the truth. I'd been given the impression you'd cooperate, given your track record. I didn't get where I am without fading a little heat, and neither did Sheriff Gables. I assumed that if we brought you back here and showed you a way out of your problems, you'd have the good sense to do as you're told and fade off into the night. I stand corrected."

"It is what it is, I guess," Cole said. "Maybe wrong is your whole business model. Y'all do whatever you want, but I doubt you can fade this heat."

Ambrose gave him a sinister grin. "I'd tell you to watch me, but you won't be here to see it."

Gables spoke from behind Cole. "You really think I got where I am without knowing a couple ol' boys could fix a problem like you? We sure as shit fixed up your buddy's problem, didn't we?"

Mandy sucked in a breath, looked at her father as if she expected outrage, but his face stayed smooth and unaffected.

"You got where you are because of my family, *Jack*," Tim Ambrose said. "Let's lay off the theatrics for a moment."

Mandy exploded out of her seat like a cannonball, was over the couch and clawing for Gables' eyes almost before anyone saw her move. "You son of a bitch!" she screamed. Gables almost lost his pistol in the chaos, had to swat at her with the barrel to try and fend off her assault.

Deputy Charles snatched her up by the back of the neck and tossed her on the floor. She came up swinging, hit him with a good right hand on the cheek. He swore and pulled her under control by the wrists, then let go of one as if to backhand her. Cole moved as if to intervene and Jack Gables backhanded him with the pistol so hard that this time he saw lightning, collapsed back down onto the couch.

"*Mister* Charles," Tim Ambrose shouted, "Lay another hand on my daughter and you'll regret it for the short duration of your life. Amanda, sit down. You're in over your head and behaving like trash."

"NO," Mandy yelled, seething now.

"I said SIT DOWN," Tim Ambrose stood and grabbed her by the bicep, yanked her down onto the opposite couch from Cole.

Mandy tried to free her arm unsuccessfully. "This asshole and his goon squad killed Caroline. His grandson *raped her*,

Daddy. Did you know that? You're going to help the men who killed your own daughter simply because you lost out on some shady business deal?"

She paused, seemed to have some sort of realization in that moment. The tension in the room seemed to have frozen everyone in space.

"Oh, my God," she said. "You *knew*. You knew they killed her, and you let it be covered up. And to think, all my life I believed you were a good businessman. That Papaw was shrewd and that's why our name meant something. Turns out it does. It means crooked. How could you let them do what they did to Caroline? If you kill Cole, you'll have to kill me, because there's no way I'm keeping this quiet."

Tim Ambrose's poker face was reduced to mild shock. He moved his lips as if to speak, then clamped them shut. Ambrose composed himself the same way Cole had seen Mandy disguise her emotions several times. The room was quiet now, beyond Mandy's broken sobs.

Tim Ambrose took Mandy's hand in both of his. She made no motion to accept or deny the gesture.

"There are things about business you don't understand," he began. "You have no idea what it takes to build all of this." He let go with one hand and gestured at the luxurious house encasing them all. "There are things you just don't do to your associates, and blackmail is one of them."

Ambrose paused when he saw the dumbstruck look on Mandy's face, then sped up his words as he went on. "Your sister was loose with her morals, Mandy. She made a false accusation that could have destroyed decades of profitable partnerships. Partnerships older than either of you. She threatened to destroy everything I've worked for and everything my father worked for. Too many people depend on me to allow that to happen. It almost killed me, but I had no choice. I tried to bring her under control. She spit in my face for the trouble, told me it would make her happy to see me go down with everyone else.

She was willing to destroy this family over her addiction. That's when I realized she couldn't be saved. She had to be sacrificed to protect the rest of us. To protect *you*, too."

"Oh Daddy, *no...*" Mandy trailed off. She slumped back into the couch and spoke in a soft voice. "You thought she was lying so you let them gut her like an animal?"

Her face displayed pain and disbelief. Cole looked around to see if anyone was watching him in case he could make a break for it, but Officer Charles was boring a hole through him, seeming not to notice the sad scene playing out in front of them, the absolute destruction of a father-daughter relationship and an entire family legacy with it.

Tim Ambrose had more conviction in his words when he spoke this time. "That wasn't how it was supposed to happen. It was supposed to be painless. They were supposed to give them poisoned drugs, but something went wrong. The men involved took matters into their own hands, and they paid for that with their lives. Believe me when I tell you that they weren't supposed to lay so much as one finger on her, or Jimmy. I would never have willingly allowed white trash like that to handle my daughter."

Ambrose pointed an accusatory finger at Cole, as if he were an example of the white trash he'd just spoken of.

"You need to think clearer than your sister did, sweetheart," Ambrose continued. "This man wants to destroy our family, everything we've worked for, everything our name stands for. Everything your sister *died* for. I can't let that happen. *You* can't let that happen. Think about your mother. This would kill her. There's no rational choice but to let me do what needs to be done to protect us."

"I can't believe what I'm hearing," Mandy said. "I won't be a part of this. If this is who we are, we don't deserve protection. Chantree Gables and Tucker Colston *did* rape Caroline. I've got her diary to prove it."

That straightened everyone in the room up except Cole, who was staying slumped over to avoid another blow to the head.

She pointed her own long, delicate finger at Jack Gables. "I bet you this sack of shit ordered his men to kill them that way because it hurt his pride to hear that his precious grandson couldn't get any without taking it by force," she shouted, glaring at Gables. "It must have killed you, watching him be rejected over and over by every name that matters. You're nothing but an errand boy, and you never will be anything else."

Gables's glare was vicious now, but he made no move to stop her from talking.

"Sweetheart, just who did you show this diary to?" Tim Ambrose said.

"Not me. Cole. I helped him. It's been sent all over, you'll never put it back in the box now. Copies of Caroline's diary entries about how she was raped by Tucker Colston are arriving in important hands as we speak. I found her journal in the spare bedroom. I used to let her crash here sometimes behind your back. Now I know why you really abandoned her."

Cole decided it was a good time to chime in. "I also sent out a signed affidavit detailing the attempted extortion I experienced with Sheriff Shithead here, which states that if I should die or disappear, it's because of said extortion. I also filed my last will and testament, so y'all go on and do what you gonna do to me, but you will NEVER see a dime of money that was rightfully mine."

Tim Ambrose's face darkened almost as much as Jack Gables's. The confused look he gave Gables was enough to get the sheriff around the couch and into Cole's line of sight.

"What do you say to that, Jack?" Ambrose asked.

"What else could I? Boy's got to go, pronto. Can't afford for so much as a piece of him ever to be found again, money or no money. No body, no murder."

Ambrose turned to his daughter. "Sweetheart, don't let this man pollute your mind with his personal problems. Whatever Caroline wrote, it was probably a lie. All she did was lie, you know that. Don't let this drug-dealing thief tear our family the rest of the way apart."

"Tucker admitted they had sex with her, and that he paid her after. If it was consensual, why did he pay to keep her quiet?"

"I won't pretend to say that I understood everything your sister did, or why. She was sick, and wild. But I loved her, just like I love you. You're not thinking clearly tonight, you're too close to it right now. Trust me, I'm your father. I know you'll come to understand when you calm down."

Mandy shook her head no, still defiant.

Gables chimed in. "This is a problem, Tim. We been at this too long to cave in on some family feud shit."

"Sit down and shut up, Jack. I know how to handle my daughter," Tim Ambrose said. He turned back to Mandy. "Sweetheart, I know you'll come around. You were always so much smarter than your sister. The sheriff tells me that this man shot one man and killed another last night over this nonsense. He's no innocent. Now go upstairs and bring me that diary so Sheriff Gables can do what needs to be done for the good of our family." He stood, guiding her by the arm. "Go on, do as you're told. It's four o'clock in the morning and you're too tired to think straight right now. It will all look different in the morning."

Mandy opened her mouth to say something, then shut it and let her head sag instead. Tears streamed down her cheeks again, but she didn't say a word as she let him guide her to the stairs. Her head hung low as she climbed them. After she disappeared into the upstairs hallway Gables spoke again.

"You sure about this, Tim?"

"Have I ever failed you, Jack? I think you can trust me when I say I know how to keep my family in line after what we've been through, no?"

"Okay. And this sumbitch here?"

"As long as no one ever sees or hears from him again, I don't care what you do with him."

Gables grinned that politicians' grin. "Okay," he said, exchanging looks with Charles. "Mister Quick, you've cost me enough money for one lifetime. And you will pay before you die. Now get on your feet. It's time to go." Gables and Deputy Charles yanked Cole up by the armpits. Charles swung him around to put handcuffs on him. Cole tried to resist, and Charles threw him to the floor, took to trying to kick the life out of him right then and there.

Cole wheezed and coughed from the kicks, tried to roll his ribs away from the blows but it was no good. He felt something crack inside him and cried out, though there was no one left to help him anymore.

"Easy, Deputy," Gables said, just as Cole thought it was going to be the end, right then and there. "Save some for later." Together they hauled Cole back to his feet as he winced in pain. "There's more where that came from," Gables said in Cole's ear.

They dragged him across the room and opened the front door to take him out. Cole was just beneath the threshold when Jack Gables's head exploded like a smashed grapefruit, spraying brain matter and blood all over Cole.

"Jesus Christ!" Tim Ambrose said.

Gables' body collapsed and flopped around on the floor. Cole almost knocked Charles over as he pushed himself away, his only instinct to flee. His face was covered in Gables' brain matter and blood. Charles snatched him by the throat and slammed his head into the doorframe, collapsing him to the bloody travertine floor. As he faded into unconsciousness the last thing he saw was Mandy Ambrose standing at the top of the stairs with Chester's pistol still smoking in her hands.

CHAPTER TWENTY-EIGHT

Cole woke up in what looked to be a hospital room, unable to see at first until his eyes cleared up. Russ Kirkpatrick sat at his bedside. Cole tried to sit up. but the man stuck his hand out and eased him back.

"You're awake, good. You took some hard shots on the head. Do you remember what happened?"

"I don't know, sort of," Cole said, his voice hoarse and foreign-sounding. "Where am I?"

"You're at Teller Regional Hospital."

Realizing he was in the hospital owned by his late wife's parents straightened him up. Bits and pieces started to come back to him. "Did Mandy Ambrose shoot Jack Gables, or did I dream that?" he asked.

Kirkpatrick leaned forward a little. His eyes had a serious quality to them. He looked tired. "She did," he said. "About took his head clean off his body. Pistol registered to your father, though. Maybe you'd also like to explain that while you're explaining all the rest of it. The FBI agents out in the hall will sure be interested to hear about it."

Cole sat up in bed, his head feeling like it was made of cotton. He touched the back of it and felt a bandage. Around it he could tell his head had been partially shaved, and there appeared to be staples in it.

He laid everything out for Kirkpatrick as best he could, the extortion, his reason for coming back to town. He even admitted to shooting Big Zach, though he wondered right after if he should have mentioned it.

But it turned out Kirkpatrick was way ahead of him anyway, appeared to have pieced things together far better than Cole might have expected. Before he could say anything else, there was a knock on the door, and a thin doctor in blue scrubs walked in.

"Mr. Quick, I see you're awake. That's good," the doctor said.

"You think so?" Cole asked. "I'm not entirely convinced. I was having one hell of a dream before I woke up."

"Well, it sounds like you've been through quite a nightmare," the doctor said. "I just want to ask you a few questions and check up on a few things with you."

"Go right ahead," Cole said, gesturing to the men in suits over the doctor's shoulder. "As you can see, you ain't the only one."

Cole spent the rest of that afternoon being questioned alternately by FBI agents Benson and Caldwell, and the doctor, a man whose name turned out to be Miller. He had a concussion to go with the staples in the back of his head, and a couple of cracked ribs as the result of the beating he'd received from Desmond Charles.

The vision in his left eye was blurry, but the doctor said that would probably pass after a week or two, if he was lucky. Otherwise, he was going to be okay, overall. They'd sedated him out of fear he might have some swelling in his brain, but it never materialized, which the doctor said was also very lucky. Cole figured it was about time he got some good luck, hadn't had much up to that point.

He'd tried to grill Kirkpatrick for information the agents might have shared with him, but was told very little beyond that they didn't have any interest in prosecuting him for shooting Big Zach, and that they considered Cole a victim, as well as a material witness.

Though it ought to have been kidnapping, it turned out that Zach had turned state's evidence, along with Desmond Charles, which sort of put him and Zach on the same team, ironically enough.

By the time Kirkpatrick left, Cole was starving, so one of the nurses brought a tray up from the cafeteria that had a rubbery ham sandwich and some green Jello on it. He took two bites of the sandwich and was picking at the Jello when someone knocked on the door. He looked up to see Mandy Ambrose, or what was left of her, standing in the doorway. She looked exhausted, with bags under her eyes and very little, if any, makeup. She wore grey yoga pants with a red Hilliard High School T-shirt.

"Do you mind if I come in?" she asked. "I heard you were awake."

"Well hey there, Mandy," he said. "Of course. Please, come on in."

Her lip quivered as she tried to speak again. "I just wanted to check on you."

"Please, come sit. I feel like I should be thanking you right now, but I know this must not be a good outcome for you. You saved my life, even if it meant..."

I didn't want to shoot him," she broke in. "Really, I didn't. I can't believe I did it." Her voice cracked, and she stopped talking until she got it back under control. "But they were going to kill you, and they might have killed me, too, all things considered. I couldn't let them get away with it. I couldn't let them just erase what happened to my sister and Jimmy."

Cole took a deep breath, felt a stabbing pain in his head as he spoke again. "When you went upstairs like he told you, I thought I was dead for sure. Wanna know something crazy? In the moment, it didn't even matter to me. Last thing I thought as they stood me up was that at least I'd be back with Kerrie. It felt peaceful. But if you shot Gables, how are you walking around free right now?"

"You want the long version or the short?"

"Start with the short, we'll see how it goes."

"My father almost lost his mind when I shot Gables. When Charles slammed your head into the doorframe I shot him too, but he lived. I held them all at gunpoint and called nine-one-one, asked for an ambulance. Then I called Mr. Kirkpatrick from your phone, had him call whatever contacts he had outside the county.

The Teller County deputies who showed up on the scene were so shocked they didn't want to do anything until backup arrived anyway, because of it being Jack Gables. By the time backup arrived, FBI agents out of Dallas had already contacted them to let them know they were on the way. EMTs took Desmond Charles away, but Gables was already dead." She wiped a tear from the corner of her eye, then continued. "They eventually did cuff me and take me downtown, but I'd already called my mother and she showed up with our lawyer before we even got there. About the time the agents got there, Mr. Kirkpatrick showed up and verified my version of the events, showed them what we'd sent over. Now everything, including Caroline's diary, is stored in an FBI evidence locker."

"What's gonna happen to your father?" Cole asked, knowing it was a sensitive question, but needing to ask it, since the man had maybe had Chester killed, too. Cole didn't feel sorry for Chester, but he felt something he couldn't explain, some sort of blood loyalty that said he still didn't deserve to die that way.

"I don't know, from what I gather it's going to take them a while to total up all the charges. When the story hit the morning news that Gables was dead, his victims started coming out of the woodwork. Apparently, a lot of people have wanted to see him dead for a long time, and the list of people claiming to be his victims is so long, it will take months to interview them all.

"Now everyone knows who was backing him up all this time, too. My mother is devastated. She's only been leaving the house to go to church and pray. My understanding is that as of right now, the FBI has arranged a special task force to launch a full-scale investigation into the Teller County Sheriff's Department's activities for the last thirty years, and also my father's company. Gables left a trail of extortion a mile long in his wake. I guess my father has one, too."

She stared off into space for a little while. Cole could see she was in pain over what had happened, would probably never get over it.

"So, they're not charging you then?" Cole asked, hoping to get her mind off her father and what was going to happen to him.

"I have immunity. My lawyer says that given the time of night it occurred, as well as the evidence you and I put together and the fact that it happened in my home, it wasn't likely to come to much anyway because of castle doctrine. This is Texas. You shoot someone who comes into your home with bad intent, you're more likely to meet a cheering squad than a firing squad. It's all over the national news, too."

"So, what happens now?" Cole asked.

"I have no idea. Right now, I'm living on a minute-to-minute basis. I suspect you'll be free to go in a day or two, provided you're willing to testify. Sounds like you're well on your way to becoming a fairly wealthy man."

"Hooray for me," Cole said. "I'd give it all back to have had none of this happen, believe me."

Mandy sniffled. "Come on now," she said in a soft tone, "Having money isn't all bad. At least you'll be able to start a new life somewhere. This was all happening long before you got tangled up in it, so it's not your fault."

"I know it. But I still can't shake the feeling that I'm responsible for destroying your life in some way."

"Don't. I'm glad I finally know the truth about my sister and my family. Living a lie would have been too damn hard to keep up."

"What are you gonna do now?" he asked her.

"I can't really say, Cole. I might take you up on your advice to get the hell out of town for a while. My father is going to prison for sure, but I don't think he'd stop me now, even if he weren't. My mother is hardly speaking to me or anyone else at the moment, but she won't make a big deal of it."

"I'm sorry to hear it," Cole said. "Anyone who would hold it against you for doing the right thing might not have your best interests at heart anyway."

"Nah, it's not like that. I think she's just jealous that I stood up to my father. I've never even heard her argue with anything he said. The only time she's not meek as a mouse is when she's at church over at Rose Meadows. It's still mostly just shock, right now. No telling what she'll do after things die down a little."

"I wouldn't blame you if you never came back," Cole said. "Personally, every second I spend here feels like another year off my life."

"I'm tempted to just go, but I can't leave, even if I wanted to. My family needs me. At least what's left of them. Jack Gables and my father were into some seriously shady stuff. It's mind-blowing how many people they bamboozled over the years. For all I know, my father was involved in every single one of them. My money is stashed away in trusts, some of them overseas, so it probably can't be touched. Gables's money will probably set off some kind of treasure hunting boom around the county or something."

Cole couldn't help but smile at that. "In this place? I bet the richest folks in town will be the first to start looking. Anyway, you've got my number. You ever need anything, just give me a call. I owe you my life, and I will absolutely help if you need it. I hope you won't take it personal if I don't come back here to see you otherwise, though."

"I certainly won't." Mandy checked the time on her phone, then tucked it back into her tiny purse. "I've gotta go, Cole. I'm picking my mother up and taking her to Rose Meadows, so she can pray some more. It's the only way I could get her to see me. Take care, I hope you find what you're looking for out there in the world."

"I just hope you find your way out there, Mandy. You're too good for this place."

Mandy smiled just a touch, leaned over and gave him a short kiss on the forehead, which made him wince a little because of the soreness. He watched her walk out of the room, wondering if he'd ever see her again.

He leaned back in the bed and was getting ready to fall back to sleep when another knock came at the door. He opened his eyes expecting to see Vernon and Millie maybe, was shocked to see Melinda Ferris standing there instead.

"Am I disturbing you?" she asked, coming in either way. "I was told you were awake, so I wanted to stop by. I've got some things to say to you."

Cole's heart raced. He could feel himself starting to sweat. After all he'd been through, the scariest thing was still facing this woman who looked so much like Kerrie.

"I—yeah, of course, Mrs. Ferris. Come in. I think I owe you an apology for the way I acted the last time we met."

"No, you don't, Cole. Actually, I owe you one. I've been doing a lot of thinking since that night, and it's been pretty painful. When I heard what all had happened to you, something sort of clicked into place, and I felt I needed to come and speak with you."

"Please, pull up a chair then," Cole said, not sure what else to say, really.

"That's all right, I won't be long," she mumbled.

He could feel her studying the bruises on his face, which made him self-conscious, particularly since she was impeccably dressed in a neat black knee-length skirt with matching jacket, rose-red silk shirt underneath and a gold locket centered on her chest that he figured had a picture of Kerrie in it.

"I wanted to come here and tell you that I think I understand now. What you said to me at the gala about Kerrie... You were right. She never did want to be that person in the picture. That always hurt me, because I wanted to share those things with her just like my mother shared them with me. She was our only child, Cole, but that doesn't excuse it. I saw in your eyes at the gala how much you loved her and it broke my heart into pieces. I'm sorry for the way we treated you, it was heartless, and it was wrong."

Cole felt himself flush, ice-cold hospital air conditioner be damned.

"It's, I mean..." Cole trailed off now, looking for the right words. "The same thing happened to me. When you came and took her body away, I wanted to die. I didn't realize it just then, not until I looked back on it. I couldn't get out of bed for a week. Lost my job, then eventually our apartment, too. I just kept moping around in some sort of fog for months, ended up living out of my truck and camping. When I found out my daddy had died, I sort of figured it was time to get down here and maybe die with him."

"I'm sorry about your father," she said. "I wanted you to know that we're not going to charge you for the care you've received. I've already spoken to my administrators and let them know not to bill you. I feel like it's the least we can do, given what's happened. I guess I understand why you wanted to leave here now, and I'm trying to understand the same about Kerrie. But I know she loved you, and the more I think about that, the more it hurts. It's strange. You and I don't even know each other, and yet we're connected for the rest of our lives through our love for Kerrie. I don't know if I can get past it."

"Me either. And I'm sorry, too, for getting her tangled up in my mess so that we had to leave the way we did. I want you to know that I tried many times to get her to call you after she got sick, to let you help her even if it meant leaving me. She refused, and looking back, I think she was too worried that something would happen to me if she came back here; that's why she didn't. I feel like I killed her just by loving her. It breaks my heart to think about that. I wish it had been me instead of her, I really do. I hope you can understand the regret I will have to live with for the rest of my life about that."

"The truth is she wasn't going to survive either way. I've seen her file. She was marked for death the day she was born, it's just one of those genetic things that no one could have stopped. How it hasn't gotten me will always be a mystery. I'm sure you understand that makes me feel responsible, too."

"I understand. Maybe it's not anyone's fault. And I want you to know that Kerrie loved you, angry as she was. She was mad for the way you treated me, even though I told her it could never hold a candle to the way my father had. I've been an outsider my entire life, Mrs. Ferris. I didn't even blame you. Some guy like me showed up and I was in your position, I might have done the same thing—especially knowing how it all turned out."

"Please, Cole, you can call me Melinda. And I was wrong. *We* were wrong. I hope someday we can have some sort of relationship, because right now it feels like you're all I have left of Kerrie. I need to know what she was like after you two left, what her hopes and dreams and desires were. It would make me feel closer to her again."

"I'd really like that, Melinda. I never totally realized how much she looked like you until I saw you face-to-face at that gala. Y'all are the only part of her I have left now, too."

They talked like that for an hour, Melinda eventually pulling up a chair. Cole answered every question she asked about Kerrie, and by the end of it they were both crying. He hadn't been able to talk about Kerrie like this with anyone since she'd died. It felt good to be connected to other people through his love for her. They exchanged contact information and agreed to talk again after things died down, Cole informing her that he probably wouldn't come back to Teller County unless he had to for court, which she understood.

But it was the last thing she said that hit him the hardest. She invited him over to their house to visit Kerrie's grave, an invitation he accepted, already feeling butterflies and sorrow in equal parts at the thought. When the conversation was over they shared an awkward handshake and Melinda went on her way, back to running her hospital or whatever role she actually played in it. Cole went back to sleep, exhausted as much by the emotion as the ordeal he'd just survived.

CHAPTER TWENTY-NINE

Mandy Ambrose gave him a ride the day he was released from the hospital. Vernon and Millie still hadn't come to see him, and he was worried they might have given up on him finally.

While he was in the hospital he'd spoken to Cecil and discovered that his first check had been issued from Chromatic Oil. Mandy drove him to pick it up, then to the bank to deposit it. As he stood at the counter he could see Randall down the hall in his office, but when Randall noticed him staring he got up and closed the door as if they'd never met. Cole just smiled, finished off his business and left. Not surprising, since Tucker was knee-deep in trouble over the whole episode.

From there, Mandy drove him over to the Chevy dealership, where he bought a two-year-old dark grey Silverado that felt so new once he was behind the wheel that he was almost afraid to touch anything. He leaned on the window of Mandy's Mercedes while they said their goodbyes, wished her well, thanked her again, and promised to stay in touch.

He didn't even get through the door at Vernon's before Millie was all over him, hugging him so tight he thought she might finish the job on his cracked ribs. He didn't doubt she could do it if she wanted. Women like Millie had been shouldering more than their share of the burden since the beginning of time, he figured, and were stronger than he could ever hope to be.

"Boy don't you ever go get tied up in that kind of nonsense again, you hear me?" Millie said through her tears. "I thought we wasn't never gonna see you again."

"I thought so too, Millie," Cole said. He reached for Vernon's hand but the big man pulled him into a hug, too.

"That was a hell of a thing you done, Cole. I ain't never thought I'd see the day someone take that Jack Gables down."

"Mandy Ambrose had a little something to do with it," Cole replied. "Without her, I'd be dead. No surprise to anyone, only thing capable of taking down this place was one of its own."

"That's what the papers say. I just can't believe y'all done that. What you gonna do now?"

"Well, I got me a new truck, think I'll point it west and head back out into the mountains, see if I can't get started living again."

"Good. That's good to hear," Vernon said. "I reckon you deserve it as much as anyone ever did."

"Not as much as y'all do."

"Nonsense, Cole. Me and Millie, we good right where we is."

"I hope you won't let that keep you from cashing the checks when they hit your mailbox someday soon."

"We can't take no money from you, Cole. We just glad you all right. We ain't come to the hospital cause we ain't want to cause you no more trouble," Millie said.

"I'm glad I'm all right, too, Millie. And y'all could never cause me trouble. To tell you the truth, I haven't felt this ready to live in a long time, bruises and all."

"Well you forget about them checks and live a good life instead, we call it all square. Don't forget to hit us up and let us know how you doin' from time to time."

"The checks are on the legal books, nothing I can do now. I guess you'll just have to learn to live with them." Cole grinned. "Of course I'll let you know where I land. I'll tell you something, though. You don't cash them checks when they arrive, I'll have to come back here and force payment on you in cash."

Vernon's face got serious lightning fast. "Don't you ever come back to this place again, Cole, you hear? You can bet that Jack Gables still got plenty of friends who ain't none too happy about what you done. We cash them checks for sure if it mean you stay the hell out of Teller County."

"Deal. When I get settled somewhere, I hope y'all will come out to see me."

"Count on that," Vernon said, "you just let us know."

Cole hugged them both one more time, then meandered slowly across the parking lot to his new truck. He turned and looked back at Vernon's place once more, almost went back inside to grab a Hunger Hanger for the road.

Instead, he climbed into the cab and drove out to the Ferris family estate, which had been in their family for five generations. Passing beneath the arched iron gates felt like entering a portal to another time and place, where Kerrie was still alive and his whole life still seemed to stretch out in front of him.

He parked the truck, gathered the three-dozen red roses he'd picked up from a stand on the side of the highway on the way over, and walked down to the family graveyard beyond a small vineyard on the east side of the property, found Kerrie's grave right where Melinda had said it would be. He placed the roses next to the polished marble headstone, the largest one there. The inscription read "Here lays Kerrie Ferris, the most beautiful rose to ever bloom in Teller County."

It hurt to see her maiden name on the stone, but he let the feeling pass, just happy to be near her again.

He sat down with his back against the headstone and stared out over the rows of grapes, satisfied that this would be the final resting place for the person he loved more than he'd ever love anyone again. Satisfied now that she would rest here forever, near people who had loved her almost as much as he had.

After a while he kissed the headstone and said his goodbyes through tears, then walked slowly back to the truck. At the Teller County line, he cranked the radio up and pointed the truck west into the setting sun, finally ready for whatever new life the next sunrise might bring.

ACKNOWLEDGMENTS

I want to thank a lot of people for this book, but I'm afraid I will leave someone out and hurt their feelings by mistake. So let's just say that I'm thankful to all my friends and family for everything they've ever done for me. I will do my best to make you proud.

MICHAEL POOL is the author of the crime novel *Texas Two-Step* and the crime noir novella *Debt Crusher*. He lives in Denver, Colorado, where he works as a licensed private investigator.

MichaelPool.net

On the following pages are a few
more great titles from the
Down & Out Books publishing family.

For a complete list of books and to
sign up for our newsletter,
go to DownAndOutBooks.com.

Silent Remains
Jerry Kennealy

Down & Out Books
March 2019
978-1-948235-66-2

When SFPD homicide inspector Nick Jarnac investigates the murder of a 19-year-old girl, missing for forty years, her skeleton found in the mud of a construction site near the remains of two dozen Miwok Indians who have been in the ground for two centuries, he becomes involved in a bizarre, complex plot that involves a Macau-based Mafia chief, several crooked state and local politicians, a cross-dressing Mongolian hit man, a 77-year-old private eye and his burned out ex-SFPD partner, who is hoping to make one last big haul before leaving the department.

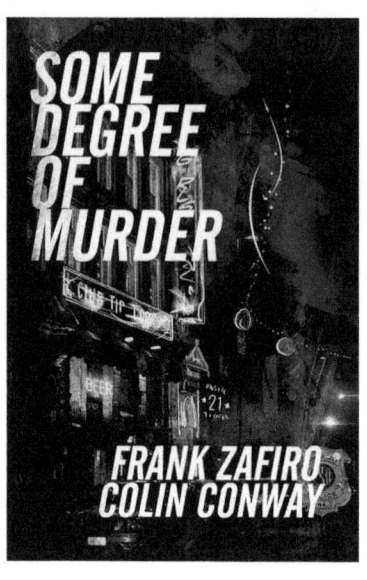

Some Degree of Murder
Frank Zafiro and Colin Conway

Down & Out Books
March 2019
978-1-948235-76-1

A young woman has been murdered in River City. Police Detective John Tower is assigned to the case but there are few clues to go on. As he digs further, he's soon picking up hints that this murder may not be the killer's first…or his last.

Virgil Kelly lives in the shadowy world of the criminal underground. He's just arrived in River City with a single-minded mission: find his daughter's killer and bury him.

Virgil Kelley and John Tower are on a collision course…and somebody is going to die…

The Hurt Business
Stories by Mike Miner

All Due Respect, an imprint of
Down & Out Books
March 2019
978-1-948235-75-4

"We are such fragile creatures."

The men, women and children in these stories will all be pushed to the breaking point, some beyond. Heroes, villains and victims. The lives Miner examines are haunted by pain and violence. They are all trying to find redemption. A few will succeed, but at a terrible price. All of them will face the consequences of their bad decisions as pipers are paid and chickens come home to roost. The lessons in these pages are learned the very hard way. Throughout, Miner captures the savage beauty of these dark tales with spare poetic prose.

Main Bad Guy
A Love & Bullets Hookup
Nick Kolakowski

Shotgun Honey, an imprint of
Down & Out Books
February 2019
978-1-948235-70-9

Bill and Fiona, the lovable anti-heroes of the "Love & Bullets" trilogy, find themselves in the toughest of tough spots: badly wounded, hunted by cops and goons, and desperately in need of a drink (or five).

After a round-the-world tour of spectacular criminality, they're back in New York. Locked in a panic room on the top floor of a skyscraper, surrounded by pretty much everyone in three zip codes who wants to kill them, they'll need to figure out how to stay upright and breathing…and maybe deal out a little payback in the process.

CPSIA information can be obtained
at www.ICGtesting.com
Printed in the USA
BVHW031709150319
542793BV00001B/88/P